Other books by Stephen Greenleaf

Southern Cross
Blood Type
Book Case
Impact
Toll Call
Beyond Blame
The Ditto List
Fatal Obsession
State's Evidence
Death Bed
Grave Error

FALSE CONCEPTION

A JOHN MARSHALL TANNER NOVEL

Stephen Greenleaf

OTTO PENZLER BOOKS

NEW YORK

**OTTO
PENZLER
BOOKS**

Otto Penzler Books   Simon & Schuster Inc.
129 West 56th Street   Rockefeller Center
New York, NY 10019   1230 Avenue of the Americas
(Editorial Offices only)   New York, NY 10020

This is a work of fiction. Names, characters, places, and incidents either are the product of the author's imagination or are used fictitiously. Any resemblance to actual events or persons, living or dead, is entirely coincidental.

Manufactured in the United States of America

10 9 8 7 6 5 4 3 2 1

Library of Congress Cataloging-in-Publication Data
Greenleaf, Stephen.
False conception: a John Marshall Tanner novel/Stephen Greenleaf
p.   cm.
1. Tanner, John Marshall (Fictitious character)—Fiction.
2. Private investigators—California—San Francisco—Fiction.
3. San Francisco (Calif.)—Fiction. I. Title.
PS3557.R3957F35   1994
813' .54—dc20   94–17371
CIP

ISBN 1-883402-87-5

To Caroline and Gerhard

FALSE CONCEPTION

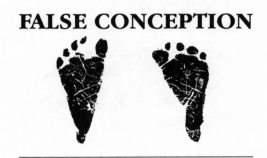

ONE

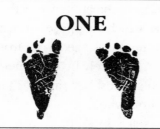

"What do you know about surrogate motherhood?" he asked, his lush black brows raised in elaborate innocence, as if the question were as offhand as a query about oat bran or Coxey's Army.

"*What* kind of motherhood?"

"Surrogate. You know, a woman having a baby for someone else."

I thought about it and shrugged. "Mary Beth Whitehead. Baby M. Plus news reports of a couple of California superior court cases that have upheld the concept. That's about it."

"That's all I knew, too, until a month ago." Russell Jorgensen clambered out of his high-tech high-backed chair and began to pace the room, his shoes scraping the polished parquet like wire brushes sweeping soulfully across a snare.

We were sitting in Russell's law office, on the northeast corner of the twenty-ninth floor of Embarcadero Four, with nothing but a sheet of lightly tinted safety glass between us and a view to the ends of the earth, or at least to the Sierras and the Trinity Alps. Cars streaked across the bridges, ships steamed across the bay, a string of cirrus clouds slipped through the sky like chiffon salmon swimming up an azure stream to spawn in the place of their birth. At one point in my life, having an office with a perspective like this one had been among the loftiest of my dreams. Now all my dreams are down to earth, which must mean they aren't dreams at all.

Worrying the silken ends of his gaudy necktie, scratching the tip of his raptor's beak, Russell was far less tranquil than the vision outside his windows. I'd known him for twenty years. He was a big man, with a big brain and a big heart and a big reputation for both courtroom theatrics and a social conscience, a combination not all that common in the world of high-priced lawyering, which I suppose was why I liked him. Like most lawyers, his ego and his temper staged a riot from time to time, and left casualties in their wake, but lately he'd seemed to mellow—I'd heard he had fallen in love, which must have also meant that he'd finally recovered from the death of his wife.

I'd worked for Russell a dozen times over the years—mostly tying up loose ends during the week before one of his trials when he was too frantic to handle minutiae himself—but this time he looked in need of more substantial assistance. "I never should have let this goddamned thing get so far along," Russell scolded himself. "I should have put a stop to it a month ago."

"Why didn't you?"

When he shrugged, his shoulders bulged like a bison's. "Stuart Colbert's an important client, and even a bit of a friend. Despite all the money he's got, and the swarms of women who hover over him down at the store, he's kind of a pathetic character, what with his old man looking over his shoulder for the slightest slip and his sister being so imposing. And besides, it isn't like they're trying to commit a felony—they just want a fucking *baby.*" He looked at me with the swollen defiance he usually reserved for a hostile witness. "What's wrong with that?"

"Nothing," I said amiably. "Theoretically."

My demeanor didn't pacify him. "Right. And even the surrogate business. I mean hell, it's not *that* big a deal—it's been around since biblical times, for Christ's sake. Abraham sired a son by his wife's maid, didn't he? When Sarah couldn't have children? Hagar was her name, I think. The maid. Am I right?"

"Beats me, Russell. But I'll check it out with Reverend Schuller if you want me to."

He ignored my offer. "There's been one surrogacy bill or another bouncing around the state legislature since 1982. I mean, this isn't witchcraft we're talking about, or even genetic engineering. It's not like they're some sort of satanists."

"Absolutely," I said, then laughed.

My chortle brought Russell up short and his skin baked even browner. "What's so funny?"

"You are. You're ranting and raving about this surrogate stuff, and looking to me for what sounds like moral support, and I don't have the slightest idea what you're talking about." I stopped grinning. "Except I'm getting the impression that you're afraid you screwed up."

Russell swore once more and looked past me toward the door, as if he was afraid someone would come through it and catch him at something. "I did screw up," he said quietly, running a hand through the hair that swept across his temples in a long black wave that was streaked with slats of gray. "It'll probably work out in the end and I'll skate by and so will the Colberts, but if not . . ." He tried for a smile but it twisted into a wince. "Disbarment isn't the worst fate in the world, is it? I mean, you ought to know, right?"

I felt myself color as I was tipped toward a past I had worked long and hard to forget. "I wasn't disbarred," I countered. "I was suspended. And you're right; it isn't the worst fate in the world." I decided not to tell him that it came close enough to cast a shadow.

I waited until he was paying more attention to me than to his doomsday projection. "Here's an idea—why don't you start at the beginning? When you're finished, maybe I can let you know if I can help you out."

Russell took one last look out the window, toward the jut of Mount Tam and the sling of the Golden Gate, then sat back down at his desk as gingerly as if he were taking a seat in a lawn chair. "This is totally work-product, Marsh," he admonished as prologue. "Privileged inside and out. No one hears about this stuff. Ever. Not from either one of us."

"Check."

"Okay. The client is Stuart Colbert."

"This is *the* Stuart Colbert we're talking about?"

Russell nodded. "Our firm represents the Colbert stores, Stuart's and his sister's both, and has since the old man founded the business after the war. We handled Stuart's prenuptial agreement and his divorce, wrote his will, and drafted the details of the compensation arrangement when he took over half the business. Bottom line is, Stuart Colbert writes this firm a pretty big check every year."

"Which means you cut him some slack."

Russell seemed relieved at what he assumed was an endorsement. "It's only natural, right, Marsh?"

"Right, Russell."

Luckily, he didn't test for sarcasm. "But Stuart's not the problem, actually. Mainly I let this thing get too far along because of Millicent."

"Who is?"

"Stuart's wife. Spouse number two. A great kid, will make a great mother, which is what she wants to be in the worst way. Problem is, she can't have children. Had an ectopic pregnancy some years back—some kind of infection had clogged up her tubes. Apparently the sepsis was so widespread that by the time they went in to take a look, they had to cut out most of the reproductive machinery to save her life—uterus, tubes, everything but the ovaries."

"Tough deal."

Russell nodded. "Especially when you're Millicent's age and think having a kid is crucial to fulfilling your role as a woman or whatever. She was crushed by this, believe me."

"So you cooked up an option for her."

Russell shook his head. "Not me, Marsh; I didn't come on the scene till the wheels were already rolling. By the time *I* got into it, all they needed was a contract."

"For what?"

"An agreement between them and the surrogate. A contract for a woman to carry their baby to term, then hand it over to the Colberts and exit their lives ever after."

Russell put his hands behind his head and leaned back in his chair and closed his eyes. On the wall behind him, a smear of graphic art made light of his predicament without knowing what it was. Beyond the windows, a 747 took another load of haoles to Hawaii. Over in Oakland, something was on fire. Something's always on fire in Oakland.

"Frankly," Russell was explaining softly, "the reason I didn't get involved with the surrogate thing more intimately was because I thought the *legislature* would take care of the situation for me. Which it did, temporarily."

"How do you mean?"

"The pols passed an Alternative Reproduction Act in Sacramento last year. Regulated this surrogate stuff up one side and down the other—insurance arrangements, psychological testing, payment terms, health exams, the whole works. I figured the law would tell the Colberts what they could and couldn't do, and I'd just incorporate the statutory requirements in the contract and that would take care of it; I just had to follow the code."

"What happened?"

"The governor fucking *vetoed* the thing."

"Why?"

"The veto message claimed that since the moral and psychological dimensions of surrogacy aren't clear at this point, the courts should deal with it on a case-by-case basis, the way they have in the past. But from what I hear, a big reason for the veto was the religious stuff—interfering with God's plan and all that. Some outfit called the Committee for Moral Concerns was lobbying pretty hard against the thing. They're worried about a domino effect—if they let people change the reproductive rules at all, the next thing you know the state will be promoting abortion and even genetic engineering. But it was also a chance for the gov to make points with the feminists, since some of them don't like surrogacy, either."

"Seems like they'd come out the other way on the issue."

"Some do, but lots of them see it as just one more instance of exploitation of poor women for the benefit of wealthy men. Although why they feel that a woman is capable of choosing whether to have an abortion but not whether she wants to be a surrogate mother is beyond me."

"Consistency and evangelism seldom occupy the same space."

"Yeah, well, the philosophical bullshit is all well and good, except it leaves *me* high and dry with two people who've lined up a woman who says she's willing to get pregnant with their kid, and I'm not sure what I can do about it. Except to have the contract track the proposed legislation as closely as possible, in case another bill goes through while the Colberts' child is getting born."

I thought about what he'd said, then held up my hand to reverse his direction. "Back up a minute, Russell. How does this surrogacy thing work, exactly?"

As though there was some spirit out there to advise him, Russell swiveled toward the window and looked out. "To make a baby, you need a sperm and an ovum. One fertilizes the other and presto, you get conception. Nine months later, you get a kid. Birds and bees and all that— propagation of the frigging species."

"I think they covered that in the Army, Russell. I seem to remember a training film."

He twirled back toward me. "Then let me bring you up to date. With the new methods of reproduction they've developed in the past decade—artificial insemination, *in vitro* fertilization, and the like—a baby can have six different parents on the day of its birth: the donors of the sperm and the egg, the mother who carries the fetus during gestation and her husband if she has one, and the man and woman who will nurture the child after it's born."

"Sounds like it could get complicated."

"Sure it can. Mary Beth Whitehead refused to give up the child to the contracting parents; another surrogate aborted the child without warning; another gave birth to twins and there was a lawsuit over what to do with the extra one. All *kinds* of problems can crop up."

"So what are the problems in your case?"

Russell rubbed his nose. "First some background. There are two basic situations. In the first, the sperm of the contracting father is arti-ficially inseminated into the surrogate. It fertilizes her egg, and she car-ries the baby to term, then yields the child to the couple who hired her and they all live happily ever after."

"Theoretically," I said again.

"Right. Theoretically. Most states that accept surrogacy don't even require an adoption procedure—the surrogate's rights in the child terminate at birth. But the process varies from state to state, and sev-eral states ban surrogacy entirely. In California, at least at this point, the surrogate isn't considered the mother in the legal sense at any time, even in cases like the one I mentioned, where her own egg has been fer-tilized so she's both the biological and birth mother. The courts gen-erally hold the surrogate's rights end at birth unless there are weird circumstances, such as the future nurturing mother dies during preg-nancy or there's some kind of fraud involved in connection with the contract. But like I said, that's one type of case. With the Colberts, there are variations."

"Such as?"

"For one thing, Stuart Colbert had a vasectomy after his first mar-riage ended, so he can't conceive by normal means. Luckily, it's not a major problem."

"Why not?"

"Because even before he got married, Stuart had some sperm put in cryopreservation storage at a sperm bank over in Berkeley."

"Why do that before he got married?"

"Because his daddy told him to after he found out that the average sperm count of the American male has fallen 50 percent in the last fifty years. The old man got worried about his legacy, so he did some checking. The medical people told Stuart that if he and his wife ever had problems conceiving, the lab guys could intensify his potency by whip-ping up an industrial-strength solution of some sort, a double shot of spermatozoa, as it were. And they *can* do that, as it turns out, although nowadays, if a man can produce even one sperm, they can inject that into the egg directly, so whole vials of the stuff aren't going to be needed anymore. The point is, the sperm that's going to make *this* kid isn't fresh from the tap—it's out of a jar in the sperm bank."

"Does that make any difference?"

"Supposedly not. Supposedly the risks to the fetus from using frozen sperm aren't that much greater than doing it the normal way."

"And what about the egg?"

"Despite the infection, Millicent's ovaries can produce eggs just fine; it's just that they don't have a place to go to get fertilized—no tubes, no uterus. So when they decided they'd try to have a kid, she went to the Coastal Fertility Center and they gave her a drug to make her super-ovulate—make a whole bunch of eggs at one time—then did something called a laparoscopy, which is when they go in with a tiny camera and look around, then suck up the eggs with a vacuum cleaner–type thing. Then the folks at the fertility center put Millicent's eggs and Stuart's sperm side by side in a petri dish—*in vitro* fertilization—and lo and behold they got an embryo. Three of them, to be exact."

"Not very romantic," I said.

"That's the nineties for you—the only romance is in Madison County. It's interesting, by the way, that for couples whose religious convictions prohibit the *in vitro* process, something called a gamete intrafallopian transfer can happen so fertilization can take place in the fallopian tubes of women even if they've had a hysterectomy. Conception occurs inside the biological mother, to track with whatever the Bible has to say on the subject, then the embryo gets transferred to the surrogate for gestation." Russell looked at me puckishly. "It's also interesting that this transfer process suggests that some day it may be possible for embryos to be implanted in the abdominal cavities of males."

I blinked. "A man could be pregnant?"

"Conceivably." He grinned. "No pun intended."

I didn't want to think about it. "An embryo is a what? A fetus?"

"More like a prefetus; it's only a fetus when it's recognizable as human, which is at about the eighth week of gestation. The Colberts' embryos are at the eight-cell stage of division, frozen at minus 196 degrees Centigrade in liquid nitrogen, ready to be thawed and implanted in the surrogate's womb the next time she's scheduled to ovulate." Russell looked at his watch. "Which is exactly five days from now."

I recapitulated. "Five days from now, one of their embryos goes in the surrogate, and from then on she's pregnant with the Colberts' kid."

"If the implant takes, as they say."

"It's spooky, sort of."

He shrugged. "The governor evidently thought so. But it's a godsend to people like the Colberts." Russell looked at me quizzically. "You got an objection to any of this, Marsh? In principle, I mean?"

I shook my head. "I haven't thought about it before today, but I don't think so."

"Good."

"How about the surrogate?" I asked. "How does she benefit in all this?"

"The biggest benefit is that she enables two people who are desperate to have children to realize their dream."

"I have a feeling there's more to it than that."

"Plus, she gets paid," he added crisply. "In this case, the surrogate will benefit to the tune of one hundred thousand dollars."

I whistled.

Russell's voice lowered to a portentous buzz. "Which brings me to why you're here."

"And why is that?"

"This woman they've come up with—this surrogate. I need you to check her out for me, Marsh. I need you to tell me she's fit for the job. I need you to tell me she's not some kind of nut who's going to do something dreadful, either to the fetus or to my clients. And I need you to do it by Monday."

TWO

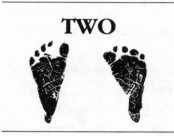

"Is that all?" I grinned. "I was afraid you figured me for a cheap source of day care from someone who isn't an illegal alien. I come cheap, but not Zoë Baird cheap."

Russell was irked at my flippancy. "This is serious, Marsh. If this woman turns out to be a charlatan, she could wreak all *sorts* of emotional havoc. For the Colberts *and* for me."

"Tell me about her," I said.

Although it was almost chilly in his office, Russell began to sweat. "This part is unusual, too," he murmured.

"How so?"

"In the normal situation, the surrogate and the parents start out as strangers. They meet through the auspices of a place like the Center for Surrogate Parenting in Beverly Hills, or the Center for Reproductive Alternatives in Pleasant Hill, and a screening process takes place— both the surrogate and the contracting parents undergo a psychological evaluation and a background check, to make sure no one's a weirdo. If the initial indications are favorable, the surrogate and the parents meet to see how they get along. If they like each other and want to go ahead with the project, they execute a contract. From then on it's a collaboration, a joint venture in which all three parties participate together, seeing each other regularly to provide mutual counsel and support until the baby is born and given over to the nurturing mother. Sometimes the venture continues afterward, as well. The surrogate sees the child periodically, keeps tabs on its development, that kind of thing."

"But that's not what's happening in your case," I guessed.

Russell shook his head. "A year or so ago, the Colberts consulted both of the centers I mentioned, but they weren't happy with the candidates they screened. They're leery, Marsh—horrible things have happened in these surrogate things, as I mentioned, and the Colberts, especially Mrs. Colbert, want to do all they can to ensure that nothing remotely like that will happen to them."

"How are they going about it?"

Russell hesitated, then fiddled with his tie once again, then looked at me with what appeared to be trepidation. "The main thing they did was dig up a surrogate themselves."

I raised a brow. "How?"

"It's a woman who used to work as Stuart's secretary when he started in the clothing business." Russell paused. "You know the Colbert story, don't you, Marsh? The stores and all that?"

"Some of it," I said.

What I knew was that if you lived in San Francisco in the middle years of this century, and decided to buy a fashionable frock or a fine suit of clothing, the odds were that you would patronize a local dry goods dynasty. If you were a businessman, the Roos brothers or the Grodins could meet your needs. If you were a stylish matron or a professional woman, the Magnins or the Livingstons would fill the bill. Over the years, these and other mercantile families became rich and powerful and prestigious, and their members contributed mightily to the legend that was the lifeblood of the city.

But as the years went by, the great retailing families began to subdivide, or feud, or go bankrupt, or all three simultaneously. The younger generation was more fascinated with cash than tradition and, under the pressure of partnership partitions and economic recessions, the dynasties began to crumble and a succession of carpetbaggers moved in to usurp them: Macy's and Saks from the East; Neiman-Marcus out of Texas; most recently the Nordstrom brothers slipping down from Seattle. It didn't take long before most of the local dry goods empires vanished, often in the wake of lawsuits and resentments, and once-vibrant buildings stood empty for decades, awaiting a commercial revival.

But somehow the Colberts held on. The flagship store on Market Street continued to hawk its wares in style and abundance despite the foreign and domestic competition, and a string of Colbert satellite stores sprang up to serve neighborhoods from the Mission to the Marina, keeping both the name and the good will alive. Several years ago, the family patriarch—Rutherford B. Colbert—had come down with some health problems and management had devolved to his kids—Stuart and Cynthia—at least it did so in name. But even though the old man is breathing with the aid of a canister of oxygen somewhere in St. Francis Wood, the word was that he still made the major decisions unilaterally, giving the children no choice but to acquiesce in public and grumble behind closed doors at the extent of the old man's continued interference in the business.

As his health continued to decline, Rutherford's children wrestled with each other for primacy, providing fodder for the local media and panic among the employees in the stores, who were in fear of a total collapse. Finally, the old man decided to make like Solomon and, in an odd experiment in cross-pollination, divided the empire in two: men's wear went to Cynthia; women's wear and haute couture to brother Stuart.

Surprisingly, the partition seemed to be working. The business page of the *Chronicle* declared the Colbert for Men and Colbert for Women chains were thriving, even while the gossip columns painted Stuart as a petty tyrant and Cynthia as a raging harridan. I had no way of separating the truth from its opposite, and since I do most of my shopping by catalog to avoid the fluorescent reality of dressing rooms, I hadn't paid it much mind. But apparently that was about to change.

"Stuart and Millicent have known each other since they were kids," Russell was saying. "Stuart was older, so they didn't travel in the same crowd, but they were raised in the same block out in St. Francis Wood. After Stuart got married and Millicent went back East to school and then to work in publishing, they lost contact. Just before Stuart's divorce, they met at the mansion at the Colberts' Christmas party and started seeing each other socially. Then they fell in love, or whatever it is you fall into at that age—they were married four years ago."

"Where does the surrogate come in?"

"Apparently the woman made such an impression during the years Stuart knew her, they decided to hunt her up and ask her to be their surrogate when the other alternatives were lackluster."

"What's this woman's name?"

"Greta. Greta Hammond."

"How old?"

"Thirty-seven."

"How old are the Colberts?"

"She's thirty-five; he's forty."

"Is Greta married?"

"Most surrogates are; she's not. But she was; she's been divorced for years."

"Kids?"

"Apparently she has a daughter."

"Where?"

"The daughter? No idea."

"Where does Greta live?"

"Kirkham Street." He gave me the number.

"Does she have a job?"

"She's some sort of technician at the medical center. Glorified orderly, it sounds like."

"Let's see if I get it," I said after a moment's thought. "The Colberts start thinking about this surrogate stuff but they don't like the women they see at the reproductive centers, so they give Stuart's old secretary a call out of the blue and ask if she wants to be implanted with an embryo that will grow to be their kid?"

By the time I was finished, Russell was shaking his head. "No call from the Colberts, Marsh. And no visit—I made the contact myself."

"How long ago?"

"Three weeks."

"That's when you laid the surrogate thing out to her?"

"Yes."

"And she was willing to do it?"

"Not at first." Russell smiled halfheartedly. "I summoned my legendary powers of persuasion."

"It probably helped when she heard it was the Colberts who wanted to hire her."

Russell's eyes focused and his tone grew insistent. "No, Marsh. That's the thing you have to understand—the Colberts absolutely *must* remain anonymous in this. Greta Hammond is not to know who the contracting parents are—not now; not ever. I'll sign the surrogacy contract on the Colberts' behalf under a power of attorney—their names won't appear on the documents, not even on the birth certificate."

I frowned. "Why all the secrecy?"

Russell rubbed his brow. "The Colberts have a high regard for Greta, or they wouldn't have picked her as their surrogate. But they want to make absolutely certain that she can't contact either them or the child once it's born. They want no interference from her at any time—no chance that the surrogate will try to void the contract and no chance that she'll try to make a claim of parental rights in the boy."

"Boy?"

Russell nodded. "This thing has been planned down to the last genetic dot—they know the sex of the child already."

"Even though it's only an embryo? How?"

"Some sort of sperm sifting procedure—apparently the lab people can isolate the sperm with the Y chromosomes and put only those in the petri dish, so a male offspring is pretty much guaranteed." Russell's look was sheepish. "It's not as sexist as it sounds—if everything works out, the Colberts want to have another one the same way, only next time they'll make it a girl."

"Sounds a lot like animal husbandry. Or maybe *1984.*"

Russell darkened. "Don't say anything like that to the Colberts,

Marsh. Not even as a joke. Besides, 1984 was ten years ago. The next stop is *2001.*"

"I think I sort of hope that science fiction stays fiction," I said uneasily. "Let's talk about me for a minute. I latch on to Greta Hammond. Then what?"

"You check her out, you evaluate her, you establish her bona fides, but by no means do you disclose what you're doing or who you're doing it for. What I need you to give me is a rundown on her habits, good and bad. Her friends and associates. Reputation in the neighborhood and at work. Extracurricular activities, including her dealings with men. Anything that might indicate a problem that would make her do something dumb. Which is to say, something harmful to the Colberts or the child."

I indicated my understanding of the task.

"There's one thing more," Russell said heavily.

"What's that?"

"The fact that the Colberts are using a surrogate must remain absolutely confidential. From *everyone,* and particularly from the media and from other members of the Colbert family. I don't suppose you'll have reason to be in contact with any of them, but if you do, not one word of this can leak out. The word will get out that Millicent's expecting a child, but no one will know of the surrogacy situation. Is that clear?"

He was so intense that it was tempting to toy with him, but I resisted. "Absolutely," I said.

Despite my assurance, Russell looked increasingly distressed. "I've gone out on a limb letting this thing get so far along without getting some assurances, Marsh. I want to know anything at all that could pop up and bite me. And I need to know it in time to put a stop to it, no matter *what* it is."

"Roger, Russell."

"We're talking kids here, Marsh. Families. Even dynasties, if you will. So don't fuck it up."

"Other people's lives I can deal with, Russell. It's only my own that I can't get a handle on."

THREE

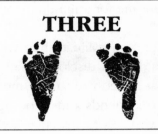

By the time I got back to the office, I'd decided the Colbert case had too many roots—too many entanglements with everything from Freud to families to the frontiers of biotechnology—and I was getting strangely nervous. My foreboding was almost as weighty as if I were deciding whether to have a child myself, and that was an issue I'd been warring with for twenty years. If I warred with it much longer, the battle would end by default.

Part of my problem was the surrogate concept—the more I thought about it, the more complicated it got. Some people saw the idea as sinful, I knew, a blasphemous abandonment of the divine design of propagation. Others saw it in feminist terms, a degradation of the bond between mother and child, a perversion of the concept of womanhood. Others viewed it from socio-economic perspectives, as part and parcel of an age-old pattern of exploitation akin to prostitution—a needful young woman persuaded to sell her body not for sex but for its by-product: impregnated artificially, then forced to endure the discomfort and inelegance of pregnancy and emerge nine months hence with a child much the way farmers emerge in the fall with a crop, the gestation in both cases financed up front by those who would enjoy the lion's share of the profits. And still others were outraged on moral grounds—womb for hire, baby-maker, child-seller, were some of the less spiteful terms that groups like the National Coalition Against

Surrogacy called women who sought to be surrogates. Cast in such harsh and unforgiving lights, surrogacy was not a pretty picture.

But seen from the side of the Colberts, the concept looked quite different. Surrogacy was unquestionably a blessing for reproductively impaired or infertile people, a chance at biological parenthood for those blocked from achieving it through usual channels and unwilling to risk the uncertainties of adoption. As for the surrogates themselves, surely many—if not most—of them were motivated not by financial desperation but by the desire to help others achieve what they considered to be the species' greatest blessing, a blessing they had already enjoyed themselves.

As with debates over other emotional issues like the death penalty and abortion, people of good will were lined up on both sides—people desperate for a child versus those convinced the process was crass and unscrupulous. Righteousness ran rampant; lawsuits raged over surrogate arrangements gone bad. Did I want to be involved in such a volatile and delicate thing? Not really.

Maybe I was reluctant because my toughest cases—the toughest on me at least—were the ones involving kids. My most frequent assignment involves a runaway, a young girl who has run off the reservation and whose parents engage me to bring her back. Even when I get the job done, which isn't always, I seldom feel good about it, because kids usually run off for reasons and often those reasons linger in their absence, or even intensify. Which is why sometimes after I find them, I decide to leave them be.

Kids are always kids, in my experience, and I imagine it's true even in the embryonic stage. When their welfare is at issue, it raises the stakes exponentially. So for reasons of inclination and history, my urge was to reject the assignment. But the imploring clutch in Russ Jorgensen's voice, and the pounding panic that had reddened his face when he voiced his fears of fiasco, made me grope for an enabling rationale.

All I really had to do was run a check on the Hammond woman, after all. If I dropped out, someone would take my place, and even if I gave her my imprimatur, I was hardly the ultimate arbiter—at most I would second a decision already reached by the Colberts. So my participation was preliminary; the trials and triumphs of parenting—the feeding and nurturing, the caring and forgiving—the rest was up to others. Just my cup of tea, in other words: when the tough stuff gets started, the stuff that makes the world go round, I make a hasty exit.

Cursing such psychic maneuverings, I fixed myself a drink and diverted myself with three chapters of the new Jon Hassler novel. Two hours and three drinks later, I drove off to pick up my date.

I've been seeing Betty Fontaine for more than two years. It's the second time around for us—the first, some dozen years back, had foundered on my reluctance to make a long-term commitment and Betty's reactive rush into the arms of an ostensibly more willing mate. The aftermath had been a brief and unfortunate marriage for her and a series of mostly unmemorable couplings for me.

When I'd had occasion to consult her on a case that involved some sexual shenanigans at an exclusive private school, we'd started seeing each other again. Now, the issues that had been nettlesome the first time around were poking their thorny canes up through the soil once again. So far, what we seemed to be doing was stepping carefully around them while pretending not to notice that if we were going to make real progress, we needed to come to terms with such obstacles. But neither of us was inclined to be that sensible.

Betty was an administrator at Jefferson, the largest public high school in the city: First Assistant Vice Principal was her official moniker. She was what amounted to the attendance cop and the job was so frustrating and dispiriting that she resisted it mightily in her head, yet couldn't bring herself to withdraw her heart from the dozens of kids that she cared about. Betty hoped to get out of the front office and back to the classroom next term, but since she'd been hoping that for five years, it didn't seem a likely prospect.

High school is hazardous duty these days, not far removed from guerrilla warfare for students and teachers alike, so when Betty and I got together I tried to lighten her mood and lessen her stress. But it wasn't always possible, and I wasn't always in shape to make the effort, because I go to war once in a while myself.

Two minutes after we'd taken our usual booth in our usual trattoria, I asked what was bothering her. She looked up from the menu and tried to look jaded. "I'm still not sure what I think about veal. Animal rights and all that."

Betty brushed her hair away from her face and dug out her glasses to decipher the menu more closely. Her lanky, often awkward, body was ensconced in a "school suit," as she called it, a beige linen jacket worn over a white silk blouse and above a pair of brown twill slacks with an ink spot in the shape of a strawberry high on the left thigh. The sleeves of the jacket were pushed to her elbows and the spectacles on her nose had slipped toward its tip. Most of the time Betty looked like the schoolmarm she was, and I liked the look as much as I liked the physical and intellectual endowments that it packaged.

"Don't kid a kidder, First Assistant Vice Principal Fontaine," I chided. "Something's on your mind besides the ethical underpinnings of scaloppine."

She paused long enough for me to decide the subject was closed, then blurted a single word. "Geranium."

She wasn't referring to a plant, she was referring to a student: Geranium Jackson—a junior from Hunters Point. Betty was in the third year of a love/hate relationship with the girl, whose IQ was as august as her domestic environment was woeful.

"What happened to her?" I asked.

"She's pregnant."

Given the realities for kids in the inner city, where suicide and homicide are leading causes of death, I'd expected worse. "How long?"

"*Too* long." She elaborated: "Four months."

"Who's the daddy?"

"A gangsta. Cool Brutha B—head of the Army Street Angolans. I know three other girls at Jeff he's impregnated, and that's without asking. But being pregnant isn't what bothers me."

I looked at her. "Not AIDS, I hope."

Betty shook her head quickly. "No, thank God. She's tested negative so far, at least. But Geranium *obviously* didn't protect herself, even though she knows Brutha B has stuck his johnson in half the girls in school, including some who turn tricks on weekends to earn money for clothes, which means . . . well, you know what it means. So the worst part is, Geranium got pregnant on *purpose.*"

"You can't be sure of that, can you?"

"She carries condoms, Marsh. I've seen them in her purse. Hell, I've even *bought* them for her. And I know she's made other guys use them—wear a hat, she calls it. But not this time. Which means she's given up."

"On what?"

"On having a normal life."

"Is she dropping out of school?"

"Not yet, thank God, but only because we've got a parenting skills program she wants to complete. But I know Geranium—she's so damned conscientious, once she has that baby in her lap she'll spend so much time with it, her grades will go straight down the toilet. Our new principal doesn't cut kids much slack—it won't take much of a drop for him to flunk her out."

"Can't you keep her in line? With her grades, I mean?"

"I've been trying for three years, Marsh. Not just with grades, but with life. You see how successful I've been."

I laughed and Betty misunderstood its source. "It's not funny," she scolded. "Geranium Jackson could have gone a long way in the world. When I was tutoring in Basic English, she wrote a story about the first day she was bused to Jefferson from Hunters Point that was so timid and hopeful and poignant it brought tears to my eyes—she made it sound as though aliens had come down and whisked her off to Pluto, and I'm sure that's how she saw it. And now she's sliding down the ghetto sewer—first the baby, then AFDC, the projects, food stamps, and some stud who beats her up 'cause he's got no other way to prove his manhood. God. She's smart enough to know how awful it is, and how much further she could have gone if she'd given herself a chance, so sooner or later she'll hate herself even more than she does already. And who knows *what* will happen then."

"Maybe she'll keep things together for the child," I offered easily, careful not to rile her further.

"It's hard enough for any black girl to make it these days, what with the recession on top of parental neglect and racism, but for girls in Geranium's position it's almost impossible. People will punish her for what they perceive to be promiscuity."

I didn't know what to say to that so I didn't say anything. "I wasn't laughing at Geranium," I explained instead. "I was laughing because you're seeing pregnancy as a curse, and a couple I heard about today would consider it divine intervention."

I explained the outlines of the Colberts' case without naming names.

"Takes all kinds," Betty said when I was finished. "What's the closest you ever came to becoming a father, Marsh?"

"The discussions you and I had ten years ago."

Her lip curled and her eyes faded to vacuous blots. "Ah, yes. The merits and demerits of bringing a child into this cold cruel world. We were so fucking rational and mature, and look where it got us."

"Where is that?"

"Nowhere."

Her look dared me to offer a more promising location. "Sounds like the alarm on your biological clock just went off," I said instead.

"Happens once a day, whether I heed it or not," she answered sourly.

"What do you plan to do about it?"

She shrugged. "Same thing I've always done, I imagine."

"If nothing else you can act unilaterally if you want to, right? I mean, single parenting is an option, isn't it?"

She gave me a look that made me wish I'd kept quiet, then questioned me with her eyes.

"I don't know," I answered truthfully.

"Same as last time, you mean."

"I suppose so."

My ambivalence incensed her. "You're so damned *casual* about it. I suppose it's because men don't *have* biological clocks. That's why it's never been *urgent* for you."

"The average sperm count of the American male has dropped 50 percent in this century," I said, repeating a statistic I'd learned that afternoon. "That's a biological clock of some sort."

"A biological hourglass, maybe. It's certainly not a siren like mine."

I shrugged. "Nature isn't equitable."

"The word you're looking for is fair. Nature isn't fair. *Nothing* for women is fair. I—" She cut off her philippic and sighed. "Sorry. The thing with Geranium makes me feel like I've lost a child myself. It makes me covet a new one, as some sort of demographic replacement."

I let her anguish dwindle before I responded. "I'm willing to discuss it, Betty."

Her laugh was brief and dubious. "We haven't even talked about *us* that much. Not in any way that's constructive. We've just been . . . skating along."

"Skating's a smooth way to travel."

"For a while, maybe, but then you get used to it, and when the road gets rough, you fall on your butt."

I smiled at our circumlocution. "Are we going to get into this, or what?"

"Get into which?"

"Us. Kids. Whatever."

"I'm pretty much always ready to get into it."

"That's not true," I said with surprising heat. "You want to at first, but whenever we start to discuss it, you throw up your hands in frustration the first time we get to where we need to talk about compromise. For example, you're around schoolkids all day. You'd think you'd know whether you want one of your own by now."

Her anger swelled red and round like a blood blister. "That's not fair and you know it—other people's kids are different from your own kids. And I don't give up, I just . . . postpone."

"You've been postponing for twenty years, Betty."

"I suppose you haven't," she countered roughly. "I mean, it's not like *you're* a beacon in the wilderness in this thing. Every time I hint that I might want to make it legal, and have a church wedding and a honeymoon in Greece and come back here and start a family, you start talking about how set in your ways you are. And how many times marriage screws up a relationship."

I shrugged. "A kid might make a difference."

"We couldn't stand it by ourselves, but maybe if we had a child in the house we could tolerate each other? Does that sound like something two sane people should *do*? Use a child as a *tranquilizer*?"

"No. But that's not what I meant."

She smiled artificially, the pain in her eyes and heart as palpable as the smell of garlic that seeped to us from the kitchen. "Back to postponement," she concluded ruefully. "So what else is on your mind, Mr. Tanner?"

"Cannelloni," I said, and stayed still while she slugged my shoulder.

FOUR

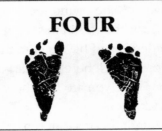

S he rounded the corner at five forty-five, and from the moment I laid
eyes on her, I was certain she was the woman I wanted. Walking with
brisk assurance, smiling at the acquaintances she encountered, carrying in one hand a plastic bag that bulged with cans and boxes and
sprouted a sprig of celery, and in the other a thin red sweater, she
ambled down the street with far more buoyancy than I'd ever felt at the
end of a working day, looking eager to move on to the next one. I don't
know what sort of aura she radiated normally, but the prospect of
serving as a surrogate mother to the Colberts' nascent child certainly
didn't seem to depress her. If I could have harnessed the euphoric
sheen that enlivened her ample eyes, I could have powered my apartment for weeks.

Athletic, even brawny, she was garbed in white synthetics from her
high stiff collar to her silent soft-soled shoes: on her, the uniform
looked less clinical than expedient. Her straight brown hair was cut short
around the base of her neck and pinked in a jagged hem across her forehead. She was strong in the arms and square in the shoulders, broad in
the hips and thighs, full in the neck and breast. In terms of physics and
physique, therefore, the Colberts had selected a Madonna from the tem-
plates of Raphael and Titian.

As Greta Hammond neared my vantage point, I could take a closer inventory. Her round face was sunny and scrubbed, simply and
attractively maintained, with a mole near her upper lip that punctuat-

ed the half-smile that seemed an indelible clue to her mood. Her green eyes were active and almost astonished, her lips full and discreetly tinted, her cheeks just this side of chubby. Her mouth moved as if she were engaged in unilateral conversation, but eventually I realized she was singing to herself, striding in time to an internal drumbeat and laughing at forgotten lyrics and her several slips off-key. If she suffered any illness or was under a cloud of stress, the signs were not apparent, unless it was symptomatic that one of the boxes in her bag was full of sugar doughnuts.

Without breaking stride, she walked to the building I'd had under surveillance for the past two hours, fished in her purse for her keys, unlocked a narrow metal box and gathered up her mail, then disappeared through the entrance. The door that eased shut at her back had a single round window in its upper center and was festooned with a sign that read FOR RENT.

I'd been waiting since four o'clock, parked at the end of her block in front of the Cambridge Market, watching a series of N Judah streetcars lumber by on the next street, on their way to and from the ends of the city. To maintain my sanity, I'd read the Hassler novel in fits and starts while keeping most of my eye on the sidewalk. To keep from nodding off, I was sipping tepid coffee from a thermos, eating Oreos from a brand-new bag, and taking a series of deep breaths whenever I felt my eyelids sag. A stakeout is to a detective what changing diapers must be to a parent: elemental and essential, but not often electrifying, or even very pleasant.

I'd spent the better part of the day determining whether Greta Hammond had ever run afoul of the law. The first thing that morning, Charley Sleet, my best friend, had run her through the cop computer and told me he'd come up empty. I wasn't sure if I was pleased by the news or not—if Greta was a felon, or even a major misdemeanant, I wouldn't have to concern myself with the caliber of my endorsement or worry about its consequences.

But she was square with the cops and with the DMV as well—not even an outstanding parking ticket. The credit bureau showed a dispute over some charges at the Emporium a few years back—apparently she'd returned some merchandise but the store hadn't credited her properly—but it was worked out in the end and that was it as far as uncivilized behavior was concerned. She wasn't delinquent with her taxes, hadn't sued or been sued for a civil offense or even an unlawful detainer. In fact, the dispute over the returned goods was the only record I could find of her—her name didn't appear in the courthouse other than on the voting lists.

After my trip through the municipal records, I'd performed one other task of relevance, just before assuming the stakeout. It was an exercise I'd been able to avoid over the course of my career, a humiliation of the sort that makes you swear you'll quit your job before submitting to it, a nadir I'd hoped I'd never descend to. But under the pressure of time and the weight of a baby's welfare, it had been the quickest way I could think of to accumulate the data I needed.

The cans were green and plastic, numbered to match the apartments, grouped in the alley in back of the building behind a waist-high wooden fence. They weren't horribly fetid, as garbage cans go, or even outrageously slimy, but they weren't fruit cups, either.

I'd cruised the alley to check them out, decided the location was too exposed to do the work on-site, and circled the block again. This time I stopped next to the corral of green cans, grabbed the one I wanted, and tossed it in the trunk of my car. Escaping unobserved as far as I could tell, I took Ninth Avenue to the innards of Golden Gate Park, drove twenty yards down a seemingly secluded lane, then examined my booty more closely.

She shopped for foodstuffs at Cala Foods and for sundries at Reliable Drugs. She had a checking account at the medical center credit union; she had a Visa card and a Chevron card; she contributed to both Special Olympics and KQED. She got catalogs from Talbots and REI and was on the mailing list of NARL. She had bills from the usual utilities and coupons from the usual merchants. I moved on to the mundane.

She ate lots of soup—Progresso and Healthy Choice and Andersen's Split Pea. She liked strawberry ice cream, onion bagels, English muffins, and Cracklin' Bran. She drank 7-Up and Crystal Light and snacked on vanilla wafers. Over the last few days she had consumed a chicken, a banana, a potato, and a pear, and another item whose entrails I couldn't decipher because they had started to decompose. She owned a Hoover that had needed a new bag—I considered opening the old one, but you have to draw a line somewhere.

On a more lofty plane, she read the *Chronicle, Newsweek,* and *Mirabella,* and drank Fetzer fumé blanc. She had received something in the mail packed in Styrofoam and bubble wrap, and a greeting card from someone with a return address on Hickory Avenue in San Bruno. She had tossed away come-ons from a record club and a credit card company without even opening the envelopes.

That was it as far as what she had. What she didn't have was a store of empty Seagram's bottles or Marlboro boxes or hypodermic syringes or Zig Zag wrappers or crack pipes or Darvon bottles or glue tubes, a void of harmful substances that would make the Colberts happy. Her only indulgences seemed to be the wine and ice cream and cookies, which put her excesses roughly on a par with my own. I doubt she would regard it as an achievement.

I stuffed the garbage back in the can and the can back in the trunk and returned it to its home behind the little fence, then found a rest room at the Owl and Monkey Café and removed the grit and the grease and the germs as best I could. When I still didn't feel clean, I considered buying some cologne and sprinkling it liberally over my person, but I'd rather smell like garbage than a gigolo, I guess. Which was why my nose was twitching from odd odors, and I was envisioning swarming maggots and deadly bacteria as the possible source of the smell as I waited to make my next move.

After Greta had a chance to get settled in, I went to the door and examined the intercom system. There were eight apartments listed, next to the appropriate call buttons, with names beside all but two of them. I copied the names in my notebook, including the name of the manager and the phone number on the FOR RENT sign, then returned to the car to wait.

What I was hoping was that Greta would emerge after dinner and go where I could observe her inclinations more closely, and maybe even eavesdrop or strike up a conversation. But three hours went by without any sign of her, so I started the car and drove home, plotting a less subtle inspection for the morning.

FIVE

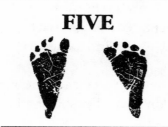

I was back on the block by 7 A.M. Just in time, too, because I was still on my first cup of thermos coffee and the second page of the *Chronicle*'s Green Sheet when Greta Hammond came out of her building and started down the street, skipping off to her daily labors. Her route was indirect; her rate of speed suggested she was eager to get where she was going; her expression suggested life was a festival or a fairy tale.

She was swathed in shiny white again, an identical outfit to the day before, except for the thin gold chain that was looped around her neck; today she didn't think she'd need her sweater. I got out of the car so I could follow on foot, bringing my newspaper with me.

She strolled blithely down Ninth Avenue, browsing in a sidewalk bin of books, waving to the boys in the body shop across the way, her first stop a drugstore on Irving Street to buy what looked like rubber gloves. Her next destination was back the way she'd come—a small café called Leo's. When I backtracked to where I'd last seen her, the smells of bacon and fried spuds that oozed out of the café opened the spigots in my mouth full force, so I tucked the paper under my arm and shoved my way inside, eager to combine business with pleasure.

The interior was dim and artless, with fake flowers on the tables and a photo montage of the regulars the primary decoration on the mirrored and paneled walls. Greta Hammond was seated at the U-shaped counter in the rear, holding a menu in her left hand as she chatted amiably with a waiter standing on the other side of the counter in front of her. The man was swarthy and muscular, a decade older and twenty pounds heavier than he hoped he looked. He wore a torn black T-shirt and a stained white apron that bulged like a jib as it bypassed his belly. The tattoo that wound around his forearm looked to be a cobra; the thing in his mouth was a match.

"Took Marie up the hill yesterday," the waiter was saying as I strolled in. "Gout. Couldn't work her shift last night, she had so much pain."

"Marie's too old to wait tables, Leo," Greta said softly. Her voice was low and well modulated, and just a little sexy, as if she and Leo were old hands at the game of double entendre.

"That may be," Leo answered. "But she's also too poor to retire."

"Isn't there something else she could do?"

"Not in here, there ain't. And if Clinton makes me stick her on a cockamamie health plan, I can't keep her on to do tables."

Greta smiled with the grace of a nun. "You couldn't fire Marie and you know it."

"Won't have to. When she sees what it's doing to the books to keep her on, she'll quit to save me from bankruptcy."

As Marie's fate was being forecast, I took a seat at the counter three empty stools down from the one that Greta was perched on. When Leo looked my way without displaying much interest in my nutritional requirements, I ordered a coffee and danish.

"Apricot's all we got; we're out of the prune."

"Apricot's fine."

"Heated?"

I shook my head.

Greta glanced at me idly as I placed my order, then looked at the menu without seeming to read it. After Leo brought her a bowl of oatmeal that was sprinkled with bananas and raisins, she started in on breakfast. As she swallowed a heaping tablespoon without much enthusiasm, I decided she had come to the café more for companionship than Quaker Oats.

I waited till I had my coffee, then opened my paper to the classifieds and took out a pen. I'd already circled three listings by the time Leo returned with my danish, which, contrary to my order, he'd heated to just below boiling. My guess was he did it on purpose.

He was about to head back to the kitchen when I stopped him with a quick question. "I don't suppose you know of any apartments for rent around here," I asked hopefully. "Cheap but decent," I amplified when he didn't seem to be giving my query much thought. "I've got a boy. Ten. So it can't be too scuzzy."

Leo looked me over long enough to make me think he was serious about his answer. "How cheap is cheap?"

I gestured toward the newspaper. "According to this, cheap seems to come at about five hundred a month. Which sure as hell isn't cheap where *I* come from." I looked at Greta. "Excuse my French."

Leo was shaking his head. "Five hundred's not cheap; five hundred's impossible. If you want decent."

"Five hundred will get you a studio," Greta chimed in the way I'd hoped she would. "But a studio's not big enough for three."

"Two," I said quickly.

She hesitated, then shrugged. "Not for two, either. You'll have to go six for a one bedroom, and that won't get you anything you'd run to get home to."

Leo was warming to the subject. "That's what you got, ain't it, Greta? One bedroom?"

She nodded.

"A studio's too small; you're right," I said. "I mean, the boy'll need privacy as he gets older. Girls and stuff." I tried to look embarrassed, then thoughtful and concerned. And then I tried to look hapless, which is the best part I play. "But it's probably worse with girls. The privacy thing, I mean. Do you have children?"

Her eyes hooded for just a moment, the way they do when you're leery or lying. "I did, but she died."

"I'm sorry. I didn't mean to—"

"It's all right. It was a long time ago."

She looked at me long enough for me to know that she'd remember me the next time we met. Which meant I might have made a mistake by following her into the café, since it was going to be tough to tail her any longer. On the other hand, since what I needed to know had more to do with mental than physical geography, tailing her wasn't going to get the job done.

I must have passed inspection. "There's a unit for rent in my building," Greta said with surprising kindliness. "One bedroom, floor below me. She's asking six-fifty, but you might get her to come down to six. It's been listed for two months—cuts into the net in a big way when it's vacant."

"Nice place?" I asked.

"It's all right. Nothing special, but handy. Streetcar. Bus. That kind of thing."

"Parking?"

She shook her head. "Not that it bothers me—I don't own a car."

"Laundry?"

"When it's working."

"Security?"

"Just the basics." She smiled. "The door has a lock and the landlady has a cat."

I looked at her uniform. "Are you a nurse?"

"Aide."

"Does that mean there's a hospital nearby?"

She laughed again. "You must be from pretty far out of town, mister."

"Redding," I said.

"Well, the University of California Medical Center is up on that mountain back there. Hospital, medical school, psych institute—you got anything wrong, they can fix you up."

I looked at Leo. "Only if I can pay for it, I imagine," I said with a shrug, indicating I couldn't pay for anything more serious than the sniffles.

"Don't worry about it," Leo proclaimed expansively. "Clinton's gonna fix that, too. Trouble is, by the time he gets everything fixed, we'll all be in the poorhouse."

"Give him a chance, Leo," Greta chided. "At least he's trying to do *something*."

"Yeah," Leo groused. "But nothing's a lot cheaper."

"Not in the long run," Greta decreed with a tease, then looked at her watch, then gobbled a last spoonful of oats. "Got to run," she said after she wiped her lips on a napkin and slid some money toward Leo. "Tell Marie I'll come see her tonight." She looked at me and smiled. "Good hunting."

"Thanks. Where's your building, by the way? Maybe I'll go take a look."

She shrugged and gave me the number.

"Are you going to be home tonight?" I hurried on. "Maybe I could call and get some dope about the schools in the area, and programs for kids and that kind of stuff. Any tips I can get will be a big help."

She hesitated, then looked at Leo, then recited her number in the shade of his massive frown. "I don't know too much about that sort of thing, but I'll be home after seven if you've got any questions." She slid off her stool and was gone.

Leo and I watched her go. "Foxy lady," he said huskily, with a hitch in his tone that was both paternal and predatory.

"Seems to be," I agreed. "What does she do at the hospital?"

"Most everything the nurses do, except she gets paid like the janitors."

"I take it she's not married."

"Not anymore."

"Boyfriend?"

"Nope. Not that she brings around." Leo's eyes narrowed to the width of Kleenex. "You don't want to mess with her, friend."

I held up a peaceable hand. "Hey. I'm just looking for a place to live."

Leo made a fist and gave the cobra some exercise. "I better not hear you tried for anything *more,* or I come looking for *you.*"

He gave me one last look at the spreading hood of the reptile that lived on the flesh of his forearm, then walked to the end of the counter and punched a key on the register the way he would undoubtedly punch me if I brought any grief to Greta.

SIX

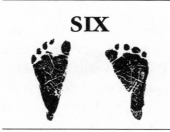

After I'd downed my danish and paid my tab and bid a meticulous good-bye to Leo, I strolled through the neighborhood for almost an hour, looking for a way to accumulate information on Greta Hammond without word of my snooping getting back to her. When I couldn't think of a guise that would fool anyone over the age of eight, I began to feel better about having approached her directly, even though it meant foreclosing most of my other options: there weren't many options, anyway.

At nine o'clock I walked up to Greta's building and punched the button next to the manager's name. The wait was long enough to make me afraid she'd gone out for the day, but the speaker finally popped and wheezed, then a voice flew at me like a startled sparrow. "What is it?"

"I'm interested in the apartment for rent."

"Six-fifty. One bedroom, no parking."

"I'd like to take a look at it."

"You got cats?"

"No."

"Kids?"

"No."

"Too bad. I'm number four in the back. If there's samples or coupons out there, bring them with you."

A buzzer opened the security lock and I dragged open the door

with the round window. The foyer was neat and dark and elemental—chair, sand urn, table and lamp, and a phony photoprint of Paris.
I didn't see a coupon or a cat or a kid—the landlady was going to be disappointed.

The hallway was dark, carpeted with a threadbare runner that
was stained in several spots and ripped from its anchors in others. The
only source of illumination was a single globe halfway down the corri-
dor, as dim as a full moon over San Bernardino. The air was a mix of
mildew and cat pee and Pine-Sol but compared to the stinks I'd been
immersed in the day before, it was comparatively pleasant.

I knocked on the door to four. It was opened by a tiny gray woman
carrying a giant gold cat. Both the cat and the woman were more oval
than oblong, and both sported a tuft of white whiskers. The cat was
wearing a sweater made with one of those knitting machines promoted on late night TV; the woman was wearing a sweat suit that fit her so
snugly and was so aptly dyed to match it was hard to tell where flesh
ended and fleece began.

The cat was asleep and the woman had obviously been in the
same state within the past hour. She regarded me through a pair of sun-
glasses that gave her a jaunty aspect, as though she were off to a casting call. "I'm Mrs. Hapwood. I own the place outright; Mr. Hapwood's
passed on. I get headaches from the TV," she added as my glance lingered on her spectacles. "These cut the light to where it don't hurt. You
the one looking for a place?"

I nodded.

"Just you?"

I almost repeated my error at the intercom. "I've got a boy. Ten."

"You told me no kids."

"I thought you meant babies." I shifted with embarrassment. "I
don't think of Jason as a child anymore, I guess. Ever since his mother
left us, he's been more like a close friend than a son. If you know
what I mean."

She looked at me so long I was afraid she'd seen through my
facade, as if there were some indelible imprint of parenthood that

fathers bear and impostors are lacking. But all she said was, "First and last up front, plus five hundred against damage and security. That's eighteen hundred all told."

I took time to measure it against an imaginary bank balance. "The deposit sounds high."

"You had shag carpet cleaned lately, mister? Or bleached stains out of porcelain?"

I was shaking my head before she finished.

"If you had, you'd know it's not high enough. But you leave it like you found it, you get your money back. I shoot straight on that score."

"I'm sure there won't be a problem; I'm a very responsible tenant."

"Last one told me that tried to make wine in the bathtub; looked like something got butchered in there. I suppose you want to see it."

I nodded. "But first, maybe you could tell me about the other tenants. I work at home a lot, plus the boy needs his rest. I want to make sure everything is sufficiently . . . *orderly* before I make my decision."

I expected her to be offended by my fussiness but she didn't seem capable of it. "In one you got old Mrs. Shifter. Widow; seventy-eight; hip replacement last March. Never goes out—gets Meals on Wheels and watches the TV with a hearing do-jingy so it don't bother anybody."

"Sounds like a considerate lady."

Mrs. Hapwood didn't second the sentiment. "Cat had fleas so I made her get rid of it. In two you got Marvin Gleaner. Never here. Drives a rig long-haul; don't know why he pays rent on a place he never uses. Used to think he was up to something but now I think he's just stupid. Three's the one that's empty—that's across from me." She patted her hair to become a more presentable neighbor.

"Sounds fine so far," I said.

"Upstairs, in five and six, you got students at the doctor school. Two males; two females—all they do is study except the night after final exams when they drink too much and yell a lot." She shrugged. "It's twice a year; one of them did CPR on Mrs. Shifter last Christmas—would have croaked without it, they said—so I put up with it."

"Handy," I said. "The medical students, I mean. In case of emergencies."

We still weren't connecting. "In seven is Miss. Hammond. Very nice; very quiet. Too quiet; Greta needs to get out more. She's up the hill, too, but a maid, not a doctor. And eight is Albert. What Albert does I have no idea. Could be a ghost, for all I know—never see him, though I hear him once in a while. Goes in for that opera-type music, but if you bang on his door, he stops. For all I know he's Italian—they're the ones that do opera, ain't they?"

I said I thought they were. "Which apartment is above number three?" I asked her.

"That would be seven."

"And that's . . . ?"

"Miss Hammond."

"And she works at the hospital?"

She nodded.

"During the day?"

"Generally. Does nights to fill in, is all."

"Does she entertain men friends very often? I'm not a prude, but in my experience women with active social lives can be rather boisterous."

I'd gone too far. "There's none of that with her at all," Mrs. Hapwood said stiffly. "Only people who come see her come by in the early evening, and even then it's seldom men. Other than the fellow asking for her last month, I can't remember the last time I heard a man up there. You want to see the unit or not?"

"Miss Hammond was entertaining a man last month?"

She shrugged. "She never laid eyes on him, far as I know. He come around asking about her for some sort of insurance thing, he claimed, though Greta said she didn't know nothing about it when I told her. Probably the government." She made it sound like a rash.

"Was it an older man or a young man?"

She squinted. "Younger than you, that's for certain."

"Did he give his name?"

She frowned. "Why would you need to know that?"

I shuffled. "No reason. I'm just extra curious, I guess." When I asked to see the unit, she led me across the hall.

The apartment was like a thousand others in the city—too much carpet, too little wood; too much Formica, too little tile; too much plastic, too little glass. The windows were the size of postage stamps; the ceiling was sprayed with gold glitter as if that would make it palatial. I'd lived in half a dozen places like it in my time, during my school years and during my early days as a detective. I didn't want to live in another one.

"It's quite a lovely unit, as you can see," Mrs. Hapwood was saying. "Remodeled four years ago. All-electric kitchen."

"Are utilities included?"

"You pay everything but water and garbage, and if we go on rationing like three summers ago, I bill you for the surcharge. It's covered in the lease."

I crossed to a pair of sliding doors and stepped onto a small patio enclosed by a wooden fence. I looked right and left and up. "It could get pretty noisy if I need ventilation and there's a party going on up there. I don't like to be picky, but I've had some bad experiences with inconsiderate people. She's not a musician, is she?"

Mrs. Hapwood had turned from gray to pink. "Greta Hammond is as considerate as the day is long. But she's human, like the rest of us. She's not a musician but she hums a tune now and then. You don't like living with human beans, find yourself a mobile home and haul it to Nevada."

It was time to back and fill. "I don't mean to be critical, Mrs. Hapwood. I like the apartment a lot—it's got great potential, as I'm sure everyone tells you. But it would make it easier if I knew more about Ms. Hammond. Just to reassure myself, you understand. Peace of mind is important in decisions like this, especially if you require a lease."

She cocked her head suspiciously. "What do you want to know?"

"Just about her . . . lifestyle."

Mrs. Hapwood refused to bend, and I admired her stalwart defense of her tenant even though it wasn't helpful. I don't run into that sort of courage very often; most people will snitch just to have someone to talk to.

"I'm not a busybody, mister," she announced. "She pays the rent; she brings me a plate of cookies along with the check; she comes and goes and no one complains about her, not even one time. That's all *I* need to know. If it's not enough for you, you know the way out."

"Is she friends with anyone in the building? Maybe it would help if I could talk to them."

"Only one I ever see her with is the woman across the way."

"What woman is that?"

"Heard Greta call her Linda. Lives in the ugly green duplex, don't know which unit. Has a child, it looks like—little girl. Don't know if she has a husband; not many seem to these days."

I walked to the door and Mrs. Hapwood took one last look around the apartment. By the time she was finished, she seemed to be considering another remodel. "You want it or not?"

"I'll need to think it over, but I'm going to try to decide by the end of the day. Will you be in this evening?"

"I'm in 'less I'm out. Number's on the sign out front—if you call before you come, you can save yourself a trip if I'm down at the Wishing Well. That's a tavern, if you don't know the area. But I always answer the phone when I'm here—I'm not like those people who let their machines do the socializing."

As I walked to the door and thanked her for her time, she put her hand on my arm. "You could do worse than get to know a woman like Greta Hammond, if you don't mind my saying so. She's younger, of course, but people with kids shouldn't live alone. Me, I was an only child. Never learned to share or take turns. Always felt it held me back."

She closed the door and left me in the piney hallway. From first to last, the gold cat hadn't moved a muscle.

SEVEN

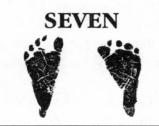

I took a stroll around the block, in case Mrs. Hapwood was keeping tabs on me, then crossed the street and rang both bells in the pea green duplex. No one responded to either ring—you can't find anyone at home in the daytime anymore—but it was probably just as well, since I wasn't sure what I would say to the woman, anyway. Tell me, Linda, is your neighbor a child molester? Dope fiend? Bunko artist? Psychopath? Or is she instead a veritable saint with a hospitable womb who would make a matchless mother?

I looked at my watch. It wasn't even noon; I had the rest of the day to kill before I could do anything even marginally productive in the Colbert case. I could have gone back to the office, I suppose, but the office was a long way off and I'd been spending too much time there, anyway—the place had started to depress me, harking back to a problematic past rather than pointing toward a fulfilling future. So I crossed the office off the list, then drove to the core of Golden Gate Park, stowed my car under an ailing eucalyptus, and purchased a pass to the California Academy of Sciences, home of the planetarium, the aquarium, and the museum of natural history. Apparently my search for a starter home for an embryonic *Homo sapiens* had piqued my interest in other forms of life as well.

As I made my way into the dark recesses of the aquarium and the museum, I fell more and more under the spell of the natural world and reverted to that magical state of youth that features a trait that deserts us all too quickly—the capacity for awe and fascination. The marvels that were seahorses and sharks and sea anemones soon whisked me off to a world far different from the one in which I made my living, a world of natural balance and functional elegance, a world of infinite variety and essential interdependence, a world in which man was ever and always insignificant. The only thing that world and mine had in common was that man was too often an enemy, even as he built monuments such as this one.

With increasing fascination, I was absorbed by the yin and yang of exhibited existence, from the giddy dolphins to the grumpy gar, from the glorious wildebeest to the skulking jackal, and a host of other creatures posed behind windows sporting far too many "Endangered" stickers.

There's a new hypothesis afloat these days, a concept called biophilia, that says that millions of years of evolution have left human beings with a genetically based need to affiliate with the rest of the living world. It's why we like rooms with a view, and go to zoos, and fawn over pets and flower gardens, and pull to the side of the road to watch deer scamper off to the forest. The natural world may in fact be a precious source of sanity, the theory suggests. I didn't know if my tour of the academy was fulfilling a genetic need, but I did know that halfway through my journey I became aware that I was grinning like one of the hyenas that was roaming a barren diorama behind a sheet of safety glass.

I sobered up and continued my tour. Much as I enjoyed the lower evolutionary orders, the children who swirled about me for a better look at the rattlesnakes and pythons, and pitched pennies onto the backs of crocodiles to prove they were alive, were an even more potent source of vigor. Youth breeds youth, Betty Fontaine liked to tell me when explaining her devotion to her work, and sharing space with so many vital minds and bodies made me feel at one with the universe of man and nature, as if I was some small part of their joint and several destinies. By the time I was sipping some Darjeeling within the cool tranquility of the Japanese Tea Garden, it was three in the afternoon and I felt better than I had in months.

I still had time to kill before I could make a final pass at Greta, so after I'd finished my tea and my almond cookie, I drove up to the medical center, a perpetually expanding empire that was engulfing its immediate environment inexorably, despite the protests of longtime residents—when it comes to health, we happily waive the rules. I stowed my car in the garage and spent enough time in the library to review articles on surrogate motherhood and alternative reproduction in both popular and professional journals, getting up to speed.

Nothing I learned was particularly surprising. It was estimated that in the past decade more than four hundred births in California, and over ten times that nationwide, had resulted from surrogate arrangements, but only six of the California births had resulted in legal wrangles, a surprisingly small number. It was also estimated that the medical risks involved—the risk to the surrogate's health during pregnancy, and the risk that the artificial insemination of sperm, or *in vitro* fertilization of the ovum, or the implantation of a previously frozen embryo, might be harmful to the resulting fetus—were only infinitesimally larger than the risks from normal conception. Which was as reassuring to me as I'm sure it had been to the Colberts.

It was also clear from my reading that the way the Colberts were proceeding—keeping their participation anonymous through the entire term of the pregnancy and the date of surrender of the child—was not the recommended approach. Nor was it the norm that the surrogate be unmarried. And the princely sum they were paying Greta Hammond was far in excess of the usual remuneration for such services, which was ten thousand dollars. There was probably a reason for all this; luckily, I didn't have to find out what it was.

By the time I'd finished my research, much of the staff was leaving for the evening. I lingered near the elevator that took people down to Irving Street, hoping to see Greta Hammond in the company of a friend or cohort I could tap for information, but my hopes went unfulfilled—I'd forgotten she planned to visit Marie from the restaurant. After half an hour of doing little more than killing time, I joined the parade of vehicles inching their way down the western slope of the hill, and ten minutes later I was back on Kirkham Street doing what I do most, which is waiting.

She came down the street at a little after six, carrying another bag of groceries, exactly as chipper as she had been that morning. I gave her half an hour, then rang her bell.

"Yes?" The voice that emerged from the intercom seemed excessively alert.

"My name is Tanner, Ms. Hammond. We met at Leo's café this morning. I was looking for an apartment and you were nice enough to mention that there was a place in your building for rent."

She hesitated, then spoke with measured graciousness. "I remember. Have you rented it?"

"No, but I talked to Ms. Hapwood, and looked at some other places in the area, but before making a decision I need to know more about the school situation. I was hoping you'd be willing to answer some questions. It will only take ten minutes," I added when she didn't say anything encouraging. "I'd be happy to talk in the lobby, or meet you at the café. Or wherever."

"I'm fixing dinner." She paused, then sighed, then relented. "You might as well come up. Number seven, second floor rear."

She buzzed me through the entrance, and opened the door to her apartment after my second knock. The look on her face was far more wary than the untroubled countenance she'd worn at breakfast, but even so, there was an expectant look about her, as though life had given her more good than bad over the years, even in the form of serendipity.

I bowed and smiled and gave her a flyer that had been stuck in her box—I think it promoted Prell. She was out of her work uniform and into a pair of faded Levi's and a snug yellow T-shirt. Her feet were bare, her eyes were greener than I remembered, and her shaggy mop of brown hair seemed more lustrous and uninhibited. If she was drained by her day with the sick and dying, there weren't any signs of it.

I wrinkled my nose and she caught me at it.

"Sauerkraut," she said with a grin. "Sorry. I fix a batch every six months or so. I'm not that crazy about it, frankly; I think I only eat it to make everything else seem better." She regarded me closely, and took a step back. "I have to check the stove. Sorry I can't ask you to stay, but there isn't enough to go round. I'm careful not to leave leftovers."

"No problem," I said quickly. "I shouldn't have come at dinnertime. I shouldn't have come at all without calling beforehand, but I was walking down the street and there wasn't a telephone in sight and my quarters were all gone anyway, so . . ." I shrugged. "I'm not big on sauerkraut, either," I added, just to be back on track with the truth.

Greta gestured at the couch, told me to have a seat, then went off to the kitchen. When she got there, she banged some pans and opened some doors and gave me a chance to take inventory.

The house was tidy but not antiseptic, cozy and lived in and comfortable. The furnishings were simple and cheap and derivative—fake Eames chair, spindly Scandinavian couch, scarred Mediterranean table, and genuine Levitz dinette. Three throw rugs diluted the relentless beige of the carpet and some Degas reproductions enlivened the off-white igloo formed by the featureless walls. There were lots of books lying around, mostly historical novels from the library, and some tapes of what looked to be primarily vintage rock and roll. I was glad to see someone besides me was holding out against the CD and living like a grad student.

Along one wall was an old oak table that served as a desk. When I heard more noises coming from the kitchen, I decided to snoop. The first drawer held bank statements, utility bills, and shopping receipts scattered among rubber bands and paper clips and broken ballpoint pens. I wrote as many account numbers in my notebook as I could, along with a phone number in San Bruno that was her only extra charge.

Near the back of the other drawer was a small stack of photographs, old and faded, bound with a rubber band that was close to wearing out. The top photo was a yellowing snapshot of two couples who looked to be in their forties, handsome, dapper, and carefree, wearing the wide lapels, elaborate neckties, and short thin skirts that dated the shot from the sixties. I thought one of the men looked familiar; the rest of them were strangers. The man and woman on the ends were gazing fondly at each other; the other couple looked straight ahead with impatience.

I extracted the snapshot and turned it over. The note on the back was scrawled in pencil, faded nearly to oblivion: "Just something I'd like you to have. Love, Dad." I looked at the photo a second time. One couple who loved each other and one that didn't any longer was my guess, and my next guess was that it wasn't relevant to what I was doing.

I was about to make a quick trip through the rest of the photos when I sensed silence in the kitchen. I eased the desk drawer closed as quietly as I could, but I was too slow and she caught me at it.

She was insulted and let me know it, with crossed arms and a withering look. But for some reason she gave me time to invent an explanation.

"Sorry," I said sheepishly. "I didn't mean to pry. I was just wondering where you bank."

Her words were as cool as custard. "Why would you want to know that?"

"I figured I'd bank there, too, if I end up in the neighborhood. You look like a person who would know the best place to do things like that. Rates and fees and all that."

I thought she bought it but I wasn't sure. She wasn't sure, either.

"I've got five minutes before I have to dish up the kraut," she informed me brusquely, far more guarded than before. "What is it you want to know?"

I resumed my role as parent and nomad; like most performances, it got easier each time.

"I spent the day walking around the area, and I like the neighborhood a lot. I don't know if I'll take the unit below—Ms. Hapwood didn't seem too happy when I told her I couldn't go more than six hundred—but there's a place over on Judah that . . . anyway, what I was wondering was where the grade schools are. And how they stack up, academically. And also whether there are any evening and weekend activities for children nearby, like a YMCA or something. Kids have so many temptations these days, I want to make sure Jason keeps active."

Greta nodded to show that she shared my concern, then compressed her lips as she drafted an answer. "Let's see. The nearest grade school is Jefferson, on Irving and Seventeenth. It's okay, but my friend Linda sends her Ingrid to Argonne. It's on Seventeenth as well, but on the north side of the park."

"Why does she go clear over there?"

"Argonne's what they call an alternative school. It's more . . . progressive, I suppose you would say—better mix of kids, wider variety of programs, greater opportunity for parent participation and special help. Plus Linda's gotten to know some of the teachers; they look out for Ingrid on the playground. Linda says these days you want all the help you can get. How old is your boy?"

"Ten. I suppose he should go to Argonne, too."

"You'll probably have to pull strings. School assignments are very political in the city these days—it's a full-time job trying to get your child in the right one."

I shook my head in wonderment. "In Redding you just find the nearest school and go to it. I hope I don't make a mistake that will set Jason back."

"You'll do fine."

"I hope so. But he's getting hard to handle."

"I imagine ten is a difficult age."

I shrugged helplessly. "Seems to me *every* age is a difficult age."

Greta's look turned gloomy. "I wouldn't know."

I waited for the explanation she seemed on the verge of making, but when it didn't come, I made our encounter more personal. "Enough about kids; how about grown-ups? Are there places to go and things to do close by? Or is that kind of action downtown?"

I'd struck a wrong note—Greta Hammond frosted fast. "It depends on what you mean by action, I imagine."

I tried to look suitably shamed. "Places to meet people, I guess."

She shrugged noncommittally. "If by people you mean women, I'm not sure what to tell you. There's Yancy's down on Irving. It's just a neighborhood bar, but it's relaxed and friendly. Sometimes you see people there. The Little Shamrock on Lincoln is nice, too."

"Do you go there yourself? Sorry," I said when her eyes hardened warily. "I didn't mean to get personal."

In spite of my impudence, she couldn't suppress her friendliness. "I do stop by Yancy's once in a while, as a matter of fact. Usually with a girlfriend after a movie. Sometimes it's fun and sometimes it's boring. And sometimes it's disgusting."

"When guys hit on you, you mean?"

She nodded but didn't elaborate.

I waited till she met my eye, then looked away bashfully. "Are you divorced?" I asked timidly.

Her nostrils flared as she searched my face for implication, so I became the innocent abroad. "I don't mean to pry. I just . . . Jason and I don't seem to be back to normal, yet. Either of us. I was wondering how long it takes."

She blinked to clear her eyes. "Years."

"My wife just up and left. Every time the phone rings I think it's going to be her, saying she wants to come back. I can't get *used* to the situation."

Her voice lowered to a comforting hum. "I know what you mean. It's difficult and it's lonely and it stays that way a long time."

"But it gets better eventually?"

"Better, yes. Perfect, no."

"Are you and your husband still friends? I think it would help if Marie and I could be friendly. If I knew why she did what she did."

Her face darkened and her lips paled. "I have no interest in a friendship with my ex-husband." It was as definite as Newton's law.

I shook my head. "I don't seem to be able to put my troubles behind me. How did you manage?"

"I ran away from them," she said without thinking.

She looked at me until I squirmed, clearly intent on seeing if I was not what I seemed but rather a mercenary from the past who had been put on her trail to reclaim her. Much as I wanted to probe the issue, I didn't think I could do it without scaring her off. Since I didn't know what to do, I didn't do anything.

The talk of her troubles had scratched old wounds and she didn't like the sensation. "I have to serve dinner now," she announced firmly, the light out of her eyes and the warmth out of her voice. "I'm afraid you'll have to go."

I hung my head and looked contrite. "I'm sorry I imposed. I appreciate the time."

"You're welcome. I hope you find a nice place."

"Thanks." I shifted from foot to foot to highlight my embarrassment. "This is awful, I know, but would you mind if I used your bathroom? I've had so much coffee, I'm floating—seems like the only place I could find to sit down was a coffee shop, and I hate to loiter without ordering anything."

"I've had days like that," she said, and pointed. "First door on the right down the hall."

I followed her directions, then closed the door behind me. After a suitable moment for nature's call, I turned on the water in the basin and began a hasty search of the drawers and cabinets.

It was a small room, and I looked everywhere there was to look, but all I learned was that her soap was Dove and shampoo was Breck and toothpaste was Crest and deodorant was Sure. She flossed, she gargled, she enameled her nails; she curled her hair and painted her lips; she put something on her flesh called Rainbath Moisturizing Body Mist and something else called an Apricot Facial Scrub. Her only drugs of choice were Excedrin PM, Anacin III, and Actifed—nothing that required a prescription.

When I'd finished with the bathroom I peeked in the kitchen. "Good night, Ms. Hammond. And thanks again." Then I hemmed and hawed. "I'll probably hang around that Yancy place till around eight or so, if you want to join me for a drink after dinner. I certainly owe you one, for all the help you gave me."

"Thanks, but I don't think so," she said quickly, then met my eye for a moment longer than was necessary. "Maybe another time."

"I'll be there till eight all the same, in case you change your mind." I waved and took my leave, the sharp sting of sauerkraut finally erasing the lingering stench of the day before.

I stayed at Yancy's till nine, but Greta Hammond never showed up. For some reason, I thought she might, and for another reason, I hoped she would. There was something about her that stirred me, one of those subtle pinpricks that, without your knowing it until after the established fact, swells and heats and itches until it feels a lot like love.

EIGHT

I spent the next morning thinking about Greta Hammond and deciding whether I should give her my seal of approval, or whether there was a reason to do other than tell the truth as I saw it. I've come across such reasons more often than you might imagine over the years, but this didn't seem to be one of those times. When I'd reached a decision, I made an appointment to see Russell Jorgensen.

By the time he could fit me in it was after six o'clock. The sun was splashing Hopperesque shadows across the pockmarked face of the city and the winds were frothing the bay like the makings of a thick meringue. As I walked into his office, Russell was gazing at the water and its environs as though he wouldn't be happy till he owned it all.

"I never get tired of this view," he said as I sat down. "When I do, it'll be time to give up the law and get into something else."

"Like what?"

He shrugged. "Sail my boat to La Paz or Acapulco, maybe. You do much sailing, Marsh?"

"None, as a matter of fact."

"Seems to me I've asked you to go out with me a time or two."

I nodded, although the correct number was more like a dozen.

Russell was trying to remember a time when we'd shared a festive outing, but he couldn't because there wasn't one. "I guess something always came up," he murmured.

The something was that Russell never expended the effort to make the invitation anything other than rote. He was one of those men, a surprising number of them successful, who project social or political undertakings without the slightest intention of consummation. It's frustrating, until you've been around them often enough to peg them for what they are and to learn that where you fit in their pantheon is somewhere near the bottom.

"Sailing's a nice combination of tranquility and terror," Russell was saying. "Gives the old motor a pretty good tune-up, over time."

"Tune-ups like that are too pricey for me," I said. "Luckily, I can get the same mix by walking around my block."

Russell laughed. "We really are going backward, aren't we? Every-day life is becoming as perilous as it was in the Middle Ages." He sighed and sat down at his desk. "Sometimes I'm glad I'm sixty-two."

"Sounds like you had a bad day."

He nodded. "That's what litigators get paid for, isn't it? To have bad days on behalf of their clients?"

"Is it anything you want to talk about?"

He shook his head. "Another Colbert problem, as it happens. Not Stuart. Cynthia."

"Isn't she sick or something?"

"She's not sick; she pigheaded. She doesn't have an objective bone in her body, which makes it hard to reason with her. That, plus the fact that she has a mind like a steel trap."

"You look like her trap just snapped shut on your foot."

"Let's just say we had a rather heated disagreement about ethics and morality."

"Yours or hers?"

"Both."

"It looks like you lost the debate."

He shrugged. "With Cynthia, that's the only option if you want to stay on good terms. So what's the verdict on the surrogate, Marsh?" he segued suddenly. "Thumbs up or thumbs down?"

I took a deep breath and said the words precisely as I'd rehearsed them an hour earlier. "The verdict is, I don't know of any reason why Greta Hammond wouldn't make an adequate surrogate mother for the Colberts."

Russell frowned. "That's a strange way to put it, isn't it? You don't sound confident of your conclusion."

"I can't be confident, Russell. No one can be confident in this situation."

"But you have to admit that's something less than a ringing endorsement."

"There are a couple of things that bother me," I admitted per my script.

Russell stopped twirling his pencil. "Like what?"

"For one thing, she's supposed to have been married, and divorced, and to have had a child, but I couldn't find evidence of any of those things."

"What kind of evidence did you expect?"

"Some data in vital statistics, for one thing. Plus there wasn't a single picture of a youngster anywhere in her apartment."

He blinked. "You got in to see her?"

I nodded. "Briefly."

"Was that wise? I don't think you were supposed to do that."

"I couldn't see any other way to get a feel for the woman, Russell."

"How did you manage to meet her?"

"I lied a little."

"That's dangerous, isn't it? What if you get caught?"

I met his look. "I'm a detective. I lie better than I tell the truth."

He looked at me as though I'd grown a horn. "You didn't *tell* her you were a detective, I hope. Sorry," he added when he saw the expression on my face.

Russell took some time to think about it. "Hell, Marsh; she probably got married in Reno and divorced down in Vegas. She could have had the child almost anywhere."

"I couldn't find a single record of anything about her that was older than a credit problem about four years back."

Russell groaned as if his worst fears were about to be realized. "What are you saying?"

"I'm not saying anything. I'm just telling you what I found and didn't find. One more thing I found was that she told me her child was dead."

"What?"

"You heard me. Based on my reading, I don't think many experts would tell you that a woman whose only child was deceased was a good surrogate prospect. Psychologically speaking."

He thought about what I'd told him. "Are you suggesting I do something?"

"Not necessarily."

"Then what?"

"Actually, she seems like a nice woman. I guess my problem has less to do with her and more to do with the concept. I feel like I've been hired to play God and I'm not qualified for the job."

"You're not playing God. The guys with the suction tubes and the petri dish are playing God. You're just playing Casting Director. Give me a rundown of everything you did," he went on guardedly. "So I can pass it on to Stuart. *He's* the one who has to decide this thing."

For some reason, I found myself editing rather extensively as I abstracted my work, so it didn't take long to run through it. "Based on all that," I said when I'd finished my summary, "what I can say is that I found no obvious problem in signing her up as a surrogate, other than the thing with her kid. She's a nice woman; she's popular in the neighborhood; and she seems to like children—she's pretty involved in the life of a little girl who lives nearby, for example. She's got a decent job but could use some extra money. And she seems happy with her life. What else do you need to know?"

"Does she drink, smoke, take drugs?"

"None of the above."

"Does she sleep around?"

I smiled. "I was going to try to get her to sleep with me but she wouldn't even meet me for a drink."

Luckily, he didn't think I was serious. "Is there a boyfriend?"

"Not currently."

"What about the ex-husband?"

"Out of her life, so she says."

It went on like that for twenty minutes more, with Russell tossing the questions and me lobbing back mostly neutral or uninformed replies. As time passed, I felt less and less comfortable with what I was doing, not on my own behalf, but on Greta Hammond's; I felt like a Peeping Tom.

"So I guess the bottom line is positive," Russell announced when he'd run out of questions.

"Let's say it's not negative," I corrected. "For positive, you should talk to a shrink."

Russell shrugged. "The Colberts can make that decision. I'll phone them and tell them as far as I'm concerned they can go ahead with the procedure. Last I heard, the implant is scheduled for Monday." He looked to see if I concurred.

I shrugged. "Whatever."

Russell wrinkled his nose and scowled. For some reason, it made me mad. "You look like you're upset that I'm not taking a paternal interest in this thing. But it's not *my* kid that will come out of this deal, or Greta Hammond's, either. You want concern, talk to a Colbert."

Russell sighed. "Sorry, Marsh. I guess I'm still nervous about this whole business. I mean, I've never done anything like this before—it's like giving the Colberts a chemistry set with a formula for making a human being. I'm not comfortable with the responsibility."

"Me, either," I said truthfully.

"But we're only agents, right? The Colberts are the ones making the decision."

"Absolutely," I said, and grinned at his embrace of my own rationale.

Russell swore at the imprecision of existence, then shook his head and returned to the window to gaze. "You have kids, Marsh?"

"No."

"Want them?"

"Sometimes, and sometimes I think it would be a criminal offense if I brought a duplicate of me into the world. Littering, at the very least. How about you?"

"Two. Boy and girl."

"And?"

"The boy is fine. Well, not fine, but okay. In school at Santa Cruz. Plays in a band called Spit. Noise like you wouldn't believe; lyrics make him sound suicidal. But we talk on the phone. And he comes home for Christmas. And cashes my checks. Which on the whole is better than a lot of families I know."

"And the girl?"

Russell blinked and looked out the window for so long I thought he'd forgotten my question. "She's crazy."

"Literally?"

He nodded. "Bi-polar. Manic-depressive. Lives in L.A., wants to be an actress on the days she doesn't want to be a truck driver. Refuses to speak to me for months, then speaks to me for hours on end without letting me get a word in edgewise. Her latest gambit is to tell people I abused her as a child so horribly that I made her sexually dysfunctional."

"I'm sorry," I said.

He blinked and shook his head. "Yes, well, that's my problem, not yours. Or the Colberts', either. I'm sure this Hammond woman will do the surrogate job just fine."

He wanted me to concur but I didn't. "How good a job will the Colberts do when Greta delivers their baby?"

Russell laughed, but the light in his eyes was cold blue. "That's not my job, either, thank God." He returned to the desk and sat down. "There's one more thing you have to do."

"What's that?"

"These surrogate contracts. Since there's no legislation that validates them in California, it's not clear how good they are—what aspects will and won't be specifically enforced, what remedies are available in case of a breach, that kind of thing."

"Which means?"

"Which means we want to make damned sure this thing stays out of court. And the only way to do that is make sure Ms. Hammond performs according to the contract."

"And the Colberts too, of course."

He ignored my bow to equilibrium. "I wrote in as much *in terrorem* language in the agreement as I could—that a failure to perform by Ms. Hammond would constitute the intentional infliction of emotional distress, that liquidated damages of twice the amount of the surrogate fee would be appropriate, that time was of the essence in the situation so the Colberts can pursue all expedited remedies in the event of a breach to ensure that their rights are protected."

"Sounds like you touched all the bases."

"Maybe. But you can be even more helpful."

"How?"

"Once the embryo has been implanted, and the fetus begins to develop, I want you to see the Hammond woman again. And this time throw the fear of God into her. Make sure she knows that if she departs from the contract in any way, or tries to contact the contracting parents during the pregnancy or at any time after the child has been born and she's given it up, her life will become a living hell. She will be sued for damages and more than that, she'll be hounded to the ends of the earth. Her background will be checked for every transgression more serious than a hangnail. Her boss will be told she's a welsher and the neighbors will be told she's a slut. Throw whatever else you can think of in there—I want this woman to be afraid to *breathe* unless it's covered in the contract."

I was shaking my head before he had halfway finished his spiel. "This is a mother we're talking about, right, Russell?"

"Right."

"Just wanted to make sure. For a moment it sounded as if you were talking about a terrorist." I stood up and walked to the door. "I won't do your dirty work for you, pal. You're going to have to have *that* bad day all by your lonesome."

NINE

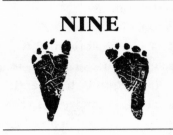

The next time I heard from Russell Jorgensen, six weeks had passed and he was talking to me over the phone. "Greetings, Marsh," he began cheerfully.

"Russell."

"How's it going?"

"Average or below. You?"

"Not that bad." He waited for me to say something, presumably about the Colberts, but I didn't. I still had a sense of foreboding about the case, a need to keep my distance, as if an inner sense was telling me that the surrogate arrangement constituted some sort of risk to me personally.

"Well, they went ahead with the implant," he said when I'd stayed silent too long.

"Good for them."

"It took the first time—rather unusual."

"Great."

"The Colberts are thrilled. They can hardly sit still when they talk about it."

"I'm happy for them."

"Good. Because there's one other thing they want you to do."

"If it's more of the *in terrorem* stuff, my answer is the same as last time."

"Nothing like that," Russell assured me quickly. "I apologize for even raising the subject—I was out of line."

"Yes, you were."

Russell seemed genuinely contrite. "This isn't like that at all, Marsh—they just want you to give them an update. You know, go back and check the Hammond woman out again, make sure things are still what they looked like two months ago."

"That's it?"

"That's it. No tough stuff, no nothing. You don't even have to speak to her, if you don't want to. Use your best judgment; just keep in mind the confidentiality requirement—she can't know the Colberts are the contracting parties."

I thought it over. Despite my disinclination to revisit the issue, I found my professional reluctance overridden by my personal desire to see Greta Hammond again.

"Okay," I said. "I'll check her out. I should have something for you next week."

"That's great, Marsh. And that should take care of it. Seven months from now, the Colberts will have a bouncing baby boy."

"I take it Stuart didn't think Mrs. Hammond's deceased child was a problem. Or the other things I mentioned."

"I guess not. He told me to go ahead, so I called Ms. Hammond in to execute the documents and the medical people went ahead with the implant."

"Well, I hope it works out for all concerned."

"I'm sure it will," he said. "Why wouldn't it?" The question was more precatory than rhetorical.

"No reason at all," I assured him.

And that was it. For yet another time, Russell invited me to go out on his boat with him and again I said I'd like to. We parted the way we always did, vowing to spend more time together.

That same evening, at precisely eight o'clock, I rang Greta Hammond's bell.

"It's Marsh Tanner," I said to the crackling intercom. "Remember me? I was looking for an apartment several weeks back. I've got a boy named Jason; you were kind enough to tell me about the school situation in this area."

"I remember," her voice said coolly. "Did you find a place?"

"No. That is, the job I thought I had lined up fell through at the last minute, so I had to go back to Redding till I got a line on something else. But I lucked out—started work last week. The job's down near the Hall of Justice, so Jason and I are living on Potrero Hill."

"It's nice down there—best weather in the city."

"That's what they say, although I was looking forward to living in your area, actually. Anyway, I was out this way on business, and I was wondering if you'd let me buy you that drink. I apologize for not calling first, but I didn't know how long my meeting would be and, well, I'm sort of phone phobic for some reason. Anyway, here I am, if you're interested."

She waited so long to respond, I was sure she was going to refuse me. But instead, she said, "I can be at Yancy's in twenty minutes. Why don't you get us a table and I'll meet you there?"

The words were agreeable but her tone was far from it—reserved, almost calculating. Still, given the circumstance, it was a better opportunity than I expected.

A part of me didn't think she'd show up, and I wasn't sure what I was going to do if she did, but it was better than pawing through her garbage. Despite my doubts, at twenty minutes after eight Greta Hammond walked into Yancy's Saloon, squinted into the gloom to make sense of the shapes scattered throughout the bar-dark that engulfed her, then waved and walked awkwardly to my table, embarrassed that far more eyes than mine were on her.

She was wearing Levi's and sandals and a sleeveless white blouse that dipped low toward her breasts and billowed saucily around her torso. Her smile was tentative but stalwart. She looked both sexier than before and more troubled. I wondered if she'd learned what I was up to, and had come to the bar to scold me, but it was more likely that she was simply plagued by her pregnancy.

I stood up. "Hi."

"Hi."

"Have a seat."

"Thanks."

She eased into the chair across from mine and arranged herself primly, placing her purse on the chair at her side and clasping her hands on the table in front of her, as though she were awaiting communion. "I can only stay a minute," she began, looking everywhere but at me. "I've got some clothes that have to be mended. But it occurred to me that I hadn't been out of the house in the evening in ages, so . . . " Her shrug established an itinerant attitude. "Here I am."

"I'm glad. What would you like to drink?"

"Sprite would be fine."

"I can spring for something more complicated—the bartender looks pretty clever."

Antennae fully extended, she sensed she was being shoved. "Sprite will be clever enough."

I gave myself a mental kick, then gestured for the waitress and ordered a soft drink for Greta and started to order a Dewar's for me, then thought better of it and settled for a beer. Hard liquor is suspect in certain circles these days, and I didn't want to foster misconceptions.

After the waitress went off to do our bidding, Greta looked at me and smiled, though not overwhelmingly. For the first time since I'd laid eyes on her, she seemed as down in the dumps as I often get. I decided she was having second thoughts about the surrogate thing, and maybe even third ones.

"Did you find a nice apartment on Potrero Hill?" she asked, without an ounce of interest in the answer.

"It's adequate. It's only five and a half, so the extra money will help. It's got lots of windows; fir floors; dishwasher."

"How's the new job working out?"

"Okay, so far."

"What type of work are you doing?"

"I'm inventory manager in a warehouse. Wholesale hardware. Not much of a job, but it pays decent money."

"Well, good luck with it."

"Thanks. I'm hoping to find something better, but these days you never know."

"That's for sure. These days you never know about anything." She unclasped her hands and toyed with her hair, as if uncertain of the image she wanted to project. The sag in her cheeks and the slump in her shoulders were so pronounced they made her a different woman from the one who had strolled down the block so jauntily two months ago. I wondered if something had happened to her in the interim, besides being implanted with the makings of another couple's child. I hoped it was only an early start on morning sickness.

The waitress returned with the drinks and we gave each other a silent toast, then sank into that slippery pit where small talk inevitably drops you. "Tell me about yourself," I began inanely.

She shrugged wearily. "There's not much to tell."

"What do you do for fun? Are you a runner? Biker? Rock climber? Fisherwoman?"

She smiled. "None of the above, although I do have a set of Supremes albums I dance to rather energetically."

I took a deeper plunge. "Do you have a significant other?"

She shook her head. "I did a while back, but we broke up. It's difficult to keep a relationship going at this stage in life, I've found, what with work, and hustling to save money every chance I get. Poverty is so exhausting—whenever he came by I was too tired to do anything fun."

"Maybe that had more to do with him than with you."

"He brought me down, you mean?" She shrugged. "It's possible. He *was* rather dour. I think it had to do with the way he was raised—his parents thought he was perfect and as a consequence they gave him the idea that nothing or no one was good enough for their pride and joy. For some reason, he began to believe it."

"Sounds like a no-win situation for the woman in his life."

She cocked her head in deference to my insight. "That's exactly what it was. I finally realized I had to get out of the situation."

"How did he take it?"

"The way men always take it—he made it seem like it was his decision."

I laughed. "So how about now? I mean, you must meet a lot of men at work."

"How do you know where I work?"

I scrambled to cover my gaffe and resolved to proceed with more caution. "After you left the restaurant that first day, I asked Leo about you. He told me you worked at the hospital."

Her brow furled. "What *else* did he tell you?"

"Not much. Leo likes you too much to gossip."

"Good. Though there's nothing to gossip about." She wrinkled her lips. "Unfortunately."

"There's *always* something to gossip about," I said. "Even having nothing to gossip about is something to gossip about."

She laughed but it was contrary to her brittle mood. "I see what you mean. And yes. I meet quite a few men in my work, but only superficially. And in my section, most of them are gay as it happens. How about you?" Her look turned impish. "Have you fallen in love since I saw you last?"

I shook my head and looked forlorn. "It's hard to meet people if you don't have a context—job, church, social club, whatever. If you don't have a context, you tend to end up looking for company in places like this."

Greta glanced around the bar with what looked like affection. "Not that this is so awful."

"It's not the place, it's the process. It's pretty ignoble to be out on the prowl."

She looked at me soberly. "You know what I think?"

"What?"

"I think you're still in love with your wife. I think until you work through that, no woman is going to look good to you no matter *what* she's like."

"You could be right," I admitted, and gave myself an invisible Oscar for my role as a jilted husband. "I take it that's not a problem in your case."

"Loving my husband? I told you, Luke and I went our separate ways twenty years ago. It was a marriage of convenience, anyway. We never would have been married in the first place if I hadn't needed . . ."

"What?"

"Never mind." Her look turned misty and wistful. "I just have to accept the fact that nothing in my life is going to work out and that they're going to keep after me until they do to me what they did to my father."

"Whoa," I said quickly. "You sound like you're mixed up in some sort of international conspiracy." We were close to something new, a corner of her life that had been hidden from me, but it had been a mistake to follow up. She came out of her nostalgic trance and looked at me with equanimity. "Don't mind me; I'm just prattling."

"It sounded sort of ominous."

"Well, it isn't. I get melodramatic when I reminisce; always have. Too much time watching the soaps in my youth."

I had a feeling she was lying and that sinister was exactly the word for whatever she had been thinking of. But I also had a feeling that Greta Hammond was the victim, not the victimizer, in the remembered drama that was spinning inside her head, and so it was not necessarily relevant to the judgment I had to make. Still, I began to wonder if I could possibly be an unwitting arm of the forces she was convinced were pursuing her.

I watched her face assume new contours as she gazed into whatever shaded realm her thoughts had taken her. "What are you thinking?" I asked after a minute.

"Nothing."

"Come on."

"It's not important."

"It is to you."

She smiled wearily. "Even if I told you my tale of woe, why would you believe it?"

"Why shouldn't I?"

"Because in my experience, women almost never tell men what they're really thinking."

"Why not?"

"They're afraid the men will get angry. And maybe hurt them. You'd be surprised how many decisions women make that are governed by the likelihood of violence their choice will provoke—what they say, what they wear, where they go, who they talk to. It's an enormous burden and most men aren't even aware of it."

"You're probably right," I said. "On the other hand, not *all* men are afraid of the truth. Not *all* men are an inch away from mayhem."

She looked at me for a long moment. "Why do you think I'm here?"

And just that quickly there was something new between us, a primitive, needful thing whose steamy vapors were rising as thickly off her as off me.

I bowed my head in mock appreciation. "Thanks for the compliment."

She touched my forearm. "You're welcome. Now let's change the subject."

I was happy to oblige, but less happy to return to the job I'd been hired for. "Do you ever do anything wild and crazy?" I asked with an appropriate leer.

I'd misread her again, and she frowned uneasily. "Like what?"

"Oh, opium dens, bowling alleys, pool halls, roller rinks."

She sniffed. "None of the above, not even remotely. Although it would be handy to have *some* sort of antidote once in a while."

"For the down times, you mean?"

She nodded.

"So what are they for you? The tough times."

She blinked at the switch in theme. "Let's see. I get so lonely on Saturday nights I could scream. Or cry, which is the more usual reaction. Then there's the little terrors that pop up now and then when you're walking down a dark street or waiting for the bus, those little brushes with psychopathy that make city life so charming. I have the most awful nightmares, sometimes."

"Me, too," I said truthfully.

"I wouldn't think Redding would furnish quite as much fuel for them as San Francisco."

"You'd be surprised," I said. So would I, I imagine—I haven't been in Redding in years.

"But I suppose my biggest fear is that I have less than a thousand dollars in the bank, which means if I get fired, I'm a month away from a homeless shelter." She paused and looked at the 49er pennant hanging above my head. "I thought that particular situation was about to improve, but now I'm not so sure."

I perked up. "New job?"

She shook her head. "Just a special project I'm involved with."

"What kind of project? Not that it's any of my business."

"If I talk about it, I'll jinx it. But if it works out, it will help my finances immensely." She made it sound more like a curse than a blessing.

"Well, good luck. I hope it comes through for you."

"Thanks," she said with sudden bitterness. "I just need to figure a way to *make* it happen. Right?"

"Right."

"A deal's a deal."

"Absolutely."

"At this age, you do what you have to do."

This time I passed on my turn. After a long look inward, Greta Hammond forced herself to brighten. "Anyway, I hope you find a better job, too, if that's what you want. Who knows, maybe we'll both end up rich."

She looked at the clock above the bar. "I have to be going." She retrieved her purse and stood up.

"I'll walk you back," I said.

"It's not necessary."

"Well, I'm glad you came over." I stood and stuck out my hand.

She gave it a brisk shake. "Me, too. And thanks for the Sprite."

"My pleasure. Maybe we can do it again, sometime."

"That would be nice."

"And thanks for the dope on schools and stuff."

"Happy to oblige. Well . . ."

"Well . . ."

She waved good-bye, walked four steps toward the door, stopped, made some sort of decision, then returned to my side and leaned toward whisper distance. "Mrs. Hapwood keeps tabs on me pretty closely, and she's such a dear, I don't want her to worry. But she falls asleep rather early—if you come by in, oh, an hour or so, I could give you a nightcap."

"That would be great."

"Just tap the buzzer, don't press it down."

"Right."

She turned away again, then pivoted and leaned even closer. "There's an all-night drugstore on Judah. Just in case you need anything."

TEN

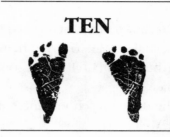

Two hours after I'd pressed her buzzer, Greta Hammond and I were making love on her lumpy sofa sleeper, smack in the center of the living room and smack on top of the slumbering Mrs. Hapwood and her furry golden sphinx. That we had come so far so fast was one of those miracles of men and women that are only explainable in the instant they occur.

Sex wasn't something I'd planned, needless to say. It wasn't something that was ethical, either, since Greta was the subject of an active inquiry, which means it wasn't something that was smart. And, given my relationship with Betty Fontaine, it was also distinctly inappropriate, in terms of morality or etiquette or even common decency, whatever the precise dimensions of that relationship might be. Which raised the usual quantum of guilt that comes with the exercise to an even more potent dosage.

But I played the hand out anyway, without qualm or resistance, with my eyes wide open and the contraindications dispatched to the cellar of my mind, for reasons that had nothing to do with ethics or intelligence or the job I'd been hired to do, but a lot to do with the electric arc that illuminated the dusky nucleus of Greta Hammond's eyes when she laughed at something I said. Most of all, what it had to do with, I like to think, was her obvious need of me.

What the motivation was on Greta's part I could only guess at, although I suspect its genesis was her state of being pregnant artificially, without benefit of emotional congress or even sticky sex, and that I was in some sense a stand-in for Stuart Colbert or Robert Redford or whomever she imagined the ghostly father to be, so that we were belatedly accomplishing the act of procreation even though the cart had come clearly before the horse. For my part, it seems that I need to be needed, enough to make me do things that will haunt me ever after.

Whatever the psychological underpinnings of our decision, in the beginning it was an engineering exercise. For some reason, Greta didn't want us to use the bedroom, so we removed and stacked the sofa cushions, then pulled the sleeper partway out, then shoved the coffee table aside so there would be room to extend the sofa fully, and finally completed the process of providing ourselves a surface. Then came the peeling of the blankets and the smoothing of the linens, Greta's apology for the clutch of blood spots on the bottom sheet the only words she offered during the entire exercise.

At this point the lights were switched off and the curtains drawn shut; then we debated music. Surprisingly, we settled rather easily on Sam Cooke and the Supremes as our opening acts, with Sinatra as the headliner. All in all, I'd made love in far less salubrious surroundings, amid far more rudimentary accessories.

The mechanics out of the way, we were left with our clothing and our laggard apprehensions. "Did you go to the drugstore?" she asked me softly, looking at something beyond the walls of the suddenly tiny room, something that doubtlessly had roots in other times with other men for other purposes.

I nodded. "Top of the line."

"Thank you. It's basically a matter of respect, I feel. In addition to life and death, of course."

"I agree."

Something in my tone made her cant her head and regard me with sudden detachment. "Are you really what you say you are?"

"What do you mean?"

"I mean are you really a guy from Redding with a job in a warehouse and an apartment on Potrero Hill?"

I laughed. "What makes you think I'm not?"

"Something about the way you look at me. And at my apartment. You seem, I don't know, analytical. Like the pathologists up on the hill."

"Well, I'm definitely not a pathologist. I'm just what I said I am— a guy with a nowhere job who lives in a cheap apartment on the wrong side of the hill," I said, all of which was sort of true.

Soothed by my lie, Greta toyed with a button on her blouse. "Well . . ."

I took her hand and kissed it. "Why don't you let me do that?"

She stiffened. "Are you sure? I'm not . . . spectacular."

"It's not a requirement." I unbuttoned the very button she'd been worrying.

"I can't believe I'm doing this," she said nervously, her breaths quick and audible above the strains of "You Send Me."

I unbuttoned another button. "Name something you'd rather be doing."

When she didn't answer, I regarded it as a license to proceed and freed another button. "The reasons you decided to meet me at Yancy's still hold, don't they?"

"I suppose so."

"Nothing's happened in the interim to make the situation less tempting, has it?"

She ran a lazy finger down my chest. "Quite the contrary."

Restrictions removed in compliance with the code of conduct in such encounters, I dispatched the final button. "Then let's not play pathologist."

I pushed the blouse off her shoulders, then peeled it down her arms and dispatched it to the floor at her back. As I drew her toward me, I slid my hands around her and began to unhook her bra in the way men always think they are managing it—without the woman noticing. It took me longer than it used to.

When the elastic strap was uncoupled, she leaned away from me to let the bra join the blouse on the carpet, then pressed an arm across her breasts. "Promise you'll be responsible? About protection, I mean?"

"I promise."

"Promise you'll stop if I ask you to?"

"Promise."

"Promise this isn't some sort of . . . trick?"

"Promise."

"Promise you won't make any loud noises?"

"Only if you promise not to tickle."

Her eyes alert to my reaction, she lowered her arm to offer me her breasts; I examined them with due diligence. They were pale and defenseless in the accusing beam of light that crossed the room from the street lamp, but plucky and willing nonetheless. The look on her face was more ambiguous. "Should I undo your belt or anything?"

"Feel free to undo anything that needs undone."

I bent to kiss a breast, then stood steadfast till she had tugged loose the buckle at my waist. After she pulled down my fly and unbuttoned my button, I did the same with hers, then kicked off my shoes and took her with me to the bed. The shakes and shudders it emitted upon arrival made me worry that it would fold around us in the middle of the proceedings and we would be immersed in its innards forever, lying frozen and contorted and surprised, like the immortal corpses of Pompeii.

As everyone knows, however, even after the belts are unbuckled and the bras are unhooked, trousers are still a problem, whether they're worsteds, like mine, or Levi's, like hers. But a man is never stronger than when he's maneuvering a woman to be rid of her clothing, nor more agile than when he's twisting to doff a piece of his own. Which was how, without excessive clumsiness or even major damage to a ligament, we managed to be naked in less than a minute.

"I haven't done this in a while," she said as I caressed the curve of her hip and watched goose bumps form along her flank and the tip of her nipple elongate. "Not in real life, at least."

"Are you afraid you've forgotten how?"

"I'm afraid I'm going to enjoy it so much I'll want to do it every night."

I found a familiar phrase. "That's not the worst fate in the world, is it?"

"It can get to be."

I slid down her chest and ran my tongue across her eager nipple. She shivered, then sighed, and then her skeleton decomposed and her musculature melted and she became a life-sized Raggedy Ann, all soft and supple and familiar, all warm and fuzzy and amenable, all comfortable and cuddly and compatible.

We turned this way and that, sampled one part and then another, then went back for second helpings. The sheets grew wet from our sweat; the steel stays of the sleeper strained to contain our contortions. Once, I almost fell off the bed; another time, Greta's head banged the sofa arm so hard I was afraid she would knock herself out. By the time I arrived at her vortex, and I began my thrusts and she began her clutches, I was as heedless as I had been in years.

And yet, through every minute of our coupling, as we groped and groaned with what was clearly authentic passion, there was something in the air as dense as desire and as active as delight. Looming above the bed, like a thunderhead that threatened to spit out a pitiless whirlwind and a blinding flash of light, was the fact of my profession and the deceptions I had utilized in pursuit of it. Despite my hunger and regardless of my greed, as we made our way toward climax I was never not aware of fraudulence, never able to entirely evade the shame it generated, never able to drown myself in the pleasure we were jointly manufacturing.

Nevertheless, I didn't stop, and all too soon I couldn't. We finished more or less in sync, and after a kiss on her nose and a pat on her hip, I rolled away and began to tidy up.

"Why don't you let me do that?" she said. "I'll bring you back a towel."

When I told her to go ahead, she rolled the condom off my penis and carried it off to the bathroom, its lifeless droop dangling from her fingertips like a mouse she'd retrieved from a trap. She didn't return for ten minutes.

Back in our clothing, sitting in the kitchen drinking tea, with the room reassembled and the sleeper returned to a sofa, Greta began to speak of matters other than the gifts we had just exchanged. She talked about how she'd always thought that some day there would be time to go back to school and be trained in what she had always wanted to do with her life, which was to become an interior designer, but that she knew now that it was something that would never happen. She talked about the loneliness and uncertainty that buffeted a woman alone, and about the vital support she received from her girlfriend Linda and her old pal Leo. She talked about her life being okay, all things considered, and she talked about how easily it could become a nightmare if she were laid off in the next round of staff reductions that were rumored to be imminent at the medical center.

And finally she talked, in sly hints and oblique references, about the consulting arrangement she'd spoken of earlier, and about how it could solve a big share of her problems if it only worked out, sounding much more hopeful than she had sounded at Yancy's. For some reason, as I looked in her eyes and listened to her muted yearning, I began to wish she hadn't signed that contract.

When I had stayed as long as was necessary to validate what we'd done, I bid Greta a brief good-bye, then promised to call when I got home, then told her I hoped we could see each other again. She told me she hoped so, too.

As usual, it was far too soon to know if either of us was telling the truth.

ELEVEN

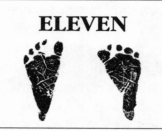

I phoned a report to Russell Jorgensen the next morning—status remains quo, all systems remained go. There were other things I could have said, of course, about Greta Hammond's altered mood, about her impassioned lunge toward me, about the compromise of my professional ethics in exchange for a helping of sex, but I didn't say any of those things, in the end, because I didn't think they were relevant.

And that was it, or so I hoped. Although a part of me wanted to see Greta again, to probe the erotic and intellectual regions to which our attraction might take us, the major part of me advised myself to leave well enough firmly alone. Greta was, primarily, a job, and now the job was finished. So I thought about her a lot, about the swell of her breast and the curve of her hip and the lift of her laugh when she giggled, and picked up the phone and called her twice, only to hang up when she answered. Finally, and not a little reluctantly, I swore to let sleeping dogs lie.

Days went by. I didn't hear from Russell, and I didn't hear from the Colberts, so I assumed the surrogate issue was over. And as far as I knew it was, except that some three weeks later, as Betty Fontaine was performing yet another autopsy on the state of our relationship, she resurrected the subject, if only indirectly.

"Is it that you think you won't make a good father?" Betty asked me abruptly, in the middle of an after-dinner stroll down a resurrected strip of Fillmore Street in a middle week of June.

"I have no idea what kind of father I'd be," I answered peevishly.

"It's like asking if I'd be brave in battle—there's no way to know till it happens."

"But you *were* brave in battle; you've got medals and stuff."

"I did what had to be done. So what?"

"I'm just saying you did fine then and you'd do fine as a father. You *like* children, don't you?"

"I don't know any children. Unless you count Charley Sleet."

"Do you like games?"

"Playing or watching?"

"Playing."

"I make my living at hide-and-seek," I pointed out, and not for the first time.

She laughed. "I guess you do, don't you? So how do you feel about pets?"

"I don't have any pets."

"I know you don't. Why don't you?"

"Because the only pets that thrive in apartments are goldfish and parakeets."

"So?"

"Birds shit and fish die."

"So do people."

"Not nearly as often."

"Which is all the more reason you should have kids."

We got to Geary and crossed the street and walked up the east side of Fillmore. I looked for a store window that would divert Betty from her course, a display of new shoes or designer eyewear or something, but nothing filled the bill.

"We're talking about having children, I take it," I mused finally, when Betty seemed sullen at my side.

"We certainly are."

"Together, or just in general?"

"Together, you dope."

"If we conceived a child tonight, I'd be sixty-seven when it graduated from high school. I'm pretty sure that's not fair."

"It's not how old you are, it's how good you are. And you'd make a great father."

"What makes you think so?"

"Because you care about people. You even care about those benighted creatures who walk in your office and ask you to keep the CIA from reading their minds or to guard their secret formula for growing hair or turning seashells into diamonds. You get all fuzzy over them and you'd go batty over a child the same way; you *know* you would."

"I didn't know being batty was the recommended approach to parenthood. Plus, I'm not sure I have the energy to keep up with kids anymore."

"We could get help. We wouldn't have to do it by ourselves."

"You mean day care?"

"Why not?"

"I don't approve of day care. I approve of it for people who don't have a choice, of course, but I don't think it's the optimum for kids."

"Optimum hasn't been an option since the seventies; no one can afford optimum anymore."

"Then maybe they shouldn't have kids."

"So the species gets dominated by the offspring of lawyers and investment bankers and computer nerds? Because they can afford to let their spouse stay home with the *kids* all day? Is *that* the world you want to live in?"

"That's the world we *do* live in."

She slugged me on the arm again, this time more than playfully. "It is not and you know it. Anyway, what I think is that the world could use a few more Marsh Tanners."

"Not to mention Betty Fontaines."

"So why don't we do something about it?"

"Now?"

She grasped my injured arm and snuggled tightly against my side. "I'm game if you are."

I stopped walking. Her expression was simultaneously endearing and intimidating, which kept me in the muddle I was in already.

"I'm flattered you want to do this, Betty," I fumbled. "I really am. But I don't think I'm the man for the job."

She sensed it was a verdict of sorts and it was a long time before she responded. By the time she did, the colors in her eyes had turned turbulent and her voice trembled with the rush of revelation. "Then I may have to find someone who is," she murmured hollowly. "Time's running out for me, Marsh. I'm going to have to make my move, with you or without you."

"I don't think I'm up to it, Betty."

Her grip on my arm intensified to industrial strength. "That's such crap, Marsh Tanner. If you want to know what *I* think, I don't think kids are the problem at all. I think *I'm* the problem."

"What's that supposed to mean?"

"It means I don't think it's kids you're scared of; I think it's making a commitment to *me.*"

"What makes you think that?"

"Because we're not *getting* anywhere. We're exactly where we were twelve months ago, which is exactly where we were twelve *years* ago. I need to be excited. I need to be *moving.* I need to be making progress."

"So do I."

"Well, you don't show much sign of it. We're in a rut a mile deep and frankly you seem pleased as punch about it. We go out twice a week, we have pleasant chats, we laugh at miscues of the mayor and the President, we go back to my place for sex, and we do it again the next weekend. It's not awful, I'm not saying that. You're funny and you're smart. I like being with you. And I love you more than any man I've ever known. But I need more than feelings, now. I need a life I can be proud of for the next forty years."

I tried to grin but didn't make it. "This is beginning to sound like we're breaking up."

She looked beyond me, at the surge of Mount Sutro toward the twisted towers that defiled its top and seemed suddenly to define our relationship. "I'm afraid maybe we are," she said softly.

"Can't we retire and think about it, at least?"

"You can do what you want. But I'm not going to see you again unless I hear some words I haven't heard from you before."

"Such as?"

"Words like love. And marriage. And family. Words like us, and we, and our. All those words that indicate you see your life as something beyond yourself, as something bigger and broader and more encompassing than it's been for the last thirty years."

She took my hand and looked at me through a sheen of tears polluted with mascara. "I have to say, I don't think you have those words in you, Marsh. I wish I did, but I don't. I don't think you feel them; I don't think you'll *ever* feel them; not about me, at least. And that truly breaks my heart. But I know you won't lie—you never lie to me, that's one thing I appreciate—so what I'm saying is, I don't think you'll be saying the words, so I don't think we'll be doing this again."

She began to sob, with typical restraint and decorum, which made it all the more painful to watch. "I just don't," she concluded dismally. She pressed her palm to her lips, then twisted away as though I was an ogre.

"Do we need to do this now?" I asked, with surprising distress. "Why can't we talk about it later?"

"Because this *is* later. This is the later we've talked about for years." She dropped my arm and stopped walking. "I can't do it anymore, Marsh. I just can't."

She looked wildly down the block; for an instant, I thought she was going to run away. In the next instant, I was certain I would never see her again and something in my chest began to shrink and wrinkle and die. "Betty. Please. Let's not do anything rash."

"I'm going to call a cab," she said brusquely. "I've got all that stuff at your place, but none of it's important except my nightgown. I like my sexy nightgown."

"So do I."

She swiped at her eye as if a bee had landed on it. "I hope very much that I'll be needing to look sexy again, so maybe you can mail it back to me."

"I'd rather deliver it in person. Actually, what I'd rather do is keep it. So we can still use it."

She shook her head. "We're past that, Marsh. We're somewhere else, now. I'm sorry, I really am, but I've been thinking a lot about this and it's something I have to do."

"That's the problem, you know."

"What?"

"Women *think* too damned much."

"Well, *somebody's* got to. And it's not a crime, you know." She turned her back and crossed her arms.

I flagged a cab and gave him a twenty and told him where to take her. We kissed on the lips, but coldly and without passion, then I waved good-bye to the woman I loved more than I had loved anyone since my secretary had gone out of my life four years ago, and things had gone to hell.

TWELVE

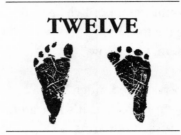

Two weeks later, I still hadn't seen or spoken to Betty since she'd disappeared down Fillmore Street in the back of a cab after eating at a Mediterranean restaurant. In retrospect, I blamed the food for the whole mess.

I'd waited two days for her to change her mind, then mailed her the nightgown, squeezed into a manila envelope and plastered with too many stamps, without an accompanying message. And that had been it—no calls, no notes, no late-night visitations featuring the cascade of tears and flood of apologies that are the stuff of reconciliation. I felt bad about the situation but not bad enough to do anything about it but mope.

Among the other activities that filled my time in the interim—in addition to renting bad movies and reading bad books—was contemplating my night with Greta Hammond. What I was wondering, quite frankly, was whether there was a way to start seeing her on a personal basis now that my professional task was completed. To that end, I spent several hours trying to calculate a way to reorient myself in her mind—to exit the guise of warehouseman and father and enter the person of bachelor and private investigator—without her resenting my initial duplicity and without my disclosing the nature of the job I'd been doing. Somehow I knew that pretending to be a parent would be the most serious of my sins in her mind and it was likely she would never forgive me.

I still hadn't come up with a plan when the phone rang one morning, even before I'd put on the coffee.

"Goddammit, Marsh," he said without preamble.

"God damn what, Russell? The Giants?"

"Fuck the Giants. You told me she was okay."

My stomach performed a tricky calisthenic. "No, I didn't. I told you I couldn't find anything wrong with her."

"Well, you must not have looked very hard."

"Why?"

"She's *gone*. That's why."

"What do you mean, gone?"

"I mean disappeared. Flown the coop. Vanished. All of the above."

"Says who?"

"Says the doctor she was supposed to see every other week for a prenatal examination, for starters. She missed the last two appointments, so he called Stuart and told him about it. So Stuart called me and told *me* about it. So last night I went out to Kirkham Street to see what the hell the deal was."

"And?"

"She's gone, sure enough. Landlady hasn't seen her in almost a month. Mail's been piling up, rent hasn't been paid, nothing. She was about to call in the cops till I paid the rent to put a stop to it. The personnel office at the med center doesn't know where she is, either . . . They've got her down as AWOL."

Russell paused for breath. "Goddammit, Marsh. I thought this thing was under control. I thought the woman was *solid.*"

Despite the implicit slur on my judgment, I held my disputatious tongue and stuck to the business at hand. "Did you look inside the apartment?"

"Landlady wouldn't let me. I'm thinking about getting a court order, if I can do it on the Q.T. The Colberts don't want this thing to go public. Especially not now."

"Let me take a shot at Mrs. Hapwood before you go to court. I talked with her before—maybe I can persuade her to let me inside."

"Sure. I'll let you take a shot. In fact, I *insist* that you take a shot. But not till you've talked with the Colberts."

"Why?"

"They're going crazy, that's why. The very thing they didn't want to happen—the thing they hired the two of us to *keep* from happening—has happened anyway. And they want some answers."

"I'm not sure I have any, Russell."

"Then at least let them ask their questions. I think the money they've paid us to handle this thing gives them that right, don't you?"

I told him I did, even though it wasn't quite that simple. Russell was right—a disappointed client has the right to ask questions—except the Colberts weren't my clients, they were Russell's. But out of respect for him and in furtherance of my personal repute and that of my profession, I was willing to accept a tangential obligation and submit to an interrogation. But only once.

"Meet me at Colbert for Women at four," Russell was saying. "Eighth floor. Tell the elevator woman who you are, so she'll take you up there. And don't talk back, Marsh; don't get self-righteous. Take your medicine like a man, then we'll figure out how to salvage this thing."

There were several points I wanted to make in my defense, but I only made one of them. "I'll try, Russell."

I hadn't been in Colbert for Women since I'd been shopping for a present for Betty last Christmas. I hadn't found anything suitable at Colbert; I'd found it at Eddie Bauer, but the current excursion reminded me of Betty, which reminded me of how hollow my life was without her, which explained why my mood was edgy and irritable even before I shoved my way through the revolving door on the main floor of Colbert for Women at four on the dot on a sunny Friday in July, when I should have been out having fun.

Long a lone holdout among the deteriorating denizens of Market Street, Colbert for Women now found itself at the core of an urban revival, with Nordstrom and the Emporium across the street and the remodeled terminus of the main cable car route right out front on Powell Street. The new mayor had vowed to clean up the sleaze that had usurped the area over the years, and now the predominant presence wasn't panhandlers it was chess players, a dozen tables of them stretched along the sidewalk toward Justin Herman Plaza, all races and colors squaring off in good humor above a bevy of knights and bishops. The street vendors and musicians gave the area a festive air, and beneath the newly paved road and the elaborately bricked walkway were streetcars on one level and BART on the level below that, one train or another rumbling by every ten minutes or so, bringing a host of suburban shoppers back to the heart of downtown to join the tourists and participate in the frolic.

Inside the triangular store, the ceiling was impossibly high as befitted the age and neo-classicism of the building, which dated to the years before the Second World War when money and materials were plentiful and architects had the guts and the budgets to use them voluptuously. The stained-glass dome in the center of the high rotunda softened and tinted the light so that the wrinkles in the faces of the matrons would magically vanish and the color in their hair would seem real. I wondered if it was doing anything special for me.

In keeping with more current fashion, the plaster walls were draped with diaphanous silks that provided a festive backdrop to the cherubs and angels that peered at me from the corners of the room, wearing red lips and gilt hair and jewelry that sparked in the light. The music in the air was Vivaldi; the smells were close to overwhelming. It took a while to get my bearings.

There were perfumes and colognes down the aisle to the right, along with a sapper squad of women assigned to inflict you with a fragrance if you showed any interest or even slowed down. I looked left. Costume jewels were the sirens that beckoned in that direction, mounds of cut glass and gold plate piled on counters that were staffed by overdressed women wearing puzzling clothes and peculiar makeup. Since my tweeds and corduroys made it obvious I wasn't a candidate for a scent or a bauble, no one wasted more than an upbraiding glance at my distance from style and flash. After a moment of reconnoitering, I braved the gauntlet of perfume girls, crossed to the rear of the store, and punched the button marked UP.

The elevator was as old as the building, which meant that, like many elderly ladies, it needed help to get where it was going. The woman perched like a gargoyle on the stool next to the brass lever that started and stopped the cage looked to be jeopardizing her Social Security by holding down a paying job; the hangdog look on her face suggested she wasn't happy with the regulations or with anything else. When I told her who I was, and asked to be lifted to eight, she consulted a list of names that was taped to the left of the emergency button. She seemed insulted to find me on it.

The directory above the door only went to seven—furs and the bridal boutique: the powers that be evidently didn't want the hoi polloi blundering into their executive domain in pursuit of a white sale. As we ascended, various clumps of customers, exclusively female, got on and off the elevator bearing bags and babies and briefcases—women are always carrying something without even noticing, while men feel slightly enslaved when forced to do the same.

After six, I was alone in the car with the grumpy operator and the dregs of too many perfumes. A needle couldn't have slipped between her lips—conversation was out of the question. Based on the sounds that echoed through the shaft as we approached its peak, so was the reliability of the mechanism we were utilizing. When the doors squeaked open at eight, the operator bid me a terse good-bye, which seemed a minimal courtesy to someone who could conceivably be launching a takeover.

In contrast to the rest of the building, the eighth floor was subdued and reclusive. With its walnut panels and Persian carpets, it looked more like a law office than a dress shop; at least it looked the way law offices looked back when the managing partners were raised on Marquand and Auchincloss instead of Grisham and Turow. A more compelling exception was the parade of women that moved across the parquet floor, gliding like seraphs from one room to another, modeling outerwear for management in preview of next season's winners. It was a while before I could absorb anything more relevant than arrogant and anorexic loveliness.

A small waiting area was arrayed in front of the reception desk; two chairs and a couch and a potted plant. Russell Jorgensen had obviously been posted there to greet my arrival, so the Colberts wouldn't have to contend with me alone. As I walked his way, he looked even less happy than he'd sounded on the telephone; he was so disconcerted, he didn't even shake my hand.

"You're going to take some heat in there, Marsh," he muttered as I sat in the chair beside him. "Stuart isn't happy with either of us."

"I can take heat when I need to take heat but I'm not sure it's deserved in this case."

"Whether it is or isn't, I want you to let Stuart rant and rave for a while. Eventually he'll calm down and then we can decide how to clean this up."

"I'll do what I can, but you'd better keep him in check. I'm not in the mood for misplaced criticism."

"I can't afford to lose the Colberts as clients," Russell said simply.

"Which makes me the sacrificial lamb."

"If you want to see it that way."

"My rate's going to double if we get into this any deeper, Russell. I don't know what happened to the Hammond woman but I know it didn't have anything to do with me."

Russell leaned toward me and whispered. "Stuart thinks she stole it."

"The fetus?"

He nodded.

"To keep or as a kidnaping?"

"Kidnaping. He thinks sooner or later she's going to ask for more money."

"I don't think a pregnant woman can kidnap her own child, Russell."

"But that's just the point. It's *not* her child. It never was. And I have a contract that says so."

THIRTEEN

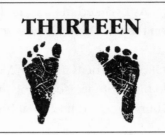

They were side by side and hand in hand, an *au courant* American Gothic garbed by Ralph Lauren and Laura Ashley instead of Penney's and OshKosh B'gosh, smack in the center of a creamy leather couch at the west end of a long and lavish office on the top floor of their very own building. The furnishings that surrounded them were on the cutting edge of European design and the photos on the walls featured the facades of various Colbert stores and a bevy of beautiful women posed in dramatic settings and modeling couturier fashions. The only window looked down on Powell and west toward Upper Market but the cerise gauze curtain drawn across its bright expanse indicated the boulevard and buildings outside couldn't compete with the human architecture on display within the store.

Because it was his office, Stuart Colbert looked comfortable and self-possessed and bursting with something to say. From the heat in his eyes and the flush to his face, I guessed it wouldn't be pleasant. He was wiry and small, with an aesthete's high forehead, a lizard's bulbous eyes, and a languid smirk that declared he was master of all he surveyed. He struck me as a cold fish—judgmental, sanctimonious, arrogant, didactic—and a trifle jejune underneath. All to be expected, I suppose, given that his only source of early nourishment had come from a silver spoon.

As Russell and I entered the room, Millicent Colbert squeezed her husband's hand, then hauled it to her lap for comfort. The movements of her eyes and hands made her seem flighty and abstracted and a bit on the manic side, which might have masked a vat of insecurity or have been merely symptomatic of a frantic mom.

She was pretty in a vague and brittle way, with wispy blond hair and a long slim body that lacked noticeable curvature beneath the many blooms of her Laura Ashley. Her fingers flew about her person like pixies, adjusting her hair and her clothes and her nose, making sure they were suitably displayed. She was so worried that her dress would wrinkle, she plucked at it the way a chef would pluck a squab, redraping it in ever-changing folds about her thighs. My guess was that she'd grown up with major money around the house and that she fell far too easily in love and had been hurt too frequently by men. I also guessed that she was less ardent than dutiful toward her mate and more needful than was healthy to possess a child.

When Russell introduced me, Stuart only nodded and Millicent only blinked: it was going to be a long meeting. When Russell offered a speech in the nature of an opening statement, Stuart held up a hand to preempt him.

"We are not pleased, Mr. Tanner," he began forcefully, his eyes on the bridge of my nose.

"I don't blame you," I said, then opted to anticipate. "But I don't blame me, either."

Neither Colbert nor his lawyer liked what they regarded as flippancy. "Nevertheless, we feel we have been poorly served," Colbert countered.

My eye was on Russell as I answered. "As I said, I don't happen to see it that way. But if you have been, I apologize."

Colbert squeezed his wife's hand and looked at her from an autocratic loftiness. "Apologies won't get our baby back."

"No, they won't," I agreed. "Neither will recriminations or aspersions."

"But they might make me feel better," Colbert responded, through clenched teeth and a tight half-smile that must have been his concept of levity.

I should have let it go but I didn't. "The balm would only be temporary," I pointed out, "unless the problem itself gets solved."

Colbert started to take his next turn, but then thought better of it. He leaned back and looked down his nose at his wife, granting her permission to speak. "Do you have any idea where Miss Hammond might have gone, Mr. Tanner?" Millicent asked breathily.

I shook my head. "And even if I did, it might not be helpful."

"Why not?"

"Because she might not have had any choice in the matter."

Millicent frowned. "I'm not sure what you mean."

"I mean she might have been abducted."

"You mean kidnapped," Stuart interjected.

"It's certainly possible."

"It's also possible it was our child that was kidnaped, and that Greta Hammond was the kidnaper."

"Have you had a ransom note? Or any other communication to that end?"

He shook his head. "But I'm sure we'll hear from her soon."

I shrugged. "Or from someone. But it's also possible that she wants to keep the child herself."

"What makes you say that?"

"Because apparently her only other child is dead. As I told Russell in my first report, that sort of past personal tragedy goes against the prevailing wisdom in these things. It gives the surrogate a motive to renege."

Colbert shook his head stubbornly. "I'm sure she just wants money."

"She was already going to get a lot of money. All she had to do was follow the contract."

"In my experience, the more money people have, the more they want. Especially poor people." His contempt was as unalloyed as only those born to the purple can render it.

I looked at him with what I hoped was insolence. "I have to tell you that based on my contacts with her, I don't think this is something she did voluntarily."

Colbert curled his lip. "Well, I think you're wrong. I think she's a conniving little bitch. I think she planned this thing all the way, from the first day Russell got in touch with her."

I was stubborn in the storm of his vituperation. "If she's that corrupt, why did you pick her to begin with?"

The question and its implications put a stop to things for a while, long enough for tempers to cool and a semblance of reason to return to the room. When a secretary came in to offer refreshment, we placed our orders as gratefully as if we'd been lost in the desert for days.

After the secretary had served us, Russell Jorgensen took charge. "We need to decide what we do now."

"We find her, don't we?" Millicent blurted, her voice splinted and reinforced, her determination virile.

Russell looked left. "Do you agree, Stuart?"

"Absolutely. Provided we proceed confidentially."

"With or without the aid of the police?" I asked.

Russell twisted my way. "What do you recommend?"

"If she left voluntarily, the police could be a help—missing persons procedures and all that. If it's a kidnaping, the FBI is usually a better choice than local law enforcement, although the S.F.P.D. has lots of experience in these things. More than makes it into the papers," I added truthfully.

Stuart Colbert shook his head. "No cops. Not yet. Not till we know what we're dealing with."

I nodded. "That's probably wise."

Millicent spoke again. "If the police aren't going to look for her, who will?"

Russell looked at me. "Marsh?"

I shrugged. "I could try my luck."

Stuart squinted. "Immediately?"

"Yes."

"Full time?"

I nodded.

"Have you ever done this type of thing before?"

"Several times, if you mean a skip. Once, if you mean a kidnaping."

"And?"

"Sometimes I found them; a few times I didn't. With the kidnap, the victim was dead before I got called in on the case. Of course we didn't know it at the time."

Millicent Colbert started to cry. Her husband murmured something I didn't catch, which made her try to pull herself together but for the moment it was a losing battle.

Her husband put his arm around her, then looked at Russell and me in turn. "You see how vital this is? To both of us? So what's going to happen is that I'm going to move heaven and earth to find that woman, and if you can't do it, I'll find someone who can." Colbert looked as though he'd just declared war; I gave him credit for his zeal.

"Maybe you should start again," Russell offered. "Find another surrogate and do another implant."

"You know the odds, Stuart," his wife protested in between her sniffles. "At every step, something can go wrong. It worked so perfectly this time, and your father seems so pleased, I just think it was our destiny. I think if we don't find Greta Hammond we'll *never* have a child and I don't know if I can bear that. I just don't." She had worked so hard to suppress them, I felt guilty bearing witness to her tears.

"We'll find her," Stuart Colbert declared above her heartache. "And that's a promise." He stood and began to pace.

I wanted to like him for his resolve and to sympathize with his plight, but nothing I'd seen so far contradicted the picture of him painted by the columnists—spoiled, tactless, humorless, dictatorial. His interest in both his wife and fatherhood seemed somehow forced and artificial, which made it likely that the baby was being manufactured to be a buffer between two people who didn't like each other much and as a glue to hold something together that otherwise would have shat-

tered. But none of that was my business. At least that's what I told myself, to keep from walking out the door.

"What do you charge?" Colbert asked in the middle of my assessment, as he helped himself to a glass of water from a crystal carafe on
the credenza.

I glanced at Russell before I doubled my usual rate. "For this type
of thing, it's seventy-five an hour. Plus expenses."

"That's outrageous."

"No, it isn't. This is a delicate problem, and the down side is a long
way down. But if you want cheap, I can get you cheap." I glanced toward
the translucent window. "There's plenty of cheap half a block from here."

"Stuart?" Millicent asked rhetorically, her high-pitched squeal reg-
istering her objection.

He wanted to spar with me some more but he relented. "Okay.
You're hired. But I bring in someone else if you don't get the job done
in a week."

"Fine, as long as I get that week on my own, before anyone else
mucks up the field of play."

He hesitated, then nodded. "What do we do now?"

"We look for motive. Basically, there are two possibilities. The
first is that she took off on her own, to keep the child herself or to ex-
tort money from you. What I need to know is if there's anything you
know that I don't that might suggest where she's gone or why."

The Colberts looked at each other and shook their heads simultaneously. "Not unless she went back to her husband," Stuart said.

I shook my head. "I talked with her about him—I don't think
that's likely. But I'll check it out anyway. Do you know where he lives?"

Colbert shook his head. "He was nothing; a common laborer.
That's all I know about the man."

"You met him?"

He shook his head. "Of course not. I just remember her men-
tioning him."

"It sounded more personal than that."

"Well, it wasn't."

He resented my prying but I was beyond caring what he felt. At some point in the meeting, I had begun working solely for his wife.

"I'm still not clear how you found the woman in the first place," I said. "For the surrogate business, I mean."

Stuart shrugged casually. "I just happened to see Greta on the street one day. It was a shock—I hadn't thought about her for years, didn't even know she was still in town. I started to say hello but for some reason the surrogate possibility came to mind and I held off till I could discuss it with Milly. We talked it over and we decided to go ahead."

"Why? Why pick Greta Hammond over all the other options?"

The Colberts exchanged looks. "We knew her, for one thing," Stuart said ambiguously. "Or I did, at least."

I waved my hand. "This building is full of women you know. Most of them are stunning; lots of them must also be smart. Why not use one of them?"

Colbert's look turned magisterial. "The models see pregnancy as a career killer."

"Not all of them, surely."

"All the ones that matter do. Anyway, Greta was a loyal, intelligent, competent employee. I relied on her a great deal in those days and, since we needed someone equally reliable to act as our surrogate, it seemed only sensible to use her."

I let his proprietary phraseology pass unchallenged. "Did you know the Hammond woman, Mrs. Colbert?"

Millicent shook her head. "I've never seen her, even to this day. But I trust Stuart's judgment on such matters."

I walked to the end of the room, then turned my back to the window. "Now comes the hard part," I said.

FOURTEEN

"**H**ard part?"

The phrase was voiced by a chorus of three, with a mixture of puzzlement, irritation, and maybe a little fear.

I nodded. "The hard part is discussing who might have wanted to harm you like this. Either of you," I added, when Millicent glanced quickly at her husband, as though he were the only conceivable target of spite.

Stuart wasn't buying. "Even assuming it's a snatch, what makes you think it's someone we know? Kidnapers and their victims aren't usually bosom buddies, are they?"

"But if this was just a move for money, why not take your wife? Or you, for that matter, since your father can presumably put his hands on more ransom than you can? Why mess with this surrogate thing?"

"And how would they even know about it?" Russell added, which was a question I was about to ask myself.

The Colberts eyed each other but said nothing.

"What I'm getting at," I went on, "is that the motive might be to wound one or both of you in the place where you're most vulnerable." I looked at Mrs. Colbert with what I hoped was understanding. "I'm sure it's no secret that you've been wanting a child very badly."

She only shook her head. "No one could be that cruel."

"I've made a career out of them," I said, then looked at Stuart Colbert. "The question is, who would want to make you miserable?"

"Cynthia," he said simply.

"Your sister?"

He nodded. "It's no secret that we hate each other. Cynthia probably sees this baby as my latest attempt to curry favor with the old man."

"How do you mean?"

His lip lifted cynically. "Line of succession and all that. Dad's a big fan of primogeniture."

"I guess you need to explain," I said.

"There's no mystery about it: Cyn and I are at war. We have been since we were kids, in one way or another, and it's been an all-out dogfight ever since Daddy gave us each a store to run. The grand prize is the entire empire, of course—the stores, real estate, all of it."

"So you don't own the women's store yourself?"

His chuckle was brief and sardonic. "Hell, no; I'm just a sharecropper. The old man gave me some property to work—the women's store. I do well if the store does well; if the store takes a beating, I take a beating. Meanwhile, the old man still owns the whole ball of wax. All Cyn and I have are some Class B shares that pay a decent return provided we net enough to pay the dividends on Daddy's Class A shares first."

"Are you on the board?"

He nodded. "But it's totally at Rutherford's sufferance. I've got no real power—my own shares are nonvoting, so the only seat I control is my own. On any issue that comes up, Daddy's got a majority in his pocket. Two of his henchmen are Russell's law partners. Right, Russell?"

"Right, Stuart."

"Your father is more likely to leave the business to you if you have a son. Is that it?"

"I hope so. But what the old man thinks, no one ever knows till it's too late."

He seemed to mean something by that, so I looked at Russell. "For obvious reasons, I have nothing to say on the subject of Rutherford's testamentary intentions," he said, then crossed his arms to close the issue.

"Why doesn't your sister have kids too?" I asked. "To stay even with you, if nothing else?"

"She hates men," the Colberts said in unison.

It seemed a silly response. I looked at Russell to see how he took it, but he only smiled and shrugged.

I turned back to Stuart Colbert. "Your sister hates men but runs a men's store. Your father must have a puckish sense of humor."

"Humor has nothing to do with it," he said, then lapsed into a fervid rant. "Have you seen the merchandise she stocks? Look at her window displays. Only a man-hater would *think* of dressing men like that. The manikins look like fops out of Edwardian England and the customers are more prissy than the manikins. If this weren't San Francisco, she'd have been in Chapter 11 three years ago."

The bitterness rolled off his tongue so easily it was clearly a theme song. I waited for his fixation to subside, then cut more closely to the chase.

"Do you have any evidence that your sister was prepared to take steps to defeat this pregnancy?"

"No more than a few hundred snide remarks."

"But she knew about it?"

He looked at his wife. "Not specifically, but in general. Having a child is all Milly's talked about since we were married."

"Did your sister know about the surrogate?"

Colbert shook his head. "I don't see how. The only one who could have told her was Russell, and he wouldn't do something like that, would you, Russell?"

Despite the veiled threat in his principal's tone, Russell only smiled and shook his head.

"Who else might see this child as some kind of threat to them?" I asked.

No one said anything.

"How about your ex-wife?" I asked Stuart. "Where is she these days?"

"Louise lives like Cleopatra on a houseboat on Mission Creek. The court makes me pay her eight thousand a month. With the help of her little capsules, she has a nice life." His tone would have been a better fit if he'd told me she had shingles.

"Capsules?" I asked.

"Louise is addicted to a variety of tranquilizing medications. She's stoned out of her mind 80 percent of the time."

There didn't seem to be anywhere to go with that, so I looked closer to home. "How about the business? Is there anyone around here who doesn't like the way Daddy is allocating the assets?"

Stuart looked at Russell, but Russell was sitting this one out.

"Harvey Gallatin is CEO of the combined stores," Colbert said. "He has 10 percent of the Class B stock, just like Cyn and I do. He'd make a mint if we went public or got sucked up in a takeover. Which he would like because he knows he's only a caretaker. No way he ever owns the business."

"How likely is a takeover?"

"Not very at the moment. But Federated made a serious pass at us back in the eighties, as did KKR and some others. Even Macy's made some inquiries, or so I'm told. Federated's offer would have made Harvey 6 million before taxes. I know because I calculated my own share down to the last penny. But Daddy wouldn't hear of it."

"Any chance there's something like that going on now?"

"A takeover? We would have heard of it, wouldn't we, Russell?"

"Probably," Russell said.

"But if the stores stay in the family after your father dies, Harvey won't get his 6 million," I pointed out.

"Not unless Daddy splits his stock and Harvey and Cyn gang up on me. *I* certainly don't have any intention of bailing out."

I took time to review the bidding, then decided to wrap it up. I was accumulating information but it wasn't objective information, which meant there was no way to gauge its value.

"Cynthia and Louise and Harvey," I repeated. "Anyone else have a stake in this?"

Stuart shrugged. "No one I can think of. Russell?"

Russell shook his head.

I looked at Stuart Colbert. "How about your mother? Is she a player?"

"My mother is insane," he said offhandedly.

"Literally?"

"Literally. I haven't seen her in months."

"Is that of any relevance to this?"

"None at all."

"How about you, Mrs. Colbert? Any sicko out there who would get a kick out of making you suffer?"

She colored, then gulped, then shook her head. "Not that I know of. Of course not."

"I can't believe there isn't someone who was heartbroken when you married Mr. Colbert. An old boyfriend or two?"

She shook her head.

"Or maybe an old girlfriend of his?"

That one brought a frown. "I don't think so. But then Stuart would be the one to ask, wouldn't he?"

I kept my eyes on Millicent. "Was your husband divorced when you started seeing each other? Or does his ex-wife regard you as a home wrecker?"

She was stung and she showed it. "They were already having difficulties when Stuart and I started seeing each other as friends. We talked about his problems with Louise—I was the only person in his life he could trust at that point and he badly needed someone to confide in. But I assure you we didn't become lovers until after they divorced."

"Mrs. Colbert might not have believed that."

Stuart stood up. "Who gives a shit *what* she believed? Louise may be capable of a lot of things, but not this. She doesn't have the fucking energy." He looked at his watch. "I'm due in a staff meeting."

I looked at the three of them in turn. "Have we covered all the bases as far as motive is concerned?"

One by one they nodded.

"Okay. I'm going to start on Greta's end. If I find a trail, I'll follow it. If I don't, I'll be talking to the people you've mentioned." I stood up. "If you need to know what's happening, ask Russell. I'll keep him up to date." I looked at Stuart Colbert. "Unless you'd rather I reported directly to you."

Colbert shook his head. "If Russell's against me, I'm screwed anyway—he can hang me out to dry any time he wants to. So go to it, Tanner. Save me my business."

"He's not saving a *business,*" his wife interrupted angrily. "He's saving a baby."

"And he'd better do it by next week," Russell Jorgensen said suddenly.

"Why?"

"Because if that woman has messed this up, that's all the time we have before we can call it off. The contract says no abortion after the first trimester of pregnancy."

FIFTEEN

At nine the next morning I was back on Kirkham Street, buzzing Mrs. Hapwood's button. I told a white lie to get inside the building and another to get her to open her door. When we were finally face-to-face, she recognized me, but from the vertical folds in her face it wasn't a happy experience. The fat gold cat didn't care one way or another, although this time it had an eye open, so I wasn't going to get away with anything.

"You may remember I was here a couple of months ago," I began when she had opened the door. "You showed me the unit across the hall."

"It's rented now," she pointed out.

"I'm sure you found a nice tenant. The reason I didn't take it myself is that my requirements of quiet are so particular, I was afraid with a young woman living overhead . . ." I shrugged to complete the excuse. "Anyway, the reason I've come is to see Ms. Hammond."

"Why?"

"She has something of mine that I need to get back."

"What?"

"A briefcase."

"Greta has your briefcase?"

I nodded. "After you showed me the unit that morning, I ran into Ms. Hammond at a nearby café. We got to talking and she was kind enough to invite me to join her for a glass of wine, which I did later that evening. We had a nice chat but, what with the late hour and the wine and all, when I left I forgot my case. Then I went out of town on business, and I moved, so this is the first chance I've had to come back for it."

"Seems like if it was important, you'd have been here before. But it's no use anyway. Greta ain't here."

I treated it as new information. "That's unfortunate. Where is she?"

"Don't know."

"Well then, when will she be back?"

"Don't know that, either. If you give me your number, I'll have her call first thing I see her."

I frowned. "Do you have reason to believe that Ms. Hammond may have . . . absconded, for some reason?"

"If you mean do I think she did something wrong," Mrs. Hapwood said stiffly, "then no. I don't have any sign of that at all."

"Nevertheless, you admit you don't know where she's gone, or when she'll get back. That worries me. She must have known she had my case but she didn't contact me to arrange a retrieval even though my business card was inside. Frankly, I'm beginning to think the authorities should be called in."

Mrs. Hapwood squeezed her cat until it purred in protest. "I hope you're not saying she stole it."

"It appears at the very least she may have abandoned it." I took time to consider the situation. "I will contact the police in five days. However, if the case is up in her apartment even as we speak, and you would be willing to let me retrieve it informally, then no such messiness would be necessary." I gave her time to reflect. "You're welcome to accompany me, of course. To see that nothing but the case is removed. It seems tragic to allow a criminal charge to loom over Ms. Hammond's head when you could have prevented it so easily."

She was clearly in a quandary. "I respect my tenant's privacy."

"I'm sure you do. But it's not like I'd be rummaging around—a briefcase can't be hidden in a cookie jar, after all."

"Well . . ."

I shrugged. "The police will be here with a warrant by the end of the week. Since that's the way you want to handle it."

Naturally, she yielded. She was too nice not to, and it's the nice ones you can manipulate easiest, which is one of the less endearing corollaries of the profession.

Two minutes later I was back in Greta Hammond's apartment, with Mrs. Hapwood and her cat chaperoning my every move. I moved through the place rather quickly, describing the case I was seeking, enlisting Mrs. Hapwood's help in the search. At one point my eye lingered on the couch as I tried to transform the woman I'd made love to into an extortionist or worse, but thankfully I couldn't come close.

What I was looking for wasn't a briefcase, of course, but an explanation for Greta Hammond's absence, and perhaps a clue to her whereabouts. Fortunately, there were indications her departure had been benign. There was no food decomposing on plates, no stagnant bathwater, no overturned chairs, no splash of blood to indicate a violent intrusion. There was only the musty smell of disuse and the normal clutter of a harried existence. I took all that as a good sign.

But there weren't indications of a premeditated departure, either—no undraped clothes hangers, no empty drawers or bookcases, no orange boxes or storage bags scattered about. At bottom, the shape and contents of the apartment seemed undisturbed, which was mysterious in itself, given the circumstances. The only sense I got was that there wasn't quite enough of everything, as though the contents had been reduced across the board by maybe 20 percent, as though Greta had taken only what she truly needed and left the rest behind. But that was at best a hunch.

I was about to give up when I remembered the packet of photos in the desk. After sidling idly to it, I directed Mrs. Hapwood's attention elsewhere, then opened the drawer for a peek. But the photos were gone, as were some of the other contents.

I paged quickly through the past few weeks in the engagement calendar on the desktop, but except for some predictable notations, there was nothing unusual but for a big black circle drawn around a day in mid-May. For a moment, I thought it marked the date of our tryst, and was indicative of its significance to her, but a run through my grainy memory suggested we had coupled at least two weeks later. As a consolation prize for my lack of progress, I slid Greta's six-inch plastic ruler into my pocket while Mrs. Hapwood was toying with her cat, then told her I'd done all I could.

"Do you have any reason to think she met with foul play?" I asked in all innocence as I headed for the door.

"Why would I think that?"

I shrugged. "Because she was worried about something; because strangers have been inquiring about her; because you overheard a mysterious phone conversation?"

She shook her head. "There wasn't anything like that. Only the fight with her friend."

"The friend from across the street?"

She nodded.

"When was this?"

"Couple of months ago, I guess. I don't keep good track of time."

"What were they fighting about?"

"I didn't hear the words, I just heard the voices. Screams and screeches. I had my hand on the phone toward the end; wouldn't be the first time I got the cops to quiet someone down."

"Well, let's hope it was only a tiff and not something serious. You did see her afterward, right?"

She nodded. "Women don't hurt women, anyway," she said in a surprising burst of gender analysis. I guess she'd never heard of Lizzy Borden.

After urging Mrs. Hapwood to be sure Greta called me the minute she got back, I walked two blocks north and took a stool at the end of the counter. The breakfast crowd had thinned, but a handful of customers lingered over coffee and the *Chronicle,* prolonging the peak of their day.

I was in the middle of an apricot danish by the time Leo came out of the kitchen. After flirting with a woman at a table, he strolled behind the counter and began to put salt in some shakers. When he had finished, our eyes met and held but it took him a while to place me. When he had, he lumbered toward me, his tattoo as sinuous as ever.

"How ya doin'?" was his opener.

"Good. You?"

"Okay. You been in before, right?"

I nodded. "Couple of months ago. I was looking for a place to live."

His smile was a smoke-stained accusation. "You was looking for some action, too."

"I was attracted to Greta Hammond, if that's what you mean."

He beamed expansively, his omniscience again supreme. "She said you come by later on."

"I did. Yes."

"She said she liked you."

"The feeling was mutual."

"She said she wouldn't mind bumping into you again. And then she didn't talk about you no more."

"Maybe that's because she did bump into me."

"Yeah?"

"Yeah."

"What happened?"

"Nice things."

That part didn't please him. He started to take umbrage, but knew he didn't have a leg to stand on. "What you after now?"

"I'm looking for Greta. I can't seem to get her by phone. I was wondering if she moved or something."

Leo looked up and down the counter, then lowered his voice to a grating whisper. "It's good you showed up."

"Why?"

"'Cause I was about to come looking for you."

"Why?"

"'Cause Greta ain't around all of a sudden."

"How long's she been gone?"

"Three weeks Monday."

"Just like that?"

"Just like that."

"Have you talked to her friend, Linda?"

"I talked to everybody."

"And?"

"Nothing."

"You think someone did something to her?"

"Yeah, I think someone did something. Till you showed up, I thought you was the one that done it."

"Has anyone called the cops?"

"Cops don't count for much out here."

"Well, I'm worried about her, too. I'm going to try to find her."

He was still leery of my motives. "Why?"

"We got along."

"Yeah. So did we."

We paused in homage to the object of our mutual regard. "So what do you think I should do first? Talk to people who worked with her up the hill?"

He shook his head. "Medical geeks is all that's up there; she didn't run much with them. But she had something in the works, I know that much."

"What?"

"Something that was going to make her some money. But I think it went sour."

"What makes you think so?"

"She was feeling real down last time she was in. And she was also pissed. Pissed at someone for fucking her over."

"Who was she pissed at?"

"She didn't say. No name, or nothing. But she was pissed and she said she was going to make him pay for what he did."

"That sounds a little like blackmail."

Leo awakened the cobra by crossing his arms. "From someone else, maybe; not her. But I figure she got involved in some scam that went south and now she's at the bottom of the fucking bay."

I tried not to shudder. "It doesn't sound like the kind of thing she'd be mixed up in."

"Maybe she didn't know what it was at first. Maybe they set her up. Maybe she was conned. But sure as shit *something* happened, because there at the end, she wasn't sounding like herself. She was sounding like a woman with both tits in a wringer."

"Do you have any idea at all who the guy is?"

"Yeah. I got an idea. He come in looking for her."

"When?"

"Week ago."

"Who was it?"

Leo woke the cobra and gave me a good look at it. "The asshole claimed to be her husband."

"What did he want?"

"Don't know."

"Where does he live?"

"Don't know that, either. All I know is, Greta's up the proverbial creek without a paddle."

SIXTEEN

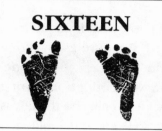

There was one more place to try, so I knocked on the door to the duplex. It was Saturday, so there was a chance she was home, and this time I got lucky.

She was blond and in her early thirties, tall and slim and attractively exhausted. She was dressed for cleaning and scrubbing and ironing, the things working women can only do on weekends, and when she opened the door she was scowling—she had programmed her day to the max and hadn't scheduled an interruption.

"Sorry to bother you," I began. "My name's Tanner. I'm a friend of Greta Hammond's."

"You are?" Her vacant look suggested that was the last subject she thought I would broach.

"I'm not a friend of long standing," I explained, "but I know your name is Linda and you have a daughter named Ingrid who goes to Argonne school and you've been a friend of Greta's for quite a while."

"So?" Her eyes thinned to a squint and she shoved her hands in her denim pockets. The middle button of her flannel shirt was missing, and a wisp of white bra peeked through the gap, a clinical contrast to the rest of her dingy outfit.

"I'm here because I'm worried about her," I said, with enough ambiguity to pique her interest. "And I'm guessing you are, too."

"Why would I be worried?"

"Because she's missing. At least everyone else in the neighborhood thinks she's missing, and unless you know where she is, I'm assuming you do, too. I was hoping we could talk about it."

The request was unnerving. She glanced back to the house as though there was someone inside who would object to my presence and get her off the hook.

"I can come back later," I offered, as fealty and anxiety collided between us. "You seem pretty busy right now."

Something in my face helped her make a decision. "No. This is as good a time as any. I need to talk about it, too." She fussed with her hair as she inspected me. "Who are you, again?"

"Marsh Tanner. I met Greta a couple of months ago, when I was looking for a place to live. Then my job fell through, so I didn't . . . anyway, I stopped by to see Greta one night, to thank her for her help, and we . . ." I left the rest to Greta's indiscretion or Linda's imagination.

The tension went out of her face. "So you're *that* guy."

"Apparently so."

"Greta was like a kid after the circus," she said with a laugh, then quickly sobered. "Is that the last time you saw her?"

"Yes."

"Shit."

"What?"

"I was hoping she'd run off with you. That was the most joyful explanation I could think of and I was praying it was true." She brushed at an aberrant lock of hair. "So now I have to think about all those other possibilities," she concluded glumly.

"I think we should discuss some of them."

She sighed and stepped back. "I guess we should. Come on in. Do you want coffee? Excuse the mess, but—" She shrugged at the state of her scattered quarters, as though her possessions had unruly minds of their own. "My daughter wanted to shift the furniture around because it was so boring the way it had been for the last five years, but of course she disappeared halfway through the project. Par for the course."

And it was true—the furniture was shoved to the center of the room, the rugs were rolled, the occasional tables were tugged to the fringes—she might have been moving out. "Coffee would be fine," I told her.

"If you can find a seat, help yourself. If not, grab a pillow and find a spot on the floor."

I found a chair in the exact center of the room and removed the women's magazines that were piled on top of it. When she returned with the coffee, Linda perched on the matching love seat that was perpendicular to me. We had to contort to keep an eye on each other.

"I don't know your last name," I said.

"Webber."

"Do you work with Greta?"

She shook her head. "We met at a local restaurant. We kept showing up at the same time every Sunday, and got to talking and discovered we lived across the street from each other. Eventually we cut out the middleman."

"Poor Leo."

She blinked. "You know Leo?"

"I was just talking with him."

"Did he know anything?"

I shook my head.

"I hope you're right," she said.

The expression prompted a question. "Is Leo okay?"

"Why do you ask?"

"He seems enamored with Greta. Do you think there's any chance he might have . . ."

"What?"

"Gone out of his gourd when she rebuffed his advances."

She shook her head. "I think it's pretty much what he does—make advances and get rebuffed. He'd have a heart attack if anyone took him up on it. But God. If you're asking if it's impossible, then no. Of course it's not. Any man on earth is capable of that."

"No, they're not."

She met my eye, then yielded a fraction. "Most of them."

I passed on my chance at surrebuttal. "I understand you and Greta had quite a fight a couple of months back."

"What?"

"The argument."

"*What* argument?"

"The one in Greta's apartment. The one so loud it made Mrs. Hapwood consider calling the cops."

She squeezed her cup with both hands. "If there was such an argument, it wasn't with me."

"Then who was it with?"

"No idea."

"Greta didn't mention it?"

She shook her head. "And for your information, Greta and I didn't argue; we didn't want to waste the time. What we used each other for was reinforcement, not the opposite, and arguing would get in the way of that. But now that I think about it, we didn't disagree about all that much." She smiled wistfully. "Except rap music. Greta likes it; I think it ought to be banned." Her final words were thick with emotion, and she paused to get a grip.

"Let's back up a second," I said. "I need to know whether you really *don't* know anything about Greta, or whether you're part of her scheme and covering up."

"What scheme?"

"You tell me."

The hurt in her eyes was palpable. "I don't *know* about any scheme. And even if I did, why would I cover for her?"

"Because she's your friend and you might think you were doing her a favor. But I assure you, you aren't. She could be in big trouble, legal trouble, and I need to find her to keep it from happening."

She bit her lip and looked worried. "What kind of trouble are we talking about?"

"I can't tell you. I'm sorry. Do you know where she is?"

"No."

"Scout's honor?"

She nodded. "I really don't, and I've been worried sick about it. Ingrid's been after me to go to the police for days."

"Why didn't you?"

"I didn't want to make things worse."

"How would that happen?"

"I don't know. But around the time you showed up, Greta started acting funny. I figured she'd fallen in love—that does weird things to people, as you probably know."

"I have a vague recollection."

"But it seemed more sinister than that."

"Why?"

"Nothing specific; she was just . . . touchy. And upset about something. I figured maybe you ditched her after a couple of dates, but now that you mention it, she did say some things that hinted of schemes and plots of some sort."

"How so?"

"She made odd references to her past, as though something she'd done a long time ago was haunting her. And she was talking so morbidly."

"About what?"

"Suicide. Murder. Euthanasia. Abortion. All kinds of sick stuff. I was getting worried about her mental health; it really wasn't like her."

"What were the references to her past about?"

"She asked me if I'd ever known anyone who was truly evil. And I told her I hadn't and that I didn't believe such people existed. And she told me they did, and that one of them had been after her for years, but she had finally found a way to beat him."

"Was she talking about her ex-husband?"

"That was my assumption, but I'm not sure."

"Have you ever met him?"

"Luke? No. All I know is what she said about him."

"Which was?"

"That he was handsome, ambitious, and dumb."

"Where does he live?"

"I don't know."

"Was Greta afraid of him, do you think?"

"She was upset, I know that. But I don't know if he was the reason."

"Leo said the guy had come around recently, asking about her."

"If he did, I didn't see him."

I changed directions. "Where was Greta from?"

"Somewhere in the Midwest, I think. Ohio. Iowa. She didn't talk about it much."

"Did she go to college?"

"Yes, but I don't know where. I don't think she graduated. If she had a degree, she'd have a better job."

"Does she have family?"

"Her father's dead, I know that. So is mine. We talked about it one time. About what effect it had on us."

"What did you decide?"

Her eyes became ceramic. "I decided it was good riddance to bad rubbish. Greta decided she was still grieving over it."

"Why?"

"I don't know, exactly. She said she was responsible, somehow. But she didn't say how. Or for what."

"What about her mother?"

"I never heard her mention her."

"Greta had a child, she told me."

Linda nodded. "It died."

"How?"

"Some sort of congenital abnormality, I think, but I don't know what. I got the impression it happened right away, that she didn't bond with it or anything."

"Did Greta ever mention working for the Colbert clothing stores?"

"No. Did she?"

"Several years ago, apparently."

"We shopped there once, I remember. She did seem quite interested in the place, come to think of it. She wore these big dark glasses, like Garbo or someone, and she tried to go somewhere that was off limits, I remember that."

"Up to the eighth floor?"

Her eyes widened. "How did you know? She got furious when the elevator operator wouldn't take us. She wanted to sneak up the fire stairs but I managed to talk her out of it."

"What was she going to do when she got there?"

"She didn't say."

"She never mentioned Stuart Colbert? Or Millicent or Cynthia Colbert?"

"Maybe in passing, because they were in the news or something. But no big deal."

"The night I was with her she mentioned some sort of business deal that was going to make her money. Did she mention it to you?"

"Yes, but I think it fell through."

"Why?"

"She flew off the handle one day, not long before she . . . left. 'Nothing ever goes right for me,' she said. 'I'm jinxed. I'm a fly in a web and I can't get out of it. I'll *never* get out of it.' Oh. And there was something about someone handing her another nightmare."

"What do you think she was talking about?"

"I haven't the faintest idea. But I know she's been worrying about losing her job and I was afraid she'd gotten herself caught up in some kind of shady scheme and so if the police started looking for her, she'd be arrested and . . . anyway, that's why I haven't done more to find her. That's what I tell myself, at least." Her words trailed off into the hush of a moral dilemma.

"Had she been threatened?" I went on. "Or followed? Or had there been odd phone calls or weird messages?"

"No. Not that she told me."

"Is there anyone at work she confided in?"

"I doubt it. There was a lot of turnover at her level. She said it was like a war zone up there—no one stayed around long enough for her to get to know them."

I took time to review everything Linda had told me, and when I finished, I decided to move on. "Well, thank you for talking to me."

"Are you really going to look for her?"

I nodded.

"Is it because you're in love with her?"

"Partly," I said, then wondered how true it was.

"What's the other part?"

"Nothing I can talk about."

She looked at me for several seconds. "All of a sudden you're scaring me."

"I'm not going to hurt her; I'm going to help her."

"How can I be sure?"

"Trust me."

"I don't trust men anymore."

"Greta trusted me," I pointed out.

"No, she didn't. If she did, you'd know where she was." She closed her eyes and shook her head. "I should never have said anything. I shouldn't have gotten involved."

"You're being alarmist and that's not going to help anybody. Is there anything else you can think of? Something she said; some strange reference she made? Anything?"

She took time to calm down, then shook her head. "No, I . . . wait a minute. It was the oddest thing. One of the last times I saw her, she asked to borrow some baby clothes."

"Why?"

"She wouldn't say. But that's not the weird part. The weird part is, I had Mrs. Hapwood let me in Greta's apartment last week? Just to look around? And I found the little sleeper I gave her."

"So?"

"It was all torn up. Ripped to shreds. It was like some animal had savaged it, a pit bull or something. It almost made me sick."

SEVENTEEN

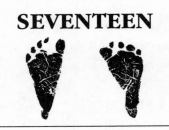

I spent ten minutes looking for a pay phone before I remembered that I had gone cellular three weeks before. When I got back to my car, I called the Central Station and asked for Charley Sleet. Even though it was Saturday, it didn't occur to me that Charley might be off duty: Charley was never off duty.

After lolling on hold for five minutes, I heard his grumble roll at me the way a bowling ball rolls down the gutter.

"Charley."

"Marsh."

"Going to be around awhile?"

"How long is that?"

"Twenty minutes."

"Twenty minutes, probably." He sniffed and cleared his throat—it sounded like he used an earthmover. "You got that sound you get when you want to make unauthorized use of the police force," he grumbled when he was finished.

"Fingerprints, is all," I assured him quickly. "Piece of cake."

"Piece of shit, is what it is. Is this something to do with your social life, like last time, or does it have to do with a criminal offense? Not that there's much difference."

"It's probably criminal, Charley."

The sarcasm went out of Charley's voice in a hurry—Charley doesn't joke about crime. "What kind of offense we talking about?"

"That's the problem—I don't know."

"Give me some possibilities."

"Kidnaping, maybe. Extortion, maybe. Murder, maybe. Or maybe just a missing person."

Charley knew me too well. "Or maybe nothing."

"Preferably, nothing," I agreed.

He sniffed. "I suppose you need it yesterday."

"Today will do."

"Monday. Things back up on weekends."

"Monday is fine."

Twenty minutes later I was double-parked on Vallejo Street in front of the Central Station. Charley was waiting out front, because one thing Charley knows is that, with him, when I say twenty minutes I mean twenty minutes.

With his bald head and stumpy neck and massive arms that were crossed like anchor chains on his barrel chest, he looked like the original Mr. Clean. Which wasn't a bad description of his personal ethic, either.

I gave him the ruler I'd lifted from Greta Hammond's apartment. He held it the way he would hold an orchid. "Whose is this?" he asked.

"That's what I want to know. Female. Thirties. As far as I know, no record."

"So we may not have a comp."

"I thought maybe an employment thing. Or driver's license."

"If you're lucky."

"If I wasn't lucky, I'd have to do legwork."

He cursed my truism. "Remind me why we're interested in the lady."

"Because she doesn't seem to have a past."

"What you're saying is she's got one but you don't know what it is."

"Close enough."

"She skipped, or what?"

"She made a deal with some friends of mine but she seems to be backing out. They want to know why. So do I."

He looked at the ruler again, as though it might contain a hint in scrimshaw. "Kidnaping can be tricky," he observed cryptically.

"I know."

"If something goes wrong, the loved ones like to have someone to blame."

"I know, Charley."

"So you should go through me if that's what it turns out to be."

"I will if I can."

His gnarled skull rumpled at my evasiveness. "Remember the last one."

"I remember."

Charley nodded to confirm that my mind was where he wanted it, which was on a kidnaping that had gone as sour as one of them can go. "Monday," he said, waving the ruler.

"Monday," I agreed.

He turned and went into the station, leaving me to remember what it felt like when we'd learned that the little girl who'd been snatched from the yard of her home in Seacliff had been buried alive before the ransom demand was called in and had suffocated before we'd found her. I hadn't had any worse day than that, except for the day my friend Harry Spring had been found dead out in the valley and I'd been there when they told his wife about it.

I stopped for coffee at Zorba's along the way, then mounted the stairs to the office. There were several messages on my answering machine; one of them was Russell Jorgensen, announcing that he was going sailing that afternoon and asking if I wanted to join him. I laughed and erased the tape.

I put on some coffee and watered the plants and sat down to look at the ledgers. Before long I was thinking about Greta Hammond, about where she could have gone and why she might have gone there. The more I thought about her, the less I liked the conclusions I was reaching, so I jotted some memos to some files, dictated some letters to some deadbeats, posted some expenses in the ledgers, and adjourned to my apartment up the slope of Telegraph Hill.

After I'd fixed a lunch consisting of a cheese sandwich and six Ore-os, and changed my clothes, I sat by the phone and thought about Bet-ty Fontaine. Thinking about Betty made me think about the reasons we'd broken up, which made me think about children and my reluc-tance to have them and what that seemed to say about the kind of man I was.

There was a range of ignoble possibilities, of course—selfishness, fussiness, listlessness, laziness—and they all no doubt played a part. But I wasn't nearly as reluctant as I was scared. Partly I was scared because I had been unhappy over much of my childhood, for a host of complex reasons, and I didn't want to inflict the disabilities that had caused or resulted from that condition on yet another generation of Tanners. But mostly I was scared of kids because over the years I'd seen too many of them in dire straits—kids shoved so far off the track they couldn't find their way back even when people who loved them hired people like me to bring them home.

They weren't the children of ogres always, either; surprisingly of-ten they were the offspring of decent people who didn't realize until too late that their children had run afoul of the wrong crowd or the wrong drug or the wrong chromosome or, as Freud suggested, had heard the wrong word at the wrong moment sometime before the age of two. It was hard enough to see the consequences as a detached observer—fif-teen-year-olds prostituting themselves, twelve-year-olds living under bridges and eating out of dumpsters, eighteen-year-olds terrorizing their grandparents to support their heroin habits—I didn't think I could bear to watch it happen to someone I had brought into being.

But that's not the way it would be, I would tell myself; the sad cas-es are only a fraction of the whole. How can you be sure? was my ri-poste. What makes you entitled to certainty? went the rebuttal. And somewhere in there I realized that what I was scared of most of all was that I wouldn't measure up, that fatherhood would be one more thing I would fail at, that it would generate yet another debacle for which I would have to take the blame.

I was still locked in an interior tussle when the telephone rang. I'd been thinking about her so much I was certain it was Betty, responding to a telepathic summons, but it wasn't Betty; it was Charley.

"I caught a break," he said.

"At the track?"

"At the lab. I took the ruler thing down there, and a friend of mine—Petey Karns—you know Petey?"

"The guy with the limp and the monocle?"

"Right."

"I know Petey."

"Anyway, Petey was in for some rush thing—another tourist mugging in the Western Addition—and he owes me a favor."

"Everyone on the force owes you a favor."

"Probably. Anyway, Petey dusted the ruler and I took it upstairs and we got a twelve-point match out of the machine."

"Greta Hammond. Right?"

"I don't know no Greta anybody. The match we got was a Clara Brennan."

"Who?"

"Brennan. Clara. Caucasian female, brown on green, five-six, one twenty-five. DOB seven eight fifty-six. Last known address, Santa Ana Way in the city."

"Where's that?"

"St. Francis Wood."

"You're kidding."

"I don't kid."

And all of a sudden the poor little waif from a walk-up on Kirkham Street had turned into a Clara Brennan from St. Francis Wood, one of the most exclusive neighborhoods in the city, the neighborhood where Rutherford Colbert still held court, surrounded by his feuding clan.

"What's this about, Marsh?" Charley was saying.

"I don't know, Charley. I don't know anything, obviously. So how come she was in your computer?"

"Driver's license. Age sixteen."

"Any record on her?"

"No." Someone said something in the background, then Charley asked me, "Is that it?"

"For now."

"Good," he repeated, then announced the going rate for cooperation. "Dinner. Chan's. Thursday. Seven."

"Clement Street; seven o'clock. I'll be there."

I hung up and called Russell Jorgensen. "About that sailing trip," I said when he answered.

"You got the message. Good. Can you come?"

"Where and when?"

"Yacht club in an hour."

"How many people are going to be there?"

"How many do you want to be there?"

"Just us," I told him.

EIGHTEEN

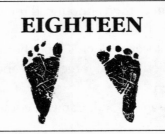

I was sure I was going to throw up. I was afraid I was going to throw up. I hoped I was going to throw up. I was afraid I *wouldn't* throw up.

That's the way it went for a while, as Russell Jorgensen's thirty-eight-foot ketch bobbed on the bay like a champagne cork. The breeze was at eighteen knots from the west-southwest, the sails were full to bursting, the hull was canted to an alarming angle, the electronic sheets and halyards were whizzing up and down, and the water that splashed off the prow was as salty as a good margarita. My stomach journeyed from my throat to my groin and back again, and again and again, like a piston in a two-stroke engine. My head spun like a flywheel. Russell was loving every minute of it and I was hanging on for dear life.

From time to time, he gave me something to do, usually involving ropes. On two occasions, he let me man the helm, or tend the tiller, or whatever you call it when you steer the damned thing. Like most aspects of sailing, it was harder than it looked to do right: things kept flapping that weren't supposed to flap.

For the most part I was left to my own devices, as Russell steered a course for Angel Island while trying to avoid the scores of other sailors who had duplicated our decision to sally forth on the bounding main. My plan had been to have a leisurely chat with the skipper about now, taking advantage of his divided attention to pierce his customary reticence. But given the exigencies of this particular form of recreation, conversation was going to have to wait until we were safely on dry land. Which, as far as I was concerned, was already overdue.

After an hour or so, the breeze seemed to subside and we came about onto a comparatively stable tack. When everything was back in trim, Russell broke out the lunch basket and I cracked open the Anchor Steam. His idea of seagoing fare was goose pâté and a crab sandwich. My taste tends more to roast beef and coleslaw but it was a good day to eat less than my fill, so I consumed what I needed to be polite, and tried to keep it down as we took a turn toward Alcatraz.

Half an hour later, we were nibbling chocolate truffles and relaxing in a reach downwind. I watched a particularly opulent cruiser knife its way toward the Golden Gate, then decided not to wait for shore.

"Clara Brennan," I blurted, apropos of nothing.

Russell only half-heard me. "What?"

"Clara Brennan," I repeated.

Russell was suddenly all ears. The sail luffed and a halyard slacked, but for the first time all day, he didn't trim them up. "What about her?"

"That's what I want to know."

He was surprised and he didn't like it—lawyers don't like surprises because that's when they make mistakes. "Please tell me what you're talking about," he asked levelly.

I waved at a woman on a passing skiff who looked even more imperiled than I was; she seemed pleased to have a sympathizer. "I need to know what Clara Brennan has to do with the Colbert case."

Russell rubbed spray off his face as he thought it over. "It would help if you'd explain why you think she has *anything* to do with it," he said finally, still reluctant to address the question.

"I can't."

"Can't? Or won't?"

"Take your pick," I said, more irritated by the moment at Russell's dodging and weaving. It had begun to look like the foundations of the Colbert case were quicksand and, if they were, Russell had probably known it from the first. I'd thought we were closer than that, close enough that he wouldn't try to take advantage of me, but then again this was the first time we'd ever been sailing.

Russell tended his boat for a few more moments, then sat back down and looked toward the looming wart of Alcatraz, which somehow had come quite close. He didn't seem to enjoy the view.

"Is there some reason I shouldn't know about the Brennan woman, Russell?" I asked in all innocence.

"Not really. It's just an unfortunate chapter in the Colbert story."

"How so?"

He sighed and shook his head, as if the subject were too dreary to contemplate. "Is the Brennan name familiar to you?" he asked at last.

"Should it be?"

"Ethan Brennan was Clara's father. He went to work for the Colbert stores as a stock boy when he was eighteen years old and just out of Mission High. Ten years later, he was the highestranking officer in the company, next to Rutherford Colbert himself."

"How did he manage that?"

"He was a genius."

"How so?"

"When Rutherford founded the store, it carried mens wear exclusively and was at best a marginal operation. Then Ethan Brennan came along, and put them into high-end women's fashion, and profits eventually soared. Apparently he had an uncanny ability to pick which of the European and New York styles would catch on out here and which the local swells wouldn't touch with a kid glove. And he was smart enough to follow up with exclusive distribution arrangements with popular designers like Balenciaga and Chanel and Schiaparelli, which meant the hot stuff was available only at Colbert's. Plus, his personality was a perfect complement to Rutherford's."

"In what way?"

"Rutherford was—is—hard as nails. He was the toughest negotiator in the rag trade on the West Coast, with suppliers, staff, ad media, everyone. The deals he cut with the New York manufacturers were legendary—his margins were bigger than anyone's. But he needed someone to smooth the feathers he ruffled and Ethan Brennan was that guy. Ethan kept the staff happy with a bonus system, the models happy with a better rate, the suppliers happy with consistently high volumes, and the customers happy by living up to the motto he came up with—'Colbert's cares.'"

"Sounds like quite a guy."

"He was. What he also did was keep the old man from making mistakes of hubris—not too large an inventory, or too rapid expansion, or too big a sales staff, that kind of thing. I think it's fair to say that without Ethan Brennan, the Colbert stores wouldn't exist today. One recession or another would have wiped them out."

From the look on his face, Russell was hoping his essay would slake my thirst. "I'm losing track of the names and numbers of the players," I said after a moment. "You've got Rutherford and his kids—Stuart and Cynthia. And Stuart's wife Millicent's family—her father worked for Colbert's too, right?"

Russell nodded. "Millicent's father, Leonard Stanley, was comptroller for the stores. He's retired."

"And now we've got the Brennans."

"Ethan and Opal. And their daughter, Clara."

"Cozy situation."

He laughed. "Rutherford was rather like a potentate there for a while—Santa Ana Way in St. Francis Wood was virtually a company town. The old man's big place came first, then the Stanleys moved in next door. When Ethan Brennan became Rutherford's right-hand man, he and his family moved out there, too. It was a pretty closed society, apparently—wives played bridge, husbands played golf, kids smoked dope and went surfing and got in minor scrapes together—you know what I mean."

I compared life in St. Francis Wood with the life I'd led in Chaldea, back in the frigid Midwest. "Vaguely. And it sounds a little incestuous."

"After they were grown," Russell continued, "Stuart and his sister each bought a house in the area, too, so they could stay close to the old man."

"Keeping their eye on the prize, as it were."

Russell grinned. "Something like that."

"Where does Clara come in?" I asked, as Russell paused to see if I was satisfied with the information I already had.

"I'm not sure what you mean."

"I'm not either," I said. "So tell me what you know about her."

"Not that much, actually; mostly just hearsay."

"Hearsay's fine."

"Clara was the Brennans' only child. She grew up next door to the elder Colberts. I think she was between Millicent and Stuart in age— maybe two years younger than Stuart."

"So Stuart has known Clara Brennan since childhood?"

"Sure." Russell frowned. "But what does she have to *do* with anything? I haven't heard her name in years."

"Tell me what happened to Ethan Brennan," I said instead of answering his question.

Russell blinked. "What makes you think something happened to him?"

"The look on your face when I mentioned his name."

Russell did some more sailing, then raised his face to the sun, as though it would bleach out the smudges in his brain. "Rutherford Colbert is not a generous man," he began.

"Titans of commerce seldom are."

"True. Anyway, as the years went by and the empire expanded, Ethan Brennan wasn't being compensated nearly as well as he should have been, given his contribution to the company. Everyone knew it, Ethan most of all. But by the time Rutherford took out his own salary and the dividends were paid on his stock and the children's shares as well, there wasn't much left for poor Ethan. It began to grate on him and he asked for a better salary, but Rutherford wouldn't give in, except in the form of a 10 percent nonvoting interest in the business. Which was marginally better, but it still left Ethan on the short end, no better off than the kids. I'm pretty sure Ethan was ready to quit—Magnin's wanted him awfully bad at one point. But for some reason, he took matters into his own hands."

"How?"

Russell's look turned grave. "Embezzlement. Big time. Hundreds of thousands of dollars."

"When?"

"Early seventies."

"Was he prosecuted?"

Russell shook his head. "Rutherford offered a deal. Ethan was fired, of course. And he agreed to turn over most of his liquid assets to Rutherford in partial restitution, and to leave the state, and to keep out of retailing forever. In return, Rutherford would keep the embezzlement under wraps and forgo any contact with the authorities. Since it was a private company, he could do that; if it were public, the stockholders would have had to be told."

"Ethan agreed to all this?"

"Ethan killed himself." Russell's face turned ashen, even in the heat of the sun. "Which I suppose is a form of consent, given the situation."

"Or confession."

Russell nodded.

"Where did this happen?"

"The suicide? At the Colbert mansion in St. Francis Wood. Ethan shot himself on Rutherford's front porch."

"Jesus."

"Indeed."

"What happened to the rest of the Brennan family?"

"Rutherford bought the Brennan house out of probate and gave it to his wife, Delilah, after they separated. Opal Brennan stayed on in the house to care for Mrs. Colbert."

"Rutherford and his wife live in separate houses?"

He nodded. "Delilah has a mental problem."

"What kind?"

"She's obsessive-compulsive, among other things, particularly about personal hygiene. It got so bad, she wouldn't let Rutherford wear shoes in the house. When she insisted he wear rubber gloves to bed, he had to move her to separate quarters. She's virtually a recluse."

"How about the daughter? What happened to her after her father died?"

"Clara was seventeen when it happened, I think. She was an only child; she and her father were particularly close. She took his death hard—started running with a fast crowd, drinking and carrying on. Not long afterward she ran off with a young man who worked for Rutherford on the estate. A day laborer, basically, named Luke Drummond."

"Where did she end up?"

"I don't know. By then there was no reason to keep track of her—it was best for the Colberts that the Brennan chapter was forgotten as soon as possible."

"Because of the suicide, you mean."

"And the embezzlement."

"Were Clara and Stuart involved when they were young?"

Russell's grip on the wheel seemed to tighten. "You mean romantically?"

I nodded.

"Why? What makes you ask that? What makes any of this relevant to *anything*?"

"I can't tell you, Russell."

"Why not?"

"For one thing, I don't know yet. For another, you've got too many clients: Stuart, and Cynthia, and Rutherford, too. Am I right?"

"But what does Cynthia have to do with Millicent and Stuart's effort to have a baby? Or with Rutherford either, for that matter?"

"I haven't the faintest idea."

"Then what's with the history lesson? You sound as though what happened to Ethan Brennan had something to do with Greta Hammond's disappearance."

"It did, I think. But I don't know what yet. I just know that Stuart

Colbert's up to something besides making a high-tech child and until I know what it is you're better off not knowing something that would create a conflict of interest."

"Why don't you let *me* be the judge of whether there's a conflict of interest?" he said huffily.

"I would, except I've got a personal and professional interest in Greta Hammond and I'm not willing to see those interests sacrificed so you can stay on the good side of the Colberts."

"I wouldn't do anything like that, Marsh. You know that."

"I know you wouldn't want to, Russell," I said. "Can we go home now?"

NINETEEN

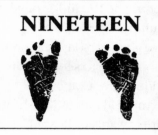

"I appreciate your seeing me on Sunday. And on such short notice," I added as she faced me in the doorway deciding what to do with me. After scratching her nose and redraping her bodice and twirling her hair on a finger, Millicent Colbert stepped back to let me into her home. She was puzzled and uneasy and more than a little apprehensive, so I tried to calm her down.

"I'm not bringing bad news," I said for the second time that day. "As I told you on the phone, this is routine." I sought the aid of my most engaging grin.

"It may be routine for you," she said, "but I'm not used to being questioned. Except by my husband," she added with a timorous smile.

"I understand. I just need to ask you about someone you used to know. Then I'll be on my way."

"But I don't understand why Stuart can't *be* here. And I certainly don't understand why I have to keep this a *secret* from him."

I gestured beyond the narrow confines of the entryway toward the accommodating expanse of the house. "May we?"

She reddened. "Of course. Please come this way. Would you care for coffee?"

"Only if it's no trouble."

"Sylvia just made a fresh pot."

"Then coffee would be nice."

After a quick pirouette, she led me to the core of her colorful lair, which seemed to have been designed to augment the gush of her clothing. After making sure I was comfortably ensconced, she went off to see about coffee. I took advantage of her absence to take a tiny inventory.

The decor was as busy as her blouse, highlighted by dozens of flowers, both fresh and dried, stuffed into a welter of wicker baskets and cut-glass vessels that were sprinkled throughout the room. There were lots of pinks and yellows and blues in the fabrics on the furniture, and plenty of pillows and padding and poufs to make it all seem comfy. The carpet was stark white, with a blue and yellow bouquet woven into the center section, beneath a chandelier that served as its sun.

As if that weren't busy enough, on the arms and backs of the furnishings were a variety of doilies and what used to be called antimacassars but probably aren't called that anymore, layer on top of layer of ever more intricate design. The shelves and occasional tables were dotted with glass and ceramic bowls containing individually wrapped pieces of peppermint candy; the walls were stamped with at least a dozen heavily framed land- and seascapes, one of which could pass for an original Monet. Except for the pseudo Monet, the room was not to my taste, but it was a definite, if somewhat labored, assertion of personality, which I suppose is what interior design is all about. Its most surprising aspect was that the personality on display was Millicent's, not her husband's.

The Colberts' house—Stuart and Millicent's that is—was smack in the center of St. Francis Wood, on the end of the stretch of Santa Ana Way that served as the Colbert compound, just north of the fountain and gateposts that formed St. Francis Circle. We were two doors down from the patriarch's ungainly mansion, a hulking stucco and tile monstrosity that simmered behind far too much wrought iron and was overrun with so much vegetation it looked like the long-lost villa of a forgotten Spanish king of the type that Velázquez used to paint, the ones whose minds and bodies were congealed by too much inbreeding.

In between the mansion and the Stuart Colberts' house was the Stanley place—Millicent lived next door to her parents, which probably accounted for her nervous nature. On the far side of Rutherford's castle was the former Brennan place, where Rutherford's wife now lived; beyond that were Cynthia Colbert's digs. I hadn't had time to inspect either of the latter homes as yet, but they were the next stops on my tour.

When Millicent returned to the living room she was followed by a Latina retainer bearing coffee and pastry on a silver tray. The woman deposited the tray on a marble table, looked at her mistress for further instruction, then vanished when no mandate was forthcoming.

Millicent poured. I sipped, then nibbled, then sipped a second time. Millicent abstained, although she seemed pleased to watch me fuel myself. I tried to think of a subject of mutual interest other than the business that had brought me to her but I couldn't come up with anything that would override her concern for her missing child. From time to time her eyelids fluttered as rapidly as a hummingbird's wings—she was desperate to know what I was up to but knew it was gauche to ask. She was probably afraid if she made a faux pas, I'd go next door and tattle.

I put down my cup and crossed my legs and tried to make both of us comfortable. "As I told you on the phone, I'm not going to ask you to reveal any family secrets, or any trade secrets, either. But it's essential that our talk remain confidential, even from your husband. Are you still agreeable to that arrangement, Mrs. Colbert?"

She blinked half a dozen times. "I suppose so. But I still don't understand why. Stuart's so good in a crisis; he's always so . . . controlled."

I smiled the way a dentist smiles when he tells you it's not going to hurt. "There's no question that your husband is a powerful man, Mrs. Colbert. Even a willful one. Which is why I'm concerned that if he gets a sense of how I'm proceeding in the search for your surrogate, he'll be inclined to take matters into his own hands. I'm sure you can appreciate that such action on his part could cause complications, and if there's one thing we don't need in this case, it's more complications."

"Yes, but Stuart will want to—"

I held up a hand. "He'll know everything in due course, you can count on it. But for now, there's no need for him to know we've talked. Is there?"

Her shoulders sagged. "I suppose not."

I took another sip of coffee, tiptoeing to the point. "Russell Jorgensen can hire any investigator in the city, Mrs. Colbert; he chose me because I'm good at what I do. I wouldn't presume to tell your husband how to sell ball gowns and we need to make sure he doesn't try to tell me how to look for a missing person. Or worse, start looking on his own."

"I understand, Mr. Tanner," she said with surprising resolve. "What is it you need to know?"

I put down my cup and uncrossed my legs. "I need to know about Clara Brennan."

She blinked her hummingbird blink, gave another twist to her hair, and finally shook her head. "I don't understand. How could *she* be involved in this? I haven't seen Clara in twenty years."

"I have reason to believe that if I can locate Clara Brennan, I'll be closer to finding Greta Hammond. Which is to say, closer to finding your child."

"But why? What does Clara have to do with the Hammond woman?"

My urge to accommodate her was so strong, I barely caught myself before blurting that they were one and the same person. "I'm not sure yet," I said instead. "But my investigation indicates there's a link between the two women. Since I haven't come up with a firm lead to Greta, it seems sensible to spend some time looking for Clara."

"I see." Millicent Colbert stood up and crossed the room and looked at a porcelain statue of what looked like albino lovers entwined on a tree stump. "Clara used to live down the street. Her mother still does."

"I know."

"Clara and I were quite good friends for a while. She used to help me make furniture for my dollhouse. I used to borrow her clothes."

"So you were always close?"

She did a quick twirl. "Till she started going out with boys. Clara was popular with boys and I wasn't, so I didn't see her very often after we were, oh, thirteen or so." Her smile was brief and rueful. "She had better things to do all of a sudden; she decided dolls were silly. I never did decide that," she added in response to a question I hadn't asked. The ache in her tone was palpable. I wondered if it was the kind of ache that produced envy, or even hatred, of its stimulus.

"Did Clara go out with any particular boys in those days?" I asked.

"All of them, it seemed like."

"But no one special?"

"They were all special. For about a month." The spark in her eye was spiteful.

"Did she ever go out with your husband?"

Her lips pursed as though she'd just sucked something sour. "I don't know. I don't think so, but I was oblivious to those sorts of things back then."

"How about the man Clara married? Who was he?"

"Luke? Luke Drummond wasn't one of us, he was just . . . around, you know? He didn't live on Santa Ana or anything. He was just a helper."

"Where did he live, do you know?"

She shook her head. "He worked at the mansion on afternoons and weekends. He didn't go to our school—I'm not sure he went to *any* school—so that's the only time I saw him, mowing yards and pruning hedges and things. His mother may have worked in the big house, I'm not sure—I didn't pay much attention to servants back then. I still don't," she added abjectly, as though it was another in a long list of failings.

"Why was Clara Brennan attracted to this Luke?"

A scrim was peeled from her eyes and they became momentarily glossy and lustful. "Luke Drummond was the best-looking boy I'd ever seen. When he took his shirt off and was digging a hole or sawing a board or something, the muscles in his back would ripple like butterscotch pudding when you pour it in a bowl." She colored and looked away. "He was beautiful, and so was she. They were a perfect match, except of course everyone was scandalized because they came from such different backgrounds. Stuart couldn't get over it; he took it as a personal affront. As though Luke didn't have a right to talk to her, let alone marry her."

Which seemed to make Stuart more than a detached observer of the Santa Ana social scene. "What kind of person was Luke? Mean? Violent? A drinker or doper?"

She shrugged. "I don't really know. I never talked to him, only to say hi to. He always looked so envious, I remember that. As though the people on Santa Ana were from another species. As though living out here was the greatest thing that could happen to a person."

"It probably seemed that way to him."

She looked toward the window and the manicured world beyond it. "Well, it might have looked enviable on the outside, but inside it was different. We certainly weren't *happier* than other people, I don't think. *I* wasn't, I know that. I was miserable in those days. So was Stuart."

"Why was Stuart so miserable?"

"Because his father was never satisfied with anything he did and because his sister was better at most things than he was. She was even stronger than he was; the kids teased him about it unmercifully. I felt sorry for him. Of course in those days, he didn't care what I felt; I'm not sure he does now." She blinked and gnawed her lip. "I didn't mean that. Of course he cares. He wouldn't have agreed to go through all this turbulence to give me a baby if he didn't care."

"Why were *you* so miserable in those days, Mrs. Colbert?"

She had stopped blinking and now seemed subdued and transfixed, the ether of the past acting on her nerves as a tranquilizer. "Because I was a gawky kid with no hips or breasts even after the other girls had them, someone who wasn't good in school, or at sports, or fast dancing, or anything else that was important at that age, including giving boys what they wanted." She blushed when she saw my smile. "I don't mean sex, necessarily, I mean the flirting, the suggestiveness, the fawning—all the stuff that makes boys want to spend time with you at that age. Or any age, I guess."

"Was Clara Brennan good at those things?"

"She was the best."

"Then why did she end up with Luke? Why didn't one of the rich kids latch on to her?"

"Because of what happened to her father."

"Tell me about that," I said.

She finally abandoned the window. "What do you want to know? He got in trouble at the company and blew his brains out when they caught him."

"Did everyone know about the trouble before he killed himself, or did that only come out afterward?"

"*I* didn't know about it, that's for sure. I don't think any of the other kids did, either. And Clara didn't seem much different till after he was dead, so . . . I *think* it came out after they found him spattered all over the porch at the big house." She shuddered. "It was awful. They painted it over and everything, but there were still spots that seeped through—Luke used to sell tickets to see them, a dollar a peek. I still get the creeps when I go over there. Not that I ever do, except at Christmas."

"What happened after Ethan Brennan died? What did people say about it?"

"There were all kinds of guesses about how much money he'd taken and what he'd done with it. People said it was buried in the yard—some kids even dug it all up one night, but they didn't find anything. There were rumors he'd done other things, too."

"What kind of things?"

She colored. "You know kids—they make melodrama out of everything."

"For example."

"Oh, they said Ethan had raped one of the models down at the store, or that he got caught trying to rob the mansion, or was trying to kill Mr. Colbert so he could take over the company himself, or that he didn't commit suicide—he was killed because he and Mrs. Colbert were lovers. All kinds of stories were going around; it must have been awful for Clara—she and Luke ran off right afterward. Luke was the only one who stood by her, what with the shame and everything." She closed her eyes and remembered more. "I would have stood by her, too, except I didn't count by then."

"Did you ever see Clara Brennan after that?"

She shook her head. "Not once."

"Did she and Luke get married?"

"I heard they did."

"Did you ever see him around here afterward?"

"No."

"How about his family? Where are they?"

"I never saw his father. His mother worked in the big house, I think, but she left right after Luke did. Fern was a nice woman," she added generously.

"What's wrong with your mother-in-law?"

She tossed a nervous glance in the direction of the house down the block. "Delilah's a hermit. Never entertains; never goes outside for anything. I hardly ever see her and I don't know anyone who does except Mrs. Brennan. She didn't even come to our wedding—she says we're unclean."

"What did she mean by that?"

Her face took on a look of abject panic. "I didn't ask her. Would you?"

I smiled and shook my head. "Did Luke Drummond have any reason to hate your husband, Mrs. Colbert?"

The question surprised her. "Why would he?"

"I thought maybe Stuart might have fired him. Or taken his girlfriend. Or beat him up. Or embarrassed him in some way. One of those things that happen when you're young and one person thinks it's trivial and the other holds a grudge for the rest of his life."

She was shaking her head before I finished. "I don't know of anything like that, but Stuart and I didn't run in the same crowd in those days, so I can't say it didn't happen." An impish smile stretched and flattened her lips. "But no one on Santa Ana was strong enough to beat up Luke Drummond, that's for sure."

She laughed a quick titter, then as quickly began to cry. "I can't help thinking about my *baby* out there, growing inside someone else, not even knowing who I am or how much I love him. Maybe being damaged by what that Hammond woman's doing to herself. Maybe being sick. I feel like such a *failure*: we should have adopted; I *told* him we should have. But he wouldn't listen. He had to have a child of his own. As if anything matters but how much you love it."

Sobs racked her body in a powerful paroxysm; I could only sit and watch. "What if I *never* get to see him, Mr. Tanner?" she continued, working the rhetoric to its gloomy end. "What if he's born and grows up and I don't ever know the tiniest thing about him? What if that's the only baby I ever have, and I don't even have *him*? What do I do, then?"

I didn't know what to say, so I told her I was going to try to keep that from happening. The bromide didn't seem to soothe either of us.

TWENTY

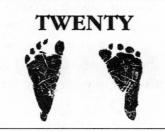

I paused in front of Rutherford Colbert's mansion long enough to absorb the message that beamed my way from within the pink stucco walls and the orange tile roof and the tangled web of foliage that wrapped the quixotic structure in a swath of leafy bondage. My sense was that the wavelengths stemmed from a source that was hostile, forbidding, and arrogant—we don't want you here, they said; we don't need you here, they announced; we are your betters in here, they bragged; we repel invaders, they warned. It was enough to keep me moving—I hurried next door and rang the bell for reasons that remained inchoate, since I was far from sure that the elder Mrs. Colbert was competent to conduct a conversation.

After the fourth ring I decided I was going to be just another worldly object shunned by the reclusive woman who had reportedly been a holdout in the house for almost twenty years. But as I turned to walk on to her daughter's residence, the door squeaked open at my back.

The woman who commandeered the threshold looked at me with a bulldog expression that suggested I was violating a cardinal principle and that if I knew what was good for me, I'd repair to a suitable temple and atone for it. For a moment, I thought it was Delilah Colbert herself determined to bar my entrance, but this woman seemed both too focused and too diminutive to be the allegedly addled mother of the one of her children I knew.

I nodded a greeting and clasped my hands at my back, bending at the waist like Groucho. "My name's Tanner. I'd like to speak with Mrs. Colbert for a moment."

She was apparently a combination security guard and practical nurse. She wore a shapeless blue smock and serviceable black shoes and her hair was contained by a net of a type I hadn't seen since I used to visit my grandmother in search of oatmeal cookies. But my grandmother didn't wear rubber gloves that reached to her elbows. Beneath their elastic sheaths, her tiny forearms were the size and density of pool cues.

"Mrs. Colbert no longer receives visitors," she said unnaturally, as though reciting directions in a foreign tongue.

"It's about—"

"Doesn't matter what it's about—no visitors."

"—her son," I finished nonetheless.

She frowned the way Warren Christopher frowns. "Stuart? What about him?"

"I have reason to believe he may be going to come to grief because of what happened in this neighborhood twenty years ago."

The barrier didn't melt. "We've all come to grief because of what happened twenty years ago. If Stuart's stirring all that up again, grief is the least he deserves."

I met her look. "Even if that's the case, it would be to the advantage of both of you to talk to me."

"Miz Colbert's got enough troubles, she's not looking to take on any more. And neither am I."

In the face of her obstinacy, I blurted more than I should have. "Even if it would help her grandson?"

She puffed like a partridge. "There's no reason for her to have anything at all to do with that boy at this point, and you can tell Stuart I said so."

The response seemed oddly heartless. "Shouldn't Mrs. Colbert be the one to decide that?"

The question seemed to penetrate a layer of her conditioning, but one layer wasn't enough. "I've got my orders."

I unclasped my hands and folded them across my chest. "What's your name?"

"What do you need to know that for?"

"I like to know who I'm pestering."

She crossed her arms to ape me. "You're not going to be pestering me any longer; I've got chores to do."

"You're Opal Brennan, aren't you?"

"What if I am?"

"If you are, then your daughter is involved in this as well."

She squinted against the suggestion. "I don't know what you're talking about. Involved in what?"

"Kidnaping, maybe."

Her right hand rose to her throat and remained like an ivory broach, of gnarled and knobby design. "Who's been kidnaped? Clara?"

"At this point it's not clear that's what's happened. But she could be in serious trouble. But if you and Mrs. Colbert cooperate, I may be able to get her out of it."

Her voice rose with the aid of twenty years of paranoia. "How do I know that? How do I know you're not a policeman? Or another of them that's working for Mr. Colbert?"

"I am working for Mr. Colbert. But I'm also a friend of Clara's and I'm trying to help her out of the mess she's in."

"That's easy enough to say. It might not be so easy to prove."

"I first knew her as Greta Hammond. She lived in an apartment on Kirkham Street. Near Golden Gate Park. I think she buys you your rubber gloves."

The conversation was going into forbidden territory but she didn't know how to confine it. "That proves you knew her. It doesn't prove you're a friend."

"She collects Supremes records and eats sauerkraut even though she hates it." I looked for a thaw but still didn't find one. "She likes vanilla wafers and her right breast is larger than her left."

Her hand dropped from her throat and made a fist at her abdomen. "Gracious." She took an involuntary step backward, into the gloomy confines of a house where licentiousness was never an issue. "What is it you're telling me?"

"I'm telling you that I'm Clara's friend," I said again, then indulged in what I hoped was hyperbole. "And I'm telling you she needs to let me find her if she wants to keep out of prison."

"I . . . perhaps you should come in."

More frightened than I wanted her to be, she let me into the foyer, then opened the door to an adjoining parlor that seemed to have been custom-made for her. The room was small and cramped, furnished with delicate chairs and tables inspired by the French provincials, each piece so reduced in scale they might have been purloined from Millicent Colbert's dollhouse. The floors were fir; the rugs thrown over them were loosely woven cottons that probably originated in Turkey. The lamps were hooded with colored glass that gave the room the inexact illumination of a church. Half a dozen bowls held discs of peppermint candy, just like the sweets down the block.

Opal Brennan led me toward matching chairs that faced each other in front of the tiny fireplace. The painting over the mantel was of the smaller man in the snapshot I'd seen at Greta Hammond's, the one who had been gazing at his mate with fondness. "Handsome man," I said when she saw me looking at it.

"Yes," she said simply.

I looked at the portrait again. Rutherford Colbert seemed pleasant and guileless and chipper, with no hint of the cruelty he was reputed to be capable of. I decided the artist was more tactful than precise, and had been paid to be just that.

"Have you spoken with your daughter lately, Mrs. Brennan?" I asked as I took a seat by the fire.

A bulb flashed on and off within her eyes. "Why is everyone looking for her?"

"Are you saying other people have asked about her?"

She started to elaborate, then didn't. "Some."

"What did you tell them?"

"That I didn't know anything about it."

"I don't believe that's true," I said.

She grew huffy at the slur. "Why wouldn't it be?"

"Because she's your daughter."

"That hasn't meant anything since she ran off twenty years ago."

I went back to square one. "As I said, my business has to do with Mrs. Colbert's grandchild."

She frowned and shook her head. "Delilah's got no interest in that circumstance whatever. Chickens coming home to roost is all it is."

For a second time, the reference was puzzling. "That's an odd thing to say about a child," I said, in an effort to draw her out.

"That's no child and never was or will be."

I still didn't know what she was talking about. "I'm afraid you're confused, Mrs. Brennan. Maybe if you let me talk to your boss, we can straighten it out."

She started to recite her exclusionary rule once more but something made her change her mind. Like a toy figure down from atop a music box, she got to her feet and returned to the foyer, then disappeared down the hall. I was as neglected as the candy in the crystal bowls.

I figured it was no better than even money she'd come back for me, but she did. "Mrs. Colbert says she can't help you," Opal announced from the foyer, proud that her stance had been validated. "She says she doesn't know anything about Clara whatsoever."

"She must know something—Clara grew up in this house and you've been her companion for twenty years."

Opal Brennan sniffed at my naiveté. "You don't know anything *about* this house, then or now, and there's no use pretending you do. Mrs. Colbert says to leave her be."

I fired my last shot. "Tell her that I've been hired to find Clara, and that if you two don't cooperate, I'll tell her husband that she has crucial information that she's refusing to disclose. And I'll tell the police as well, since they'll be involved in this sooner or later."

I'd gambled that Rutherford's name would be more galvanizing than his son's, and I was right. Opal gave my threat some thought, then disappeared down the hall once again.

Minutes later she was back. "Take off your shoes if you're coming."

I stepped into the foyer and did as I was told. In my stocking feet I felt four feet tall, which put me on a par with Opal Brennan, which might have been the idea.

"Washroom's in there." Opal pointed at a narrow doorway to the left of the staircase. "Clean your hands, then put these on." She handed me a seersucker bathrobe, a white gauze mask, and a pair of rubber gloves.

"Why the garments?"

"Miz Colbert doesn't like germs."

"I don't have any germs."

"Everybody has germs."

"Then why aren't you wearing a mask?"

She straightened like a soldier. "The germs I have are too old to do damage—I haven't been outside this house since 1974."

I went in the bathroom and did my duty. When I came out, I felt like an amalgam of Ben Casey and the Lone Ranger.

"Did you wash up?" Opal demanded. "She'll smell your fingers, to see if you used the soap."

I told her I'd used the soap.

Satisfied with my ablutions, Opal led me down the hallway, past a music room and a utility closet, and opened a door that admitted us into a chamber that was as different from the rest of the house as gypsum is from mud.

The floor and walls and ceiling formed an igloo of enameled white, unmarred by ornament, antiseptic in aspect. The vinyl floor had been cleared of everything but a bed and a chair and a tungsten floor lamp that was bright enough to illuminate any germ that blundered by. The only other objects in view were an electric humidifier, some sort of air cleaner that purred like a cat in a corner, and a table next to the bed from which dangled what looked to be an old-fashioned douche bag. The odors were of rubbing alcohol and disinfectant; the aura was distinctly creepy.

Some newspapers were stacked by the bed as well. Newspapers are clean, supposedly; they're what you wrap babies in when you have them in the backseats of taxis or the aisles of airplanes. Which made them one of the few suitable companions for the woman who occupied the bed the way a corpse occupies a coffin.

"This is Delilah Colbert," Opal Brennan said, as if there were some other option. "You're to state your piece and move on."

Propped at an angle by a mound of foam pillows, Delilah Colbert wore a white satin gown that buttoned at the neck and wrists and fell well below her ankles. There wasn't an alien object on her body—no makeup, no jewelry, no article of clothing other than the shimmering raiment. Her skin was as white as the walls and eerily unlined, as though it were a piece of lingerie she'd slipped into when she heard I was coming. Her lips were a bloodless buttonhole in the center of her stolid face; her hair was as white as her gown and wrapped in a black net much like her companion's. Her eyes were drips of ink on a page of blank parchment; her fingers were raised off the bedclothes the way a pianist raises his hands at the end of an étude.

I decided to go with the truth. "My name is Tanner, Mrs. Colbert. I'm a detective. Your son has hired me to find Clara Brennan." The words were muffled and modulated by my mask.

I had half-expected her to be a drooler, or a mute, or a raver, or some other form of half-wit, so when she responded with perfect sense it was jarring. "What does he want with her?"

"She made a deal, then tried to run away from it."

"That shouldn't have been a surprise."

"Why not?"

"She's run away from him before."

Mrs. Colbert made an infinitesimal adjustment to her position—it seemed to absorb all her attention. When she was comfortable again, she regarded me with a clinical detachment that duplicated the immediate environment. "You're the first person to enter this room since my daughter came looking for money at Easter," she said, as though it was some sort of accomplishment.

"I appreciate the honor."

"It's not an honor, it's an indulgence. You mentioned my husband's name to gain admission."

"I thought it was the only key to the palace."

"Indeed. And what does he want with Clara?"

"I wouldn't know."

"You're not working for him?"

"No, I'm not. I'm working for Stuart."

She closed her eyes; the lids were as thin as rice paper. "So Stuart is looking for Clara as well. Does that mean his marriage to Millicent has foundered so soon?"

I shook my head. "They're fine."

"I doubt it," she demurred meanly. "What does he want with Clara?"

"As I said, he hired her to do a job for him and he's afraid she won't finish it."

"What kind of job?"

I was more circumspect than I had been with Opal Brennan. "That would be up to him to disclose."

"That will be difficult—I don't communicate with Stuart."

"Why not?"

Her back arched against the feathers. "He defied me over a matter of importance. I can't forgive him for it."

"What did he do?"

Her smile was surprisingly sassy. "That would be none of your business."

"It would be in your family's best interest if Clara were found, Mrs. Colbert," I projected doggedly. "And in her mother's best interest as well." The face beneath my mask was wet with sweat and spittle. I was beginning to feel like a felon.

"Are people trying to harm Clara?" Delilah Colbert asked. "Is that what you're implying?"

"I don't know," I said truthfully. "All I know is, she's disappeared and no one from her new life or her old life admits to having seen her. Do *you* know any reason why that might have happened?"

"I know nothing about Clara's life as an adult, but she was born in trouble and she was raised in trouble and she was in trouble the day she left Santa Ana Way. She has always had a shadow over her; I wish she didn't, but she does. I would guess her life remains clouded."

"What kind of trouble are you talking about?"

The women exchanged glances that reeked of a confederacy that I wasn't party to. "That's none of your business, either."

"I think it is."

"That's not for you to say, I'm afraid. How is Nathaniel?"

I blinked. "Who?"

Mrs. Colbert looked at me for several seconds, then lowered her chin to her chest, which I took as her signal she was preparing to sleep. "It's time," Opal Brennan said at my back.

I didn't take the hint. "Have you heard from Clara in the past few weeks, Mrs. Colbert?"

She spoke through the muffle of her bodice. "If Opal hasn't heard from her, why would I?"

My frustration won out. "What happened out here twenty years ago? Why do you two *live* like this? Why are you both estranged from your children?"

Delilah Colbert didn't speak and didn't move. Opal Brennan put her hand on my biceps and tried to spin me away from her boss. "It's time," she said again.

As she tugged me toward the door, I hurried to empty my quiver. "Do you know a woman named Greta Hammond, Mrs. Colbert?"

Delilah Colbert's bosom rose and fell like the tide. "Do we know such a person, Opal?"

Opal lied and said they didn't.

"How about Clara's ex-husband? Do you know where I can find Luke Drummond?"

Her shrug made the satin gown ripple like a lake of milk. Opal gave me another tug. "One last thing," I said as I was towed toward the door. "Did your husband ever get back the money Mr. Brennan stole from the stores?"

Delilah Colbert raised her head off her chest and looked at me as though I'd quacked like a duck. "Ethan Brennan didn't steal a dime," she snapped. "That was a calumny cooked up by my husband. And everyone around here knows it."

She closed her eyes and returned her chin to the swell of her satin chest. Opal grasped my arm like a truant officer and led me to the solace of a normally infectious environment.

I took off my mask and gown and put on my shoes, then leaned against the door as Opal Brennan waited with increasing impatience.

"Who's Nathaniel?" I asked her.

"You leave Nathaniel alone."

"Maybe I would if I knew who he was."

She didn't go for the bait; her look branded me a malefactor. "He can't help you. You'd be ugly to try."

"What's Nathaniel to Clara?"

She shook her head without speaking, then opened the door to the street.

I didn't budge. "Your daughter took her father's death pretty hard, but that doesn't seem enough to justify disappearing from your life, too. What else happened out here? Why did Clara take a new name and seal herself off from her past?"

She shook her head as though to launder all memory of it. "It's over and done with."

"Did you see it happen, Mrs. Brennan?"

"What?"

"Your husband's death."

She shook her head. "I was in my room—napping. I was groggy when they came and got me. I didn't believe it till I saw the body. And even then . . ." She mopped at the corner of her eye. "He was a wonderful, kindly man. He didn't deserve what was done to him."

"What *was* done to him?"

"Everything he cared about got taken away by the Colberts."

"Except you."

Her laugh was high and inappropriate.

"Did anyone witness your husband's death, Mrs. Brennan? Did Clara, for example?"

She gave it half a thought. "She might have. It was about then that she started acting strangely."

"In what way?"

"She turned hateful to me. And to everyone else on the street as well."

"Except Luke Drummond," I reminded.

She nodded agreement. "She ruined her life by running off with that boy."

"Why did she do it?"

She blinked. "She wanted to get away; he was the only one who would take her."

I groped for something else of significance. "Was your daughter dating Stuart Colbert at the time your husband died?"

She nodded. "He was smitten to his toes. They didn't think I knew, but I did. He came home from that fancy school in the summer and started sneaking around, taking her off in that big car he drove, necking in the driveway till all hours. They didn't know it, but I watched them. Little by little he wore down her upbringing. I knew what was going to happen, but I didn't know how to stop it. By the end of the summer he had what he wanted."

"What was that?"

Her look turned hateful. "What his father told him to take. You have to leave now," she added before I could ask what it was.

She turned her back and stood by the door; I moved with the pace of a pallbearer. "Did your husband know Clara was dating Stuart Colbert?"

"Not for a long time. But in the end he did."

"How did he find out?"

"I told him."

"How did he feel about it?"

"He wanted to kill him."

"Stuart?"

"Rutherford."

Her eyes strayed to the portrait in the parlor. When I asked another question, she shook her head and crossed her arms. The door locked at my back with a thud.

TWENTY-ONE

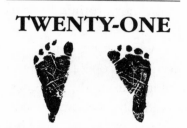

Cynthia Colbert was spending her Sunday walking her dog in Stern Grove. Or so her maid informed me when I rang the bell of the sprawling Cape Cod house and asked to see her employer. When I asked what kind of dog it was, she told me it was a Russian wolfhound.

Since Stern Grove was only a few blocks away, and since I didn't have anything better to do on my Sunday afternoons now that Betty Fontaine had discarded me, I pointed my car toward the ocean, cranked it into a parking spot on Sloat Boulevard just west of Nineteenth Avenue, and entered the overgrown grounds of the park on a path between the tennis courts and the putting green, through a WPA gate built in 1935.

The odds of finding Stuart Colbert's sister within the expanse of the grove weren't good, but it was a nice day—cool, bright, and snappy—and I hadn't communed with nature since I'd visited the Academy of Sciences while waiting to spy on Greta Hammond, and even that had been a taxidermic substitute for the real thing.

Biophilia notwithstanding, I don't commune with nature all that much since nature seldom talks back to me, but once in a while an organic flush of my corroded urban pipes seems called for, if only from the standpoint of preventive maintenance. So I strolled down the steep path toward the core of the grove, was soothed by the breezy songs of conifers and ferns and buoyed by the sharp scent off the eucalyptus that soared overhead as I ambled with a host of others of similar inclination, keeping an eye peeled for a woman with a wolfhound. I didn't know what a wolfhound looked like, exactly, but I figured there was a good chance that it was big and ugly and resembled Rasputin. From the descriptions I'd gotten from her brother, Cynthia Colbert must have been a twin.

Stern Grove is the venue for a concert series during summer months—everything from jazz to opera to mime. The performances are staged at a natural amphitheater in the center of the grove. Along the eastern edge of the amphitheater are several picnic areas, complete with tables and benches and fire pits. Perched on a hollow log in the center of one such glade was a woman with a dog. The dog looked more like a collie than a mastiff, but I figured she was a possibility.

I sat on a nearby bench and observed her. She was a large woman but not corpulent, ruggedly handsome and aggressively self-assured in the masculine manner far too many women adopt these days for reasons more Freudian than feminist. Her image was augmented by her outfit, a riff on the bush hat and safari suit motif that could have been plucked from a rack at Colbert for Men—if an emu had happened by, Cynthia Colbert would doubtlessly have gunned it down. On closer inspection, she seemed less a great white hunter than a metaphysician, her blinkless eyes raised to the treetops, looking into her soul or maybe into the solar system. She was oblivious to her surroundings, including her dog, who seemed content to lie at the end of his leash and slobber on the tuft of grass that cushioned his pointed jaw.

After some minutes of procrastination, I strolled toward where she was sitting and positioned myself where she was forced to engage me. "Miss Colbert?"

Her lips furled unattractively as she inspected me up and down. "I don't know you, do I?" she said when her sneer didn't get the job done.

"My name's Tanner. And no. You don't."

"Then please respect my privacy. If you've got a quibble about our merchandise, take it up with the manager at the store where you made your purchase."

If she wanted me to be ashamed, she was going to have to pick a target more crucial than my attire. "When I have problems with my wardrobe, I take it up with parcel post."

"I get it," she said. "You're a voluntary member of the underclass. How noble. We running dogs of capitalism are forever in your debt."

"If the running dogs really felt that way, there wouldn't *be* an underclass."

She shook her head the way she would have if her wolfhound had swallowed the neighbor's cat. "Spare me the dialectic. If you don't leave me in peace, I'll be forced to call the park police."

"I'm not here to debate utopian economics, Ms. Colbert. I'm here about Clara Brennan."

She had been scouting the grove for a policeman, but when she heard the name she stopped. "Who?"

"Clara Brennan. Your childhood pal."

"I haven't . . . who did you say you were again?"

"Marsh Tanner."

It took a minute, but she came up with it. "The detective." The label evoked images that discomfited her.

"Do you happen to know what I'm doing these days, Miss Colbert?" I asked with as much nonchalance as I could muster, which was quite a bit.

She recovered enough equilibrium to resume her aristocratic distance from both me and the world I live in. "Not precisely."

"I'm trying to find Miss Brennan."

"Why?"

"Because she's missing."

She shrugged with more indifference than she felt. "She's been missing for twenty years, hasn't she?"

"That was from her former life. Now she's missing from her new life as well."

Cynthia Colbert lifted her hat off her head, adjusted its bent brim, brushed hair away from her eyes, then fitted it back in place again, tilted at a more rakish angle. "Am I supposed to know what you're talking about? If so, I'm flunking the course. Not that I give a damn."

"I'm asking if you know the whereabouts of Clara Brennan."

"I do not. There. Can I go back to my walk now? Calvin's arthritis sets in when he stays in one place too long."

"So does mine," I said. "Is this Calvin?" I gestured toward the dog.

"Calvin Coolidge Colbert, at your service."

"A fine animal."

"He's a mess. But then, what man isn't?"

I decided she was serious. "Does the name Greta Hammond mean anything to you?" In the echo of Clara Brennan's pseudonym, I thought I saw a flicker in the eyes beneath the brim of the bush hat, but I didn't know what it meant yet.

"I know lots of women professionally," she said. "It's possible the woman worked for me at some point, or we met at some sales thing or something. She's not anyone I know socially."

"You weren't arguing with her in an apartment on Kirkham Street a couple of months ago?"

"I was not." Her entire physique was summoned behind the denial, which probably meant she was lying.

"When's the last time you saw Clara Brennan?"

"Eons ago."

"You don't know where she lives—what she does?"

"No idea. But I'm sure it's something laudable."

"What makes you say that?"

Her smile was both arch and belittling. "Everyone always thought Clara was so fucking special. Teachers, my mother, the minister, everyone always went on and on about how sweet she was. And smart. And beautiful—Clara was the whole package, as opposed to the rest of us mere mortals. I figure she must be either a nun or a novelist by now. Is she?"

"Not that I know of," I said, and tried not to remember that my original assessment of the woman had contained many of the same adjectives. "Why did her father blow his brains out?"

She was momentarily startled but her answer was elaborately offhand. "He was a thief and they caught him at it."

"Who caught him?"

"My father."

"Did he report the theft to the cops?"

She shook her head. "He handled it in-house."

"If it was handled, why did Ethan Brennan kill himself?"

She shrugged. "I don't know and I don't care. And if you're think-ing of asking my father, don't."

"Why not?"

She looked at me impatiently. "He's seventy-four and has ad-vanced emphysema. His lungs barely pump enough oxygen to maintain his motor functions, which means he doesn't know much of anything anymore. Which, in the case of the Brennans, is a blessing. They caused him a lot of grief."

"It still might be in his best interest to talk to me before this thing blows sky high."

"*What* thing?"

"Sorry. Can't say."

"Well, Father's not capable of knowing what his best interest *is*, so forget about it." She yanked her dog to its feet; it grinned for the first time all morning. "Our tête-à-tête is finished, Mr. Tanner. Next time bring a picnic lunch." She started to walk away.

"Luke Drummond," I said to her back.

She jerked the dog to a stop so quickly he looked back and bared his teeth. I felt like doing the same thing. "Who?" she asked.

"Luke Drummond. The family factotum."

She looked around with such open eagerness it was clear she was hoping Luke would be beckoning at her from the underbrush. "What about him? Is he here?"

"No."

"Where is he?"

"I don't know. I was hoping you did."

She cocked her head. "You sound as if something's happened to him."

"Not to him; to his ex-wife."

"Clara? I thought you said she ran away."

"I said she was missing. I'm not sure how she got that way, but it could be something serious."

"*How* serious?"

"Kidnaping, possibly."

She retrieved her scowl and patted her dog, who seemed unmoved by the experience. "The Clara Brennan *I* knew wasn't anyone a kidnaper would find enticing. By the time she left Santa Ana, she didn't have a dime to her name and neither did anyone else in her family."

"What makes you think she didn't end up with the money her father embezzled?"

She looked at me closely for the first time, her eyes sighting down her narrow nose, probing for the extent of my knowledge. "Daddy got the money back."

"Before Ethan Brennan killed himself? Or after?"

"Before, of course. So like I said, who would want to kidnap Clara?"

I didn't mention that Clara Brennan's major asset was growing inside her womb and that a man like Luke Drummond might regard interfering with that gestation as a way to retaliate for wounds that had been inflicted on him a quarter-century ago, wounds arising from a caste system that goes all but unacknowledged in this country but which wreaks havoc nonetheless.

"You're assuming Clara's the victim," I said, and waited for her reaction.

"You're saying Clara Brennan *kidnaped* someone?"

"I'm saying she may be involved."

"But who's been kidnaped? Not one of the family, surely. I mean, someone would have told me." She suddenly seemed to realize that wasn't a necessary corollary and glanced uncertainly around the grove, searching for reassurance.

"Let's get back to Luke," I said.

"What about him?"

"For starters, did you like him?"

She smiled salaciously, at details known only to her. "You could say that."

"Did he like you?"

"He liked my taste, at any rate. I bought him enough cowboy clothes to outfit a rodeo."

"Did you go out with him back when you were in school?"

Her chuckle was both earthy and disparaging. "Let's say we ended up in the same room a time or two."

"A bedroom?"

"That's nobody's business but my biographer's."

"It sounds like you and Luke had a fling."

"Luke had lots of flings. Having a fling with Luke was something you did in those days—like chugging beer or smoking grass or making love while you were on the rag."

I let the crudity pass. "Did Millicent Stanley partake of Luke's charms?"

She laughed. "I very much doubt it, not that she would have resisted. In those days Milly was pretty much the bottom of the barrel. She's made quite a comeback, as you probably know." She wound the leash around her hand, ready to drag Calvin off by force.

I hurried on. "I've been wondering about Luke and Clara."

"What about them?"

"Were you surprised when she took up with him? Given the difference in their backgrounds?"

She thought about it, then shrugged. "For a one-night stand, no. Luke was a hunk; any woman with a hormone could love him to death for one night, or even one summer. But permanently? Of course I was surprised. But Clara was completely shattered by the time she took up with Luke. It was any port in a storm by that time, I imagine."

"What was her problem?"

"Her father disgraced himself and blew his brains out. How many more problems do you need?"

"Did you talk to her about it? About her father, I mean?"

"Some; not much. It was considered treasonous for a Colbert to be seen with a Brennan by then."

"Did you like her?"

"Clara? I guess I did. More than anyone else on the block, at least. She had a sense of humor and a brain and a body guys got wet dreams over. It was fascinating to watch her operate. I picked up some valuable tips."

"Tips about what?"

"About how to get men to do what you want without them knowing they've been had."

"You make her sound pretty manipulative."

"Manipulative was her middle name."

"Who was she manipulating when she ran off with Luke?"

She smiled. "You'd have to ask her. I was doing my own manipulating by then—I didn't pay much attention."

Cynthia Colbert was lying—Luke Drummond had obviously been a lure for her back then, an erotic and powerful narcotic. But I didn't see what difference it made at this point, so I decided to wrap it up. Cynthia was one of those people whose opinion of herself is so all-encompassing it sucks all the air out of the immediate environment and makes it exhausting to occupy the same space.

"Have you seen Luke since he and Clara ran off together?" I asked.

She shook her head, then leaned down and patted Calvin. "Clara's mother works for my mother, you know," she said, for some reason suddenly accommodating.

I nodded. "I just talked to both of them."

Her temper ignited like tinder. "You've been interrogating my *mother*? My mother isn't competent to *dress* herself, let alone talk about our past. How *dare* you invade this family behind my back like that." She wrapped the leather leash around her hand a second time, as if to cushion her fist for a fight. "Does Russell know about this? What are you up to, anyway? What are you trying to *do* to us?"

"All I'm doing is trying to find Clara Brennan."

"But why are you going into the old stuff? Who's telling you to dig up the family skeletons? I know it's not Russell."

"I can't tell you," I answered.

"Ethics?" she sneered.

"Policy. Does the name Nathaniel mean anything to you?"

"You mean Ethan."

"I mean Nathaniel."

She shrugged. "No idea."

And just that quickly, Cynthia Colbert was bored. She looked at her watch, tugged the dog to its feet, and said, "I've got a date," as she started marching up the path toward the street like a tour guide on the way back to the bus.

When she'd gone ten yards, she tossed me an admonition. "If you're smart, this will be the last I see of you. We don't take kindly to snoops."

"What if I come up with Luke Drummond?"

She stopped walking long enough to consider the question. "It might be worth money for a phone number."

I laughed. "I'd heard you didn't like men."

"The men I don't like shop at Colberts. The men I like wear shirts with snaps." Her smile got lazy again, and this time its loop reached me. "You could deliver that number in person, if you have the inclination."

"I haven't been a delivery boy in years. And I don't think Russell would like it."

As her cheeks reddened to confirm my hunch, she resumed her march and I hurried to keep pace. "What about you and your brother?" I asked as she and Calvin waited at the light to cross Nineteenth Avenue. "How do the two of you get along?"

"The way the Muslims and Serbs get along. I'm going to cleanse his ass right out of the retail business."

"Who's going to make the decision?"

"My father."

"You just said he's not competent."

"Even a lunatic can pick the winner in this fight. I've been besting my brother for years. Now even Daddy will have to acknowledge it."

The light changed and she started to cross the street. When I didn't accompany her, she came back to where I was standing. "I do hope you'll let me know if you turn up Mr. Drummond."

I told her I'd think about it. "Why were you asking your mother for money a few months back?" I added.

"Who told you that?" she bristled. "Mother? Well, fuck her. And fuck you, too."

She looked up and down the street as traffic streamed by in a torrent of sheet metal.

"How did your brother feel when Clara Brennan ran off with Luke Drummond?"

"He was crushed. I couldn't have been happier."

"So Clara dumped Stuart for Luke. Is that the way it went?"

"That's what it looked like." She laughed. "It would make sense if you'd ever laid eyes on Luke Drummond. My brother literally pales by comparison."

"Something Mrs. Brennan said made me think Clara might have been pregnant when she left home. Do you know anything about it?"

Her expression became supercilious. "That's what I meant when I said Clara was looking for any port in a storm. I don't think anyone knew she was knocked up but me. And Papa Luke, of course, the bastard. So maybe if you find the kid, you'll find the mother. That's the way it's supposed to work, right? With the maternal bullshit?"

TWENTY-TWO

I waited for Cynthia Colbert to disappear up the block, then drove back to Santa Ana Way and parked down the street from her house, in the shade of an elm and a cypress.

Five minutes later, she and Calvin rounded the corner and marched down the sidewalk to her home and went in the side door. Ten minutes after that, a blue Mercedes pulled into the drive. There are a lot of Mercedes in San Francisco, but only one with the vanity plate JORGY; from the way he slithered out of the car and slunk into the house, Russell might have been calling on Calvin instead of his mistress. Armed with a new set of questions, and maybe a few explanations, I drove to the office to take advantage of some Sunday silence.

My plan was to dictate enough correspondence so the temp who comes in on Mondays would earn her keep for a change but, before I'd finished even one letter, I gave up. I can't be alone in the office these days without thinking about Peggy Nettleton.

Peggy had worked for me for ten years. We were employer and employee, then colleagues, and soon fast friends. Then we got snarled in a case involving a creep who was harassing her over the telephone. As an antidote to the frustration and embarrassment that are part and parcel of harassment, we added sex to our mix in the hope it would serve as a tonic. But the tonic turned out to be toxic, and the anomaly proved sufficiently awkward that Peggy exited my life in a huff once the creep was hauled to jail.

For good reason, I suppose—there are always good reasons to dissolve a relationship if that's what you're looking for—but I wished she was back and that things were the way they had been before we had sacrificed our friendship on the altar of what it had been easy to believe was love. But that's the problem with sex: its leavings aren't easily eradicated and mistakes tend to be terminal. So I swore at the gods that make men and women need each other in ways they can't define until it's too late and made myself some coffee even though it was so late the caffeine would keep me up.

It was still Sunday and the only person I wanted to talk to who was dependably available was Charley Sleet. It took them an hour to track him down—he was out in the Richmond District, busting a counterfeit ring. What was unusual was that it wasn't currency that was being counterfeited, it was food stamps.

"Sleet."

"Tanner."

"What?"

Charley always sounds as if talking to me is the last thing on earth he wants to do, but if I don't call him once a week, and we don't get together for a ballgame or cards a couple of times a month, he sulks and calls in his markers, which are the meals I promise in trade for the official information he dispenses when he knows I really need it.

"I request the pleasure of your company," I told him as cheerily as I could manage.

"When?"

"ASAP."

"Where?"

"Your pick."

"Bohemian. One hour."

An hour later, we were sipping Sunday beers in the triangular confines of the Bohemian Cigar Store, a venerable North Beach establishment whose prime attraction was its equidistance from the Central Station and my apartment. Charley and I try to keep things on an even keel between us, and somehow we've managed to keep our friendship from capsizing for nearly twenty years. Mostly it amounts to paying attention to both sides of the equation, just like with algebra.

I bought the beers at the counter and took them to a table that was the approximate size of Charley's fist. "What's the occasion?" he asked when his draft was half gone. "More prints?"

"Just a little history."

"Of what?"

"The life and death of Ethan Brennan. Emphasis on the latter."

"I thought you were after the girl."

"It might help find the girl if I know why her father got his brains blown out."

"The file says suicide."

"He was found on the front porch of another man's house, Charley."

"Rutherford Colbert's."

I smiled. "You've been boning up. You must have known I was going to spring a pop quiz."

Charley didn't say anything but I knew he was thinking—his ears get red when he's thinking.

"Colbert displaced a lot of weight in this town in those days," I observed while he worked with his general disinclination to gossip.

"Still does," Charley said. "So what?"

"Maybe enough weight to turn a homicide into a suicide."

Charley's face darkened to match his ale. "No one carries that much weight."

"Bullshit. There were rumors, Charley."

"There always are with the gentry."

"So you don't know anything?"

He shook his head. "Not firsthand. I remember when it happened, but I didn't get the call. I was on vice in those days."

I smiled. "You've got that look in your eye, Mr. Sleet."

He hates it when I read him.

"After you had me run the print, I came up with a little hearsay," he admitted.

I slapped his shoulder. "That's my boy. So what was it?"

"Homicide."

"Just as I thought."

"*Not* as you thought. It was homicide, but not murder. Justifiable. Brennan came gunning for Colbert, and Colbert had to blast him to keep from being shot himself. Open and shut."

"So where did the suicide notion come in?"

"That was a fable that got started by someone off the record and no one saw any reason to stop it before it spread to the media."

"There was no inquest?"

"No request for one, and no need. Check the Government Code if you don't believe me—the cause of death wasn't at issue. Family didn't want to go public with their dirty linen and the department was satisfied there was no crime committed so it got taken off the board real fast."

"Speaking of dirty linen, why was Ethan Brennan gunning for Rutherford Colbert?"

"Something about the business; missing money, I think."

"But Brennan was the bad guy, not Colbert."

Charley shrugged. "That's all I know and it's all anyone else in the department knows, too. You got a different story?"

"Just a lot of guesses. Has old man Colbert been in any trouble that you know of? Particularly trouble with women?"

Charley's brows lifted the way garage doors lift. "Not that I heard. You know something?"

I shook my head. "How about the rest of the family?"

"Seems to me the kid had a beef a while back."

"Stuart?"

Charley nodded. "Domestic thing, I think. Shoved his wife around. I don't think he was charged."

I drank my beer in a contemplative shell while Charley debated a guy at the next table over the relative merits of Bonds and Canseco.

At eight the next morning I was on the phone to my broker. What Clay Oerter brokers for me aren't the stocks and bonds he buys for his regular clients; what he brokers for me is information. What I give him in trade is a vicarious walk on the wild side, plus a regular income stream that flows across the Friday night poker table we share with four of our friends, Charley Sleet included.

Charley usually breaks even; I'm usually a loser and Clay Oerter invariably quits winners. I really hope he cheats—it would violate my sense of the universe for anyone to be that lucky that often.

"Clay."

"Hey, Marsh. That was fun last week."

"Not for me, it wasn't."

"How much were you down?"

"Sixty."

"Could have been worse."

"It was worse, till the last hand."

"Bad cards wouldn't matter if you'd let me put you into a stock once in a while. If you'd gone into Starbucks when I told you to, you'd have doubled your money by now."

"Two times zero is zero, Clay. Tell me about the Colberts."

"The stores?"

"The people."

"Rutherford Colbert opened the store on Market Street after he got back from the war. Mens wear first; now both genders. Rumor was, he made his money running a whorehouse in Rome, but who knows?"

"I'm more interested in the current picture—who owns what."

"Three years ago, the old man came down with emphysema. Saw the writing on the wall, naturally enough—someone was going to inherit his baby. To figure out who, he split the stores between his kids and told them to have at it. He claimed it was just an efficiency shuffle, but everyone knew it was a grudge match for the big prize."

"Who's winning?"

"Cynthia, I hear. Of course any bottom line data on the Colberts is soft—they're not public companies, so no one sees their financials outside the boardroom. And probably not even there, the old man plays it so close to his vest. But if Cynthia really is on top, it would be a surprise."

"Why?"

"Because the men's side was a mess before she took charge: obsolete inventory, overstocked warehouse, lousy store layouts, grumpy sales staff. If she comes out on top in this thing, it's going to make her a retailing legend in this town. Everyone thought Stuart would win going away, since the women's side had been the cash cow ever since Ethan Brennan came on board."

"So why isn't Stuart on top?"

"Because he spends more time complaining about the old man's interference than tending to business, is what I hear. A big whiner, Stuart. Poster boy for the Peter Principle as well. But whatever the reason, he's let Nordstrom and Saks and Neiman's, plus the boutiques like Wilkes Bashford, run off with most of the couture trade in this town."

"How about the old man? I hear he's lost it, pretty much."

"His mind, you mean? No one knows. He's like that Mafia guy who wanders around Brooklyn in his pajamas—no one knows if he's nuts or if he's just setting the stage for an incompetency plea for when the Feds decide to lock him up."

"You saying Rutherford's committed a crime?"

Clay laughed. "Not that I know of. Although some of the things I see on those manikins probably violate an ordinance or two."

"Who takes over the stores after the kids are gone? Neither of them has children, as I understand it."

"That's up in the air, I guess. Supposedly, Rutherford will decide by his birthday in '95 which of the kids will take over. After that, it's pretty much up to how that person wants to handle it, I imagine. If no one has an heir, they'll probably go public and bring someone in from outside to run things."

"There's no heir apparent in the company now?"

"From outside the family? No. A guy named Gallatin handles the financial end, but no way he can head it up—even you've got more fashion sense than he does. The only cream that can rise to the top in that bottle has Colbert blood in it."

"What happens if Rutherford drops dead before he chooses between the kids?"

"Beats me. You'd have to ask whoever drew up his will."

In other words, I'd have to ask Russell Jorgensen. "How about Ethan Brennan? What kind of role did he play?"

"In the business? Crucial. Rutherford has the charm of Pat Buchanan on a bad day, and Ethan put a human face on the operation—charmed the staff, cultivated the rag manufacturers, that kind of thing. His main contribution was getting the stores into high-end women's fashion, where the big margins are, then doing what it took to make it work."

"Such as."

"Seducing the well-heeled customer, is what it came down to. Stocking the hot lines, training the sales staff to talk the talk and walk the walk so the locals will think they're as chic as New Yorkers. Plus the accessories—tea room for the ladies who lunch; private showings in the store or at home for the women who are busy, busy; day care for their kids; lingerie boutique where ladies can try on teddies and peignoirs without worrying about men popping in; no-questions-asked returns policy; personal shoppers who know their principals well enough to take care of the small stuff by phone. Plus Ethan was the spokesman for Colberts in their first TV ads—everyone assumed he was a Colbert himself. Nice guy, they say."

"Why did he kill himself?"

Clay hesitated. "He tapped the till and they caught him was the story most people heard."

"You sound like there was more than one version."

"Let me put it this way—they say that if you worked for Rutherford Colbert, the only thing you'd have more of than reasons to kill yourself would be reasons to kill him."

"Hear anything specific along those lines?"

"You know how people talk. I heard because Ethan got so much press for his work at the company, Rutherford got jealous and decided to rub him out. I heard Ethan was mad at Rutherford for sleeping with his wife and I heard vice versa; I heard Ethan did something even worse than embezzlement though I never heard what it was; I heard Opal Brennan really pulled the trigger because she was crazy or because she was in love with Rutherford, take your pick; and I heard Stuart was really the one who did it because he was afraid Ethan would take over the company before Stuart could claim it for himself. I probably heard half a dozen other things, too, but I don't remember them."

"Which one of them do you credit?"

"None, particularly. Except Rutherford was a swordsman in his day. Cut a wide swath through the salesgirls down at the store."

"So Mrs. Brennan might have been a conquest?"

"Any woman in town might have been a conquest."

"Any rumors about him and young women?"

"How young?"

"Teens."

Clay laughed uneasily. "Jesus, Marsh. What kind of case are you into?"

"I haven't the slightest idea," I admitted, then thanked Clay for his trouble.

An hour later, Charley Sleet was on the phone. "Colbert the Younger was booked in May of '84 for domestic assault."

"Who was the complainant? Millicent?"

"Louise."

"What happened?"

"Charges dropped. Physical evidence inconclusive; complainant opted not to testify. Just another smear on the blotter."

"You don't happen to have Louise Colbert's maiden name there, do you?"

"Frankel."

"Address?"

"Santa Ana Way."

"Not anymore," I told him.

TWENTY-THREE

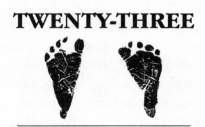

I found Louise Frankel where Stuart Colbert had told me I'd find her, on a houseboat chained to a dock that ran the rim of what was left of Mission Creek at the point where it poked its way into China Basin. I thought I knew San Francisco pretty well after being a resident for almost a third of a century, but the existence of a houseboat community smack in the heart of the city—all legal and proper and authorized—was news to me.

I parked next to the Mission Bay Golf Center—a driving range for Yuppies to while away their noon hours hitting shag balls and for Japanese businessmen to keep their swings well grooved while doing their deals on the road—then passed through a gate labeled Mission Creek Harbor and made my way down the narrow dock to the third boat from the end. As I stepped onto the deck of *Frankel's Folly,* the entire structure sagged beneath my weight and a gentle splash of displaced water slapped the hull of the next boat down. I took two steps to the door and knocked, but not before I paused to admire the variety of storybook architecture that seemed an island of uncommon gaiety and good sense in the midst of a world filled with landlubbered nonsense, and to imagine the sort of people who would occupy a neighborhood that as far as I knew was unique to the city.

I knocked twice, then twice more. A man watering his petunias two boats down looked at me without any sign of friendliness. A woman on the sun deck above him raised up, pressed a bikini top against her previously unwrapped breasts, then lay back on her padded chair after assessing my place in her universe. Strangers were either irritants or intruders, apparently; my mental picture darkened a couple of shades.

I was still gazing up at the last-known address of the bikini when the door opened. The woman who opened it was sultry in countenance and demeanor, by design more than by accident. She wore cut-off Levi's, a red tube top, glossy red lipstick, and not much else except a wall-eyed interest in my business. Her legs were long, her breasts full despite the constrictions of her top. Her hair was gathered behind her head with a blue ribbon except for the wisps that danced like charred confetti across the expanse of her well-tanned forehead. Her hands were dirty with what looked like potting soil and her face was smeared with a stripe of black above the bridge of its narrow nose. The grime only added to the sense of abandonment she projected, a bucolic eroticism I found to my liking.

"Are you Ms. Frankel?"

"Yes, I am."

In contrast to the neighbors down the dock, she seemed happy to have company. She tugged her top an inch higher on her torso, then looked at her hands to see if they were clean enough to extend my way. She decided they weren't and made do with a smile instead of a handshake.

"My name's Tanner," I said.

"First or last?"

"Last. The first is Marsh."

"For?"

"What?"

"Marsh. It must be short for something."

"Marshall. And it's not my first name, actually; it's my middle. The first is John. But I haven't used it since third grade."

"What happened in third grade?"

"The other John in the class beat the crap out of me one night after play practice."

"Why?"

"Because I was a Knight of the Round Table and he wasn't."

She gave the contretemps some thought. "So show business changed your life, basically."

"That's one way to look at it. Another is that I've been beaten up so many times since, it was sort of an apprenticeship."

She frowned. "Why are you assaulted so often?"

"Because I get on people's nerves."

"Are you going to get on mine?"

"Probably."

The prospect seemed to excite her. "How about the play? Did you win the hand of the fair maiden?"

I shook my head. "It's probably just as well."

"Why?"

"Because I seem to make a mess of things as far as fair maidens are concerned."

"Well, lucky for you there's always a woman ready to give a man a second chance."

After issuing the interesting aphorism, she asked me what she could do for me. The smoky look in her eye made me remember Stuart's slur about the tranquilizers, but on her they looked good.

It's like that sometimes—with some people you never strike a spark and conversation never moves beyond toil; with others, it makes a blaze right off. Three minutes after I laid eyes on her, I liked Louise Frankel a lot—enough so that I hoped my business wasn't going to amount to anything worse than a nuisance.

I asked if I could ask her some questions. She asked me what about.

"Stuart Colbert."

The smile fell off her face the way a picture falls off a wall. "Do I have to?"

"No."

"You're not a policeman?"

I shook my head.

"Then what are you?"

"Private investigator."

"What are you investigating?"

"I can't tell you. Other than to say that it involves your ex-husband."

The possibilities seemed sufficiently extensive to cheer her. "Has Millicent finally wised up? Has she hired you to get the goods on him, dissolution-wise?"

I smiled a smile that let her guess be as true as she wanted it to be. "No comment."

"In that case, please come in. If what you're looking for is dirt on Stuart Colbert, you've come to the filthiest place in town." She looked at her grimy palms, then displayed them as proof of the point.

She made room for me inside the superstructure of the houseboat, which in layout and design was more like a greenhouse than a cruiser. Three of its sides were glass—sliding doors that opened onto the narrow deck that surrounded the living area and to the larger patio out the back. A circular staircase climbed to what was presumably a sleeping area above, and a series of shoji screens divided the first floor into nooks for reading and eating and watching TV. There was a small bathroom in one corner and the kitchen crossed a part of the rear and opened onto the back deck as well. The breeze that moved without opposition through the room had its origins in fish and salt and fresh flowers and maybe the sweat off the naked breasts upwind.

"You want to sit outside?" she asked as I looked around. "Or do we need to be clandestine?"

"Clandestine, I think. Especially if you're going to dish dirt."

"If it's about Stuart, you'll need a bulldozer." She pointed toward a club chair next to a potted cactus that was as pert and prickly as its owner.

Louise Frankel sat on a pillow across from me, tucked her legs beneath her, and regarded me as if I were a long-lost relative with news of a family fortune. "What exactly do you want to know?" she asked. It was increasingly obvious that regardless of what had happened in the years since the divorce, Stuart Colbert remained a fixation.

"Let's start with the old days. Were you one of the crowd that lived out in St. Francis Wood?"

She laughed. "The Santa Ana Saints? No, thank God. I never laid eyes on Stuart till I was twenty-five. I grew up in Morgan Hill."

"Where did you meet?"

"At the store. I was a lingerie model. We were doing the fall showing and I was wearing a body suit that ripped down the front and all my goodies fell out. Stuart was very chivalrous—gave me his sport coat and escorted me off the runway as though things like that happened every day. It seemed cute at the time." She made a face that suggested that the words cute and Stuart Colbert hadn't been paired since.

"Did he talk much about his youth? Particularly his teenage years?"

"He talked about the old man, if that's what you mean; him being such a tyrant and all. Stuart was working in shipping and receiving when he was ten years old, if you can believe it—the whole thing was Dickensian. And he complained about Cyn, of course. She rattled his cage and still does. They were the only kids I ever heard of who, when they played house, the little girl was the doctor, not the patient. Anyway, Stuart hates both of them with a passion; with good reason as far as I can tell. I used to feel sorry for him till I had more reason to be sorry for me."

"Why so?"

"He wasn't happy and he blamed me for it. Sure, I gave him some grief, but I was *way* down the list of contributors."

"His father was the worst?"

"Big time."

"Why didn't they get along?"

"Stuart wasn't what Rutherford wanted him to be."

"Which was?"

She shrugged. "Anything except Stuart, as far as I could tell."

"Did you get the impression Stuart had done something wrong in those days?"

"Like illegal? No. Something dumb, maybe. But we all did something dumb in those years, didn't we? Or maybe you're the exception that proves the rule."

"Dumb and I have always been intimate."

Her eyes made mischief and tossed some at me. "My IQ would double if I didn't need a big hug first thing in the morning."

There was a place to go with that and it was probably a nice warm place once you got there, but I decided not to make the trip quite yet. "I was wondering if Stuart ever mentioned a woman named Clara Brennan."

"Sure he did."

"What did he say about her?"

"He said she was the most—"

She cut off the sentence, then stood and strolled about the room as though visiting for the first time and wondering if the vessel would stay afloat if the breeze picked up or an earthquake hit.

When she stopped pacing, she put her hands on her hips and gave a speech. "It's Monday morning. I'm not at work, I'm home repotting plants. I live in this weird little place, I've got a new blue Beemer parked in the lot, a diamond on my finger that would choke a horse, and a wardrobe Cindy Crawford would kill for. And I've got no visible means of support. How do you think I manage it?"

"I give up."

"I got one hell of a divorce settlement, that's how. Know why?"

"Why?"

"There were things about Stuart he didn't want known. Not big things, necessarily, but things. We were heating up for the biggest cat fight the superior court's ever seen and he knew if we went to trial it would all come out and then some. So he said if I'd promise to keep quiet, no matter who asked what, he'd pay me handsomely for my silence. When he named the figure he had in mind, I put my hand over my broken heart and swore to zip my lip."

"Stuart Colbert and Clara Brennan are part of what you're keeping quiet about?"

"*Everything* about the Colberts is part of it."

"And you're being a good scout?"

She lowered herself to the pillow and extended her legs in front of her. They seemed far more naked than when I'd boarded the boat. "Can't you tell?"

"And I thought you were going to dish dirt."

"Oh, that's just my reaction whenever Stuart's name comes up. Then I remember the deal and do my duty."

Although the words were blithe and even self-mocking, she seemed to take her pledge seriously, so I approached from a different direction. "What happened to your marriage?"

She shrugged. "Lots of things. Mostly kids."

"I didn't know you and Stuart had kids."

"We didn't. Stuart wanted them. *Insisted* on them would be more accurate. When it didn't happen even when we did the wild thing every time the sun set, he tried to get me to go through some rigma-role."

"*In vitro* fertilization?"

She blinked. "Is that the flavor of the month, or something? What the hell do *you* know about it?"

"Not much. Did you do it?"

"Hell no. I told him it was God's way or the highway. I guess he finally found a woman who would let some guy in a white coat stick a turkey baster up her twat. Me, I prefer something with a little more blood in it."

She tossed me a smoky look but I ignored it. "Did you ever have tests to see why you weren't getting pregnant?"

She started to say something, then stopped. "I can't talk about this. I'm sorry. If you weren't so damned rumpled, I wouldn't have said *that* much. Maybe it's a delayed reaction to my years in the fashion game, but lately I get all creamy for rumpled."

"Then I must be the man of your dreams."

After we shared facetious smiles, I looked at a container ship steaming south down the bay. I remembered the afternoon with Russell Jorgensen and was happy to be tied to dry land, even though I wasn't getting anywhere.

"You said your divorce was getting nasty before Stuart offered the settlement," I reminded her.

"Nasty isn't the word for it—*brutal* is the word for it. Mostly because of the lawyers."

"Did you go through discovery—depositions, interrogatories, production of documents, and all that?"

"That was the fun part. We were in court every day, it seemed like, fighting over every piece of property we ever owned and every dime we'd ever spent. He told the judge I abused the cat and sold his paintings; I claimed he was stealing my jewelry and killing the plants. It was like a kung fu film there for a while. Why?"

"I'm wondering if you still have any of those documents lying around. I'm especially interested in your husband's financial records."

She thought about it. "There's a box full of stuff in the closet I keep meaning to throw out."

"May I see them?"

She thought it over. "Why not? In fact, you can *have* them. I only promised not to talk; I didn't promise not to clean house."

She led me up the circular staircase to the loft-like bedroom overhead. It, too, had sliding doors on all sides and came complete with a fireplace and a clutch of fishing gear canted in a corner—Louise was prepared for guests. There was a deck off the side like the one in the back and a nook on the end to sit in and read or to contemplate the fickleness of fate. I decided I could live there just fine except for the concrete slash of the off-ramp that defiled the view toward the city.

She opened a closet and disappeared in its innards. A moment later she backed out tugging a Bekins box marked DIVORCE—STUART'S SHIT.

"Help yourself," she said. "If anyone asks, I threw this all out years ago."

I put the box under my arm and got down the winding stairway without falling on my face. "Come back and see me some time," she said when I was at the door. Her voice was as thick as the freeway risers. "The sunrises are beautiful."

"I don't get up that early."

"Maybe you never had a good reason." Her entendre kept me company all the way back to the car.

When I got back to the office, I thumbed through the files and pulled out one that looked promising—a folder filled with photocopies of what seemed to be Stuart Colbert's personal check register. I flipped through the pages idly, looking for oddities or outrages.

Nothing jumped out at me at first—he had charged about five thousand a month to his credit card and paid four grand a month to Louise, presumably for mad money. The rest of the payees were predictable, albeit at exalted levels compared to my own, except for one item: each and every month, Stuart Colbert wrote a check in the amount of three thousand dollars payable to Luke Drummond's mother, Fern.

TWENTY-FOUR

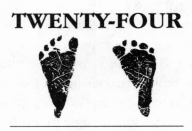

When I'd finished with the Frankel files, I called Russell Jorgensen to see if there was any news in the form of a ransom demand or otherwise. He told me no one had heard anything from anybody.

"How's Stuart holding up?" I asked.

"He's more agitated than I've ever seen him. But compared to Millicent, he's as serene as Gandhi."

I didn't tell him that I'd witnessed Millicent's jitters myself the day before. "Has he said anything about the Drummonds?"

"Why should he?"

"I thought he might have mentioned Mrs. Drummond to you at some point."

"What on earth would Stuart Colbert have to do with Fern Drummond?"

"I was hoping you could tell me."

Russell swore, then coughed, then asked what I'd been doing since he'd seen me last.

"Poking around."

"Poking in the Colberts' dirty laundry, you mean." His voice was strained and exasperated. "I'm not sure I like you buttonholing every member of the Colbert family you can find, especially without warning. You're acting like Mike Wallace, for Christ's sake. They don't like it. And if they don't like it, I don't like it."

"Shall I tell you what *I* don't like, Russell?"

"What?"

"Your sub-rosa relationship with Cynthia."

"I—"

"Don't bother to deny it, just tell me if there's more to it than money."

He got huffy. "Certainly there is. There's love, for one thing."

"Is there more to it than that? Control of the Colbert empire, for example?"

"It's got nothing to do with that. If it did, why would I be helping Stuart and Millicent to produce an heir? Christ. I don't know why you're so upset about this."

Russell's divided loyalties had singed my nerves. "I'll tell you why. I've got a job to do and you're the one who hired me to do it. Maybe you remember. Well, the more I get into the situation, the more it seems to have roots in what went on twenty years ago on Santa Ana Way."

"How can what happened to the Colberts twenty years ago have anything to do with Stuart and Millicent trying to have a baby?"

"I don't know, yet. But we're dealing with elemental issues here—families, generations, dynasties. In my experience, problems with elemental issues don't materialize overnight; they're always grounded in history."

"No offense, Marsh, but I don't see how history is going to help you find out who kidnaped Greta Hammond."

"It might tell me who would want her out of the way, or more likely, who would want to keep Stuart and Millicent from producing an heir to the Colbert stores. On the other hand, if it's *not* a kidnaping, which seems increasingly likely, then history might tell me who Greta Hammond is running from."

"But why would she run from the Colberts? She didn't know they were *involved* in the surrogate business."

"I hope you're right," I said, then hung up and did something I don't do enough of in the middle of an active case—take time to think.

Panning the waters of the Colberts' fractious past yielded several nuggets. For one, it seemed that Ethan Brennan was not a suicide, as had been commonly accepted, but had been murdered, or at least killed, by Rutherford Colbert. Her father's death at the hands of the Colberts—*any* Colbert—would give Clara/Greta a motive to throw a wrench in Stuart's plans to rent her womb to hatch an heir to the killer's dynasty, once she had learned of those plans from someone who might have wanted to provoke that reaction. Which would mean her disappearance was both obstreperous and voluntary, and that she would resist any efforts to bring her back.

Except for interrogating Rutherford Colbert himself on the past and its implications, I wasn't sure how to find out what had happened to Ethan Brennan twenty years ago, or why, and Rutherford was either incompetent or off limits, depending on whom you talked to. The only other path to enlightenment involved three disparate scraps of information I'd uncovered. One was a name—Nathaniel; one was a place—Hickory Avenue in San Bruno; and one was a woman—Fern Drummond, the recipient of a healthy stipend from the bank account of Stuart Colbert. If I was lucky, and the Colbert case congealed the way my cases sometimes do, those three scraps might combine to form a single magic carpet provided I could come up with the right incantation.

Since Stuart Colbert had been sending her a check for many years, the obvious approach was simply to ask him where Fern Drummond lived. But Stuart hadn't been forthright from the beginning, and I didn't know whether he was friend or foe at this point. Until I had time to find out, I opted for another source.

Her boss didn't like it, but I made it sound official, so he hunted her down and put her on the line.

"Mrs. Webber?"

"Yes?"

"This is Marsh Tanner. I spoke with you in your home several days ago. About Greta Hammond."

"I remember. What do you want?"

"First of all, I was wondering if you'd heard from her since we talked."

"I promised to call if I did."

"Then you haven't."

"No."

"Have you asked her landlady, or Leo, if they've heard from her?"

"No, but I'm sure they would have told me if they had. They know I've been worried."

"You don't sound worried now."

"Well, I am. Extremely."

"Have you come up with any information at all that might help locate her?"

"I said no, didn't I?"

"Yes, you did."

"So is that all? They don't like me to do this on company time."

"One thing I was wondering was if Greta ever mentioned her mother-in-law to you. A woman named Fern Drummond."

"Her mother-in-law? No. I'm sorry." She paused so long I thought she'd hung up. "Come to think of it, I think Greta mentioned that she lives back East somewhere. Massachusetts, maybe."

I laughed.

"What's so funny?"

"You've gone above and beyond the call of duty, Mrs. Webber."

"I don't know what you mean."

"I'm sure all she expected you to do was play dumb with me. I doubt if she expected you to send me on a wild goose chase."

"I have no idea what you're talking about."

"Sure you do. You've talked to Greta. Maybe even seen her. And she's told you not to cooperate with me."

"She hasn't told me anything. I—"

"She's your friend," I interrupted. "You should do as she asks. But I want you to give her a message."

"But how can I? I haven't seen her."

"Greta signed a contract. She made a promise and she agreed to all sorts of penalties if she breached it. She could end up bankrupt or in jail if she doesn't cut some kind of deal. If she's done what I think she's done, she could be charged with murder."

Her voice became a screech. "You don't even *know* her. She could *never* murder anyone. *Never.*"

"Not even if it was called an abortion?"

I'd hoped to provoke her and I did. "Abortion isn't *murder,* you bastard, abortion is . . ."

In the echo of Linda Webber's furious grope for an adjective, I offered a quick spiel. "Tell Greta I know who she is. Tell her I know about her father and her first pregnancy. Tell her I'm working for Russell Jorgensen, but that he doesn't know what I've learned as yet. And tell her I'm the only one who can get her out of this."

"But I don't . . ." She traded her protest for information. "Are you saying Greta's pregnant?"

"She got pregnant several weeks before she disappeared."

"But she's had an abortion?"

"I think it's possible."

"I don't understand. Who was the father? You?"

"My client."

"Who's your client?"

"I can't tell you that. What I can tell you is that I think Greta disappeared so she could arrange to have an abortion. By now, she's probably had it. She may be ready to come back to her old life again but she should talk to me before she does. If I understand everything that's been going on, maybe I can get her out of the fix she's in. But it's going to be up to you to persuade her to let me."

I didn't expect her to yield without thinking it over and she didn't. All she said was, "I don't know. I don't know *what* to do."

"There's obviously a lot about this you don't know, Mrs. Webber, and some I don't know, either. So give Greta the message. And my phone number. She can call me any time. I can meet her any place she chooses."

I recited the digits and waited. When Linda didn't say anything, I made my final plea. "And tell her one more thing."

"What?"

"Tell her I was off duty the night I spent with her. Tell her that was real."

"I don't think she's going to believe you," she said.

TWENTY-FIVE

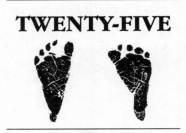

I was about to leave the office when the phone started ringing. "Hi," she said.

"Hi."

"How are you?"

"Fine. You?"

"I'm good. Is this a bad time?"

"No. It's fine."

"You use that word too much."

"What word?"

"Fine."

"What's wrong with fine?"

"It's a nothing word. Empty. It doesn't communicate anything helpful."

"Sorry. I'll try to do better. The next time I'm inclined to be helpful."

Betty Fontaine coughed nervously. "You don't *sound* sorry. You sound mad. Maybe this wasn't a good idea."

"I'm not mad."

"Really?"

"Really."

"Good."

"Fine."

Betty laughed and finally I laughed, too. "I've missed you," she said, the knot of feeling that clogged her throat a match to the lump in mine.

"I've missed you, too."

"I don't have a reason to call, really, it's just that this weekend was particularly lonely for me and I was thinking about you and trying not to believe that we weren't ever going to *see* each other again, so I thought . . . I don't know, I guess I thought I'd try to remedy the situation."

"Are you asking me for a date?"

"I don't think so. Not exactly. I mean, that was basically our problem, I think."

"Dating?"

"Yes. We dated. And held hands. And had sex. And did all kinds of things to try to pretend we were lovers, when really what we are is friends. *Good* friends. But friends." She paused. "Does that make any sense at all to you?" she asked when I didn't say anything.

"I suppose it might if I thought about it."

"What I'm saying is, I want us to go *on* being friends. I want us to do things together. I want to talk on the phone. I want to go to movies."

"Friend stuff."

"Right. So do you think that would be possible? Maybe not right away, but some day?"

"Probably. But I'm sure going to miss your nightie."

She laughed even though she wasn't amused, and paused long enough to get back on an amiable track. "Do you want to do something Saturday night? There's a play at Marine's Memorial that sounds interesting."

"As long as you don't get mad if I back out at the last minute. Things are heating up in the case I have going—it may start to get busy in a day or two."

"That's okay. I'll put Lucy on backup. She likes doing things at the last minute."

"What time?"

"Six? I'll fix something light to eat, then we can go on from here."

"Is friend food different from lover food?"

"I don't think so."

"Good. Do that thing with the skewers. If you feel like it."

"As a matter of fact, it's what I had in mind."

I thought she was finished, but there was one more caveat coming.

"I appreciate this, Marsh. You know I care for you. And enjoy being with you. It's just that I need something with more texture right now. I need something *brewing* in my life, something taking shape that I don't entirely understand but that feels like it might turn into something important. Something I can be proud of."

"I know what you mean," I said, and I did up to a point.

"I've got things in me I haven't used, Marsh."

"I know you do, Betty."

"So I'm going to start looking for someone who's willing to help me use them," Betty continued tonelessly. "And I was thinking it would be nice if you could help me with my search."

"Sort of a guide dog, you mean."

"A guide guy."

"Do I need a pith helmet?"

"All you need is some compassion and a sense of humor."

She said good-bye and hung up. I leaned back in my chair and let my mind roam over the conversation, then blended it with the months and years I'd spent with Betty, comparing my evaluation of our relationship with Betty's new interpretation of it. And she was right, of course. I hadn't been in love with her, not really, nor she with me. There had been other women in my life during the time we'd been together, not for lengthy periods, but for significant ones—Greta Hammond was only the most recent installment. For all I knew, Betty had indulged herself as well, which meant we weren't . . .

No, she hadn't. That was a rationalization—Betty would never do that. On the other hand, I hadn't been a total cad. We had never pledged fidelity, never passed beyond the loose reins of dating into the bit and bridle of permanence. That stasis had to mean something and it probably meant what Betty said it did: women know those kinds of things, sort of the way men know where the fish are likely to bite.

A shadow inched across the office wall. I watched its snaily slide for several minutes, my mind wandering in and out of sense, until I grabbed my coat and headed for Zorba's, which is where I eat, then moved on to Guido's, which is where I drink. By the time I trudged up the hill toward my apartment, it was after 10 P.M. and I was feeling lonely and sorry for myself in the moments when I wasn't feeling angry at Betty for the large hole that seemed to have formed at my core, somewhere between my belly and my heart.

Maybe I would have known he was there if I hadn't been distracted by my interior debate with Betty, or maybe he was just good. Whatever the reason, all of a sudden there was a rope around my chest, a scratchy lariat that bit deep into my flesh and pinioned my arms to my ribs. Before I could shrug it off, I was yanked off my feet and dragged on my back down the walk toward a person standing in the dark of a commercial doorway, a block west of my home, wielding a lasso as skillfully as Tom Mix.

Like a champion roper, he worked his way toward me down the wire-taut line, a pair of pigging strings clenched in his teeth like strands of cooked pasta. His tugs on the rope kept me from regaining my feet or creating enough slack to slip out of its disabling cinch. When he reached me, I tried to strike out with my fists, but I was tied too tight to move, arms snug at my sides, hands flapping impotently at my waist like a pair of stunted wings. When I tried to get to my feet, he kicked them out from under me.

"What the hell are you doing?" I asked as he loomed over me, the rawhide cords still leaking from his lips like streams of brown spittle, his cowboy hat and boots so anachronistic I couldn't suppress a laugh. "You must have taken a wrong turn at Salinas, pal," I said as I tried and failed to roll away from him.

Instead of answering, he kicked me in the side with the needle nose of a lizard-skin boot, then flipped me onto my belly and put a foot in the small of my back, the high heel impaling me as effectively as a spear. I realized what he was going to do the instant he did it, which meant there wasn't time to keep him from grabbing one leg, slipping a leather string around it, then cinching the other to it as though I was a hapless calf yanked off his feet ten yards out of the chute.

I was still trying to twist away from his boot when he bound my wrists behind me in the same manner. The excuse I awarded myself was that he was younger and faster and stronger than I was, but such truths have never kept me from feeling like a dolt, and this was no exception.

When he had me where he wanted me, he rolled me onto my back again. There was enough moonlight falling through the fog for me to see that he was tall and lean and handsome, more of "Gunsmoke" or "Bonanza" than *Unforgiven*. The grin on his face told me he was enjoying his work; the bandanna in his hand indicated he wasn't finished.

"Do I need to use this?" he asked when he was certain I was helpless. "Or are you going to be sensible?"

"I'm going to be whatever you want me to be," I said.

"Good." He stuffed the bandanna in his back pocket. "Let's go where we can talk."

"How about the police station?"

His lips didn't stretch a millimeter. "I suppose that's funny."

"It is in this neighborhood."

"I don't like funny."

"I'll curb my impulses."

With the ease that comes with strength and experience, he grabbed a wrist and jerked me to my feet—my arms threatened to pop off my shoulders. When I was standing at his side, he gave me a shove. "The F-one fifty."

I banged against a tree to keep upright. "What?"

He gestured. "The pickup. Get in it. We're going for a ride."

I considered the situation. "How do I get there?"

"Hop."

And I did, making like Christopher Rabbit as I was shanghaied off a city street within screaming distance of my home. The wiry wrangler herding me along and the rusty pickup that was my destination gave the scene an air of silliness that allowed me to be less intimidated than I should have been.

He opened the dented door and shoved me inside the truck. "Where are we going?" I asked as he lifted my feet into the cab. "Laramie?"

Ignoring my quip, he went to the other door and got in beside me. The engine fired with a noise loud enough to provoke calls to 911 on any street north of Market.

The first bad sign was geographical—he drove in the wrong direction, not north or west, toward civilization, but south down Third, toward the abandoned hulks of industry and the eager menace of gangland. When we were someplace south of Potrero Hill and west of Candlestick Park, he took some turns on streets that lacked visible names or lights and I lost my bearings in the dodge. When we pulled to a stop a few blocks later, we could have been in Hiroshima in the summer of '45.

The air smelled of salt and fish and something far more fetid; the sounds were of speeding vehicles and climbing jets, which put us near the Bayshore and the airport. Somewhere someone was playing riffs and runs on a trumpet. I hoped his repertoire didn't include taps.

The cowboy leaned against the door and looked at me. In the feeble light from the dashboard, his features were clean-cut and seamless, his eyes hooded and wary beneath the brim of his brown hat. His mouth was curled down in petulance, as if he were a TV star I'd failed to recognize even though his series had just been picked up for a second season.

"Know who I am?" he asked, a faint twang adding to the filmic aura he projected.

"I'd say you were Luke Drummond."

"Right."

"What can I do for you, Luke? Give you some tips on rustling?"

"I told you I don't like funny. What you can do is stop messing with my life."

"I wasn't aware that I was."

"We had everything fixed up, then you come along and get every-one all excited and turn everything upside down. So now I'm telling you to quit. Just back off and wheel your horse around and go the other way. Leave us the hell alone."

"I'm not sure I can do that, Luke. The situation on Santa Ana has been ignored for too long already—it's time for the truth to come out. Plus, I have a contract."

His smile was thin and nerveless. "So do I."

"Really? Who with?"

"Never mind. But if the money don't start up again real soon, it's gonna be your ass."

"It would help if I knew what money you were talking about. Is it the money Stuart was paying your mother? Or the money Ethan Brennan embezzled?"

"You don't need to know about any of that. All you need to know is that the Colberts are none of your affair anymore."

"Even if I quit, it doesn't mean things will be back the way they were."

"They'll get there in due time. Just so you keep out of it."

"Who are you working for, Luke? Rutherford Colbert?"

"I'm just keeping things straight, like always. Which is what they were till *you* came along."

I shrugged as best I could. "It would help if I knew exactly what you want."

"Money."

"What money?"

"The money we been promised."

"What for?"

"For what we did for them. Where's Clara?"

"Clara who?"

"You know damned well."

"I don't know where she is. I was hoping you did."

"Well, I don't. They think I do, but I don't. I'm about to find her, though; you can bet on it."

"What are you going to do when you do?"

"That's none of your concern. Where is she?"

"I told you I don't know. Who is it that thinks you know where she is? Cynthia?"

He didn't acknowledge the question. "Get out of the truck."

When I didn't move, he got out of his side and trotted around to mine and opened the door and dragged me onto the street. When I was standing beside him he reached into the truck bed and pulled out another length of rope, this one coiled as if it had been slung from a saddle.

"Guess I got to jog your memory," he said as he flipped out a length of ten feet or so.

"I don't know where she is, Luke. I've been looking for her myself. Ask anyone. Ask your mother-in-law."

I might as well have been talking with Trigger. With practiced ease, Luke threaded the second rope around my chest and under my arms, then formed a loop and cinched it tight above my sternum. "You see many cowboy movies, mister?" he asked as he worked.

"Double feature every Saturday for a dime," I said.

"Who's your favorite?"

"Of the old guys? Hopalong Cassidy."

"Who else?"

"Rex Allen."

"Who else?"

"Johnny Mack Brown."

"Bullshit. Nobody liked Johnny Mack Brown."

"I did," I objected. "How about you?"

"Lash LaRue," he said. "He had the best outfit."

He tugged on the end of the rope and towed me toward the rear of the pickup. I was still searching madly for an escape route when Luke leaned down and tied his end around the trailer hitch. Suddenly I started to sweat.

"You don't need to do this," I said.

"Mom says I do."

"You'll end up in jail."

"Not if you learn your lesson."

He got back in the truck and started it up. As I yelled for him to stop, he rammed the truck in gear, popped the clutch, and spun the wheels to get purchase on the dusty pavement. An instant later I was jerked off my feet and dragged down the street just the way they used to do in the movies, when the guy being towed behind the horse usually ended up dead.

I was too frightened to feel pain, too desperate to do anything but twist and writhe to keep from being pulverized by the pitted slabs of concrete on which I bounced like a tin can being towed behind a limo with JUST MARRIED on the window.

The cement tore at my clothes like the fingers of a frenzied mob. Rocks stabbed my chest like a dozen pointed darts. The dirt and dust were blinding, clogging my nose and mouth, stinging my eyes, creating the sensation of drowning in a vat of evaporated milk. Bit by bit my clothes wore away at the hip and calf, and then my shoes were gone and my flesh was scraped away as well. I rolled from belly to back to belly, trying to minimize contact with the pavement, trying to stave off concussion as the fumes from the exhaust pipe threatened to kill me more quickly than the road.

As the truck turned a corner I skidded across an impromptu shortcut until I was knocked back to the center wake by a collision with a fire hydrant; I figured I'd be lucky if only my leg was broken. In the aftermath, I traveled for half a block on my elbow and hip. About then I switched my focus from trying to stay alive to trying to escape before I collided with something that would render me senseless.

The principles of martial arts advise you to use your opponent's strength against him. At the moment, my opponent was a rock-hard expanse of concrete. Clearly the thing to do was use its rough-hewn surface to tear away something besides epidermis. Didn't it all seem simple?

The effort was all-consuming. I used muscles I didn't know I had, muscles that hadn't been summoned to full force in years, muscles that burned and knotted and screamed against me. Fueled by fear and instructed by pain, when the truck slowed at the next intersection I managed to twist to my side, then roll a half-turn up the tow rope and hook it with my legs, so that the strand that attached me to the truck was between my shoulder and the roadway.

The task was to stay there long enough for the street to serve as a scalpel. Which it did, eventually, although this particular scalpel was blunt and dull, so it seemed to take forever to make its cut. But as my muscles were about to break down under the strain, and I was about to yield to my fate and let my predicament have its way with me, the rope was severed with a sigh and I rolled to a stop somewhere in the middle of a mine-dark block of loading docks in the nether reaches of a city that seemed as alien as Mars. The only stars I could see were inside my head.

I don't know if Luke knew or cared that I'd escaped, but no brake lights flashed and no gear ground into reverse and eventually the truck swerved left and disappeared. I was alone with my heaving lungs and scalded flesh and a cascade of pain the like of which I hadn't experienced since I'd been gut-shot and left for dead in an alley south of Broadway some dozen years before.

I had problems other than pain to deal with: my hands and feet were bound; my clothing was more a net than a garment; my eyes were filled with grit. I tugged against the leather thongs without result, then scraped my ankles against the curb to slide the hobbles off them. The latter process was the more productive and in less than five minutes my feet were free and I could stand, but it was not a painless process.

I was staggering down the block, working at the tangle of wrists and leather behind my back and looking for an edge sharp enough to cut my bonds, when a car turned the corner and crawled my way like a panther downwind of fresh blood. The car was a black Infiniti, lowered, chromed, and tinted, its occupants a blur behind the smoky windshield. When it got to my flank, it stopped; the window wound down with a whine.

"Hey, dude. What's happening?" he asked with exaggerated friendliness, his eyes whipping left and right to make certain we were alone. With no rescuers in sight, he focused on my clothing. "Taking the grunge thing too far, dude."

I wanted to laugh but decided I shouldn't.

He was Asian, as were his three associates, his eyes as bright as his black satin shirt, his Giants cap backward on his head, the hands on the wheel shoved into gloves with no tips on the fingers.

"Just a stroll in the moonlight," I said. "But I appreciate the fashion tip."

"You're fucked up, man. Got blood all over you."

"I'm a little fucked up," I agreed.

"Tied up, too. Who rattled you, man?"

"Some cowboy."

His eyes flipped left. "A crip? Where is he?"

I gestured south with my chin. "Try the Cow Palace."

He paused to think it over. One of his buddies gave him some advice in a language I didn't understand.

He reached for something on the seat beside him, then held it out the window and flipped it open for me to see. "You probably like to make a call. For a cab, or something." The cellular phone fit in his hand like a sap.

"A call would be nice."

"Yeah, well, the thing is, this is a pay phone."

"I thought it might be. What's the toll?"

"All you got."

I looked at my ragged pants. "I'm not sure I have anything anymore."

"Tommy will check it out."

The passenger door opened and Tommy got out. He was a clone of the driver except his shirt was a numbered pullover and it hung below his knees. He frisked me quickly and I didn't resist. As his hands roamed my hip and ribs, it felt like I'd been boiled.

When he found my wallet, he got out a knife and cut it out of my pants. He took out all the currency, then looked for credit cards. "Where's the plastic, man?"

"Don't use it."

"Why not?"

"Too many pay phones in the world."

Tommy was pissed enough to cut me but the driver called him off. "Too many cowboys, too, looks like. Here. You bought it." As Tommy climbed back in the car, the driver tossed the phone at me. As it hit my chest and clattered to the pavement, he buzzed up the window and eased down the street as efficiently as an eel.

I flipped the phone on its back with my stockinged foot, then got down on my knees and used my nose to call an ambulance.

TWENTY-SIX

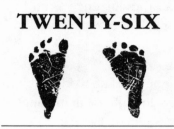

My leg wasn't broken; nothing was fractured but my pride. My skin was scraped and scabbed, my joints strained and hyperextended, my muscles cramped and pulled, my tendons stretched, my ligaments torn. But I was whole, if warped and wounded, and I was cleaned and disinfected and stitched and bandaged, and I was allowed to go home even though I had sustained a mild concussion. I told the nurse I'd fallen off my bicycle, but she didn't believe me for a minute.

I didn't confront a mirror till I got to my apartment. When I did, I thought I was looking at a Christmas tree with too much flocking and too many felt bows and red ornaments. Forbidden Scotch because of the pain pills they'd given me for my contusions, I made do with a cup of hot chocolate and a bag of Fig Newtons as pacifiers. Since there was no way I was going to be able to sleep, I scanned the TV listings to see what they offered as an anesthetic at 2 A.M.

My home number is listed. Most private eyes don't do that, for the same reason cops and lawyers don't do it, but I figure it's more important to be available when someone needs me than to avoid the occasional jolt of jeopardy that comes from a dissatisfied customer on the other end of the line. People who need help generally need it now, and people with a bone-deep grudge won't let an unlisted number keep them from extracting a pound of flesh in atonement.

All of which is to say, when the phone rang as I was in my pajamas and settling in to a reprise of *Touch of Evil* on AMC, I almost didn't answer it. I figured it was Betty, in one of her bouts with insomnia, and although my initial reaction was to hope she was calling to suggest that our new relationship might have room in it for some recreational sex, in the next instant I knew that, at most, she just wanted more talk. To tell me what and why I did what I did, which of my childhood traumas were pivotal and what they forecast for my future, and why men are such layabouts and louts when they're not cuddly teddy bears in the interim.

I answered anyway; it wasn't Betty.

"Mr. Tanner?"

"Speaking."

"The detective?"

"During normal business hours."

"It's late; I know. I'm sorry. This is—"

"How are you, Ms. Hammond?" I interrupted. "Or are you back to Brennan these days?"

"I understand you've been looking for me." Her tone would have drilled through tooth enamel.

I put the phone in the hand that wasn't bandaged. "Among other people," I said.

"You mean you're looking for someone else as well?"

"I mean other people are looking for you."

"Oh? Who?"

"The entire population of Santa Ana Way, for one. Your ex-husband, for another."

"I see."

"I hope you're not surprised. Given what you've done."

"No. I suppose not." Her tone turned hostile. "The only thing I'm surprised about is you."

"How so?" I asked, though of course I knew the answer.

"When you found me before, you were checking me out for Stuart, right? Just taking care of Colbert business."

My face reddened and my skin prickled even through the pain pills. "I . . . sort of, I admit. At first. But I wasn't—"

Her voice was as cold as my nurse's hands. "You had a job to do and you did it. I understand completely. I'm sure your employer was titillated by the details."

"He didn't get that kind of detail. It wasn't part of the job."

Somewhere in the background, a siren wailed. Which meant she could be anywhere in the world.

"It would be nice to believe that, I suppose," she said softly. "Less humiliating, at least."

"That night wasn't anything *close* to humiliation. Not as far as I'm concerned."

"Well that's neither here nor there. Is it?"

"I'd say it's wherever we want to put it. So how are you?" I asked when she didn't respond to my prompt.

"I'm fine."

"I guess what I'm asking is whether you left Kirkham Street on your own."

"Of course I did."

"No one kidnaped you?"

"What? Why would they?"

It seemed pointless to list reasons. "No one's listening to this conversation? No one's telling you what to say?"

"Does it sound like it?"

"No, as a matter of fact."

She paused. "Well *you* sound kind of funny, come to think of it."

"I had a meeting with Luke this evening."

"What about?"

"Your whereabouts, among other things."

"What did you tell him?"

"Everything I knew. Which is nothing." The final word fell victim to the recalcitrance of my swollen lips.

"Did he hurt you?" she asked.

"Yes."

"Badly?"

"I look worse than I am. But I look awful," I added with a laugh that wrecked my ribs. "Where are you?" I went on, keeping the ball in my court for as long as I could.

"Where I am is no concern of yours."

"It's a *primary* concern of mine."

"You may wish it was, but it's not. And I'm in a phone booth, so there's no use trying to trace this. The reason I'm calling is to ask you to stop looking for me."

"I can't do that."

"Of course you can. And you have to."

"You made a deal, Ms. Brennan. You agreed to all kinds of penalties if you reneged on your promise to be a surrogate. It'll be best if you come in from the cold and settle it. Otherwise you could face a kidnaping charge."

"Who am I supposed to have kidnaped?"

"The Colberts' unborn child."

Her laugh was borderline hysterical. Then she was silent so long I thought she'd dropped the phone.

"When I signed that contract, I didn't know who the father of the child was going to be," she said finally.

"But you do now."

"Yes."

"What difference does it make?"

"It makes all kinds of difference."

"It would help if I knew why."

She paused to consider what to tell me. "Let's just say certain people don't want this child to be. If I come back where they can get at me, I could be risking the baby's life. *Both* our lives."

"Then how do you want to handle it?"

"I just want to vanish for a while."

"Like you did the last time you were pregnant."

She hesitated. "You know about that?"

"I talked to your mother yesterday. And her buddy, Mrs. Colbert."

Her lungs made a sizzling grasp at air. "My God. What *are* you, some sort of incubus? First we have meaningless sex and now you try to suck secrets out of the past and parade them in front of the whole world. Why are you *doing* it?"

"Because you made it necessary."

"How did I do that?"

"By not living up to the terms of the contract."

Her scoff occupied the phone line like a clot. "You sound like every lawyer I've ever known. Which means you sound like slime with lips. How's Opal?" she asked before I could rebut her accusation.

"Okay, I think. It would probably help if she heard from you more often."

"Yes, well, it didn't seem like a good idea while I'm on the lam, as it were; Rutherford probably has the phones tapped. Lucky for me, she understands why I'm doing what I'm doing."

"What *are* you doing, Ms. Brennan?"

She laughed and cursed me.

"Who's Nathaniel?" I asked abruptly.

Her voice solidified and became repellant. "No one. You leave him out of this. I mean it."

"He's the child you had by Luke, isn't he?"

"That's nothing to *do* with this." She swore again. "I'm going to hang up. It's been nice talking to you. You're not a bad guy, actually, even though you're as crooked as Lombard Street. Maybe when this is over we can meet for champagne cocktails and make wry observations about life and death and be thrillingly sophisticated about the whole thing. Take care of yourself, Mr. Tanner."

"I need to be clear about one thing," I said quickly.

"What?"

"Are you still carrying the child?"

"Yes."

"That's good."

"You sound surprised."

"I am, a little."

"Why?"

"I thought part of this might be to give you a chance to abort it."

"Why would I want to do that?"

"I thought maybe Stuart did something that made you want to . . . but it doesn't matter now, I guess. Are you getting medical attention? Healthy baby stuff, or whatever they call it?"

"Of course. I'm just not using the Colberts' in-house obstetrician."

"I'll have to take your word for it. What's the name of the doctor who did the implant, by the way?"

"Why do you want to know?"

"For my files."

"I don't give a shit about your files."

"Humor me, Ms. Brennan. You weren't exactly aboveboard with me either, you know."

"Bradshaw," she muttered. "He's at the fertility clinic."

"So what now? Are you planning to materialize before the baby's born?"

"I'll make the baby available to the Colberts two days after it's delivered. That's all that matters."

"I'm not sure Millicent will see it that way. It would help if I could give her a guarantee."

"The guarantee is that if I don't show up in six months with a brand-new bambino, you'll track me down and do whatever you do to people who break their word."

"If the Colberts decide they don't want to wait that long, they'll just hire someone else to hunt you down."

"Not if you persuade them to stop."

"How can I do that?"

"Tell them just what I said—I'll deliver the baby when the time comes. Until then, they need to leave me alone."

"Why?"

"Because if they don't, there won't *be* a baby."

I hoped the threat was idle. "That's extortion. On top of which, I don't think you'd do something like that."

"You don't want to try me, Mr. Detective."

There was enough raw and eager menace in her voice to convince me to relent. "These people who don't want this child to happen."

"What about them?"

"Who are they?"

"You're the snoop. You figure it out."

"Are Cynthia Colbert and Russell Jorgensen trying to sabotage the pregnancy?"

She laughed bitterly. "That's the last thing in the world they want."

"Then what *do* they want?"

"What they want is for history to repeat itself."

TWENTY-SEVEN

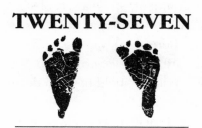

I spent a fitful night, wrestling with sheets, dueling with blankets, fending off waves of pain with the aid of prescription pharmaceuticals and a secret vice—my videotapes of *Amos & Andy.* The healing ritual was only partially successful, however, and I was still teetering like a gimpy octogenarian when I entered Colbert for Women at 10 A.M. to do Clara Brennan's bidding for reasons I was too damaged to decipher.

When I asked the operator to take me to eight, she mimicked a bulldog sucking a lemon. "I don't have my list yet."

"I was here before, remember?"

Now she looked like a ferret with the flu. "I'm not sure."

"Sure you're sure."

"Even if I am, I can't take anyone to eight unless they're on the list."

"You don't have the list."

"I know."

"So how do you know I'm not on it?"

"But how do I know you are?"

I got out a business card and stuck it under the inspection certificate. "There's a list. My name's on it. Now take me to your leader."

She looked at my scabs and bruises, she looked at the people who were clamoring to get into the elevator car but couldn't because I was blocking the way, and she looked at my card, which was stuck to the wall like a leaf on a wet window.

After her microprocessor had worked through all that, she

shrugged. "It's none of my business who comes and goes," she said, nullifying her *raison d'être*. "People want privacy, they should stay home."

Stuart Colbert's secretary was straight out of Mickey Spillane but she wasn't only an ornament, she was an obstacle. "He can't be disturbed," she told me with her nose at half-mast.

"If he knew I was here, he'd want to be."

"My instructions are, 'no calls; no visitors.'"

"If he knew I was coming, he'd have made an exception."

"That's what they all say."

"I'm a detective," I tacked, assuming my most daunting mien, which was a pale imitation of the elevator woman's.

"What kind of detective?"

"The kind that knows things other people don't want them to know."

"Like what?"

"Like how you got your job."

The heat in her cheeks told me my hunch had paid off.

"You can sound skeptical," I instructed, "as though you're sure he's too busy to see a lowlife like me but you thought you'd better check. Or you can say I threatened to spit on the carpet. But pick one and get moving."

Two minutes later I was sitting across a barren desk from Stuart Colbert, who was as nervous as he was natty. "What happened to you?" he began.

"I ran into a door."

"It must have been revolving." He looked beyond me. "Is Russell coming?"

"I thought we'd keep this between ourselves."

"Why?"

"Because at last count Russell was serving at least four people named Colbert; it could get tricky if interests start to diverge. Which they did forty years ago."

"What's that mean?"

"It means you and your sister have been on a collision course since the day you were born and you both knew it by the time you were adolescents."

"What does that have to do with you?"

"The latest battle in that war is being fought inside Greta Hammond's body. You and your lawyer made me a part of it. I have a feeling you're going to wish you hadn't, but you did."

Colbert considered what I'd said. "I've been thinking about getting separate counsel, as a matter of fact. Everything always seems to go Cynthia's way these days and I'm tired of it. I think Russell has chosen sides."

As though to remind himself of the stakes in the game, Stuart swiveled to look at the photographic array of storefronts that enlivened his office wall. "Why are you here? Have you found the Hammond woman?"

"Not yet."

"Are you close? Do you have any leads? Surely you've come up with something."

"I've come up with lots of things."

"For instance?"

"I've come up with the fact that Greta Hammond wasn't kidnaped."

He swiveled my way and frowned. "How do you know?"

"She told me so. I also came up with the fact that Greta Hammond isn't Greta Hammond."

He did a good job of looking bewildered. "Then who is she?"

"Greta Hammond is Clara Brennan and she grew up next door to you on Santa Ana Way. And you've known it all along."

He started to protest, or exonerate himself, but the look on my face announced that both were useless. To avoid my look, he put his elbows on the desk and lowered his head to his hands. "How did you find out?"

"It doesn't matter. What matters is, Clara is fine, but she seems to be running from everyone who ever lived in St. Francis Wood. Mostly the person she's running from is you. I want to know why."

He closed his eyes. "She found out; she must have."

"Found out what?"

"That I was the contractor—that I hired her to carry the child."

"You did more than hire her—you tracked her down and had Russell recruit her as your surrogate."

He lifted his head off his hands and looked at me. "You're implying I did something wrong."

"I'm not saying you did something wrong, I'm saying you did something fishy. Which probably means it's wrong as well—why else would she have absconded, if there wasn't something illicit about all this?"

"But there wasn't. The only thing fishy was that I didn't tell her who I was."

"Why did you want her for your surrogate? Why not use a stranger?"

"I told you before—we heard horror stories about women reneging on the deal and Clara was someone we trusted."

"*You* trusted. Millicent didn't know anything about Clara Brennan being the surrogate, did she?"

He sighed and shook his head. "I thought it was better not to tell her."

"You trusted Clara Brennan to carry your child even though you hadn't seen her for twenty years?"

He nodded. "People don't change. Not that much."

"Nonsense. Angelic little kids become insider traders overnight. I don't think it had anything to do with trust; I think it had to do with what happened in the old days."

He dared a peek at me. "What old days?"

"The St. Francis Wood days. I think the reason you used Clara Brennan is because you're in love with her and have been since she was in high school and you were in college."

I waited for him to deny it but he just looked the way a schoolboy in love often looks—disconsolate and forlorn and powerless to do anything about it but mope.

"I think another reason you used her is because of what happened the *first* time she got pregnant."

His eyes bulged and his neck swelled. "What the hell are you talking about?"

"I'm talking about Nathaniel."

"Who?"

"Nathaniel."

"I don't know anyone by that name."

His confusion seemed genuine. "That's rather odd, since I think he's your son."

Stuart Colbert looked the way people look when they've just been shot. "I don't have a son," he said softly. "Except the one Clara is carrying."

"I'm talking about the baby Clara Brennan gave birth to twenty years ago."

He got up and walked to the window that looked down on the scruffy hubbub of Market Street. "I never saw that child. I never even knew for sure it existed."

"It existed. It still does."

His voice was dazed and abstracted. "Where is he? Have you seen him?"

I shook my head. "I've only heard his name."

"From whom?"

"Your mother."

He twirled toward me so awkwardly he almost fell over. "My *mother* knows where he is?"

"Apparently."

"But why? How? Why didn't she ever . . ." The quantity of conceivable questions made enumeration impossible: He didn't know what he needed to know. "I want to see him," he announced with sudden strength. "I want you to find him for me."

"Why?"

"So I can do something. *Say* something. Be a father to him in some way. Will you do it? I'll double your rate."

He'd already doubled my rate. "I'm not sure if I will or not," I said, uneasy that the conversation was centered on the wrong child.

"What reason would you have to refuse me?"

I scrambled to assemble my thoughts. "I'm not sure it would be good for the boy or your wife, either one. Things are precarious enough in your family. The existence of another child, an adult by this time, one you've never met and your wife's never heard of, might cause some sort of collapse."

I was thinking of Millicent, of course, but from his look, the infirmities I spoke of could apply equally to Stuart.

"Collapse?" he echoed. "I don't know what you're talking about. How could meeting his long-lost father make more problems for the boy? Nathaniel, is it? Nathaniel. It's a nice name." He looked eagerly toward the door, as though the boy had just walked into the room.

He wasn't thinking straight and I told him so. He was upset at my comment but didn't say so. I watched him work with it for a minute, watched fact and fancy play with his face the way kids play with putty.

"Why was having a child with Clara Brennan so important that you had to go through this subterfuge?" I asked when he seemed back within his senses.

His voice fell to a miserable hum. "I loved her. I still do. I love Millicent, too, of course, but I've never gotten over Clara. She was the most wonderful thing that ever happened to me. My father and sister were such monsters. I'd spend all day hearing them criticize and taunt and demean me, but all of a sudden it didn't matter because Clara would be so loving and accepting, it was like she was my therapist or something. And then she did something like *that*."

"You mean get pregnant?"

"I mean run away. It wasn't *her* fault she got pregnant; it was mine."

"So you're admitting you're the child's father."

He nodded. "I just didn't know he existed. I thought she, you know, got rid of him."

"And you're certain you're the father."

He thrust out his chest. "Of course. Who else would it be?"

"Luke Drummond, for one."

He shook his head. "Clara and I were going steady. She wouldn't have been with Luke as well; she wasn't that kind of girl."

I was tempted to check the calendar to see if we'd slipped back to the fifties. "Then why did she run off with him?"

"Because of what happened to her father. Because after that she thought *all* the Colberts were murderers."

"Was one of them?"

"What do you mean?"

"Did your father murder Ethan Brennan?"

"Of course not. That was just a figure of speech."

"That's the way Clara thought it happened."

"She was crazy. She loved her father very much; she lost her mind for a while."

"Is there any chance her *father* was Nathaniel's father?"

Clearly the idea had never occurred to him. As my suggestion took form in his mind, his eyes seemed short-circuited by its implications. "What do you think we are?" he exclaimed. "My God. It wasn't *Tobacco Road*."

I didn't bother to mention that incest had moved uptown a long time ago. "Did Clara run off because you refused to marry her?"

He shook his head violently. "I *wanted* to marry her. I *begged* to marry her. And she was willing, I thought—we were talking about eloping to Las Vegas, then taking a honeymoon in Europe before she got too big to travel. The next thing I knew, she was gone."

"If you loved her so much, why didn't you go after her?"

"I did. Or started to. But my mother told me to stop."

"Why?"

His expression was confused and uncertain, as though the subject had switched to biophysics. "She didn't say, but she was adamant about it. She said if I found her and married her it would haunt me the rest of my life. She was very firm. For some reason, I believed her." He shook his head. "Poor Clara. I think mostly she was ashamed and afraid."

"Of what? Of who?"

"Ashamed of what we did. Afraid of what else he might do."

"Luke?"

"Rutherford."

It wasn't the name I expected and I blurted an idea that had been percolating all morning. "What did he do, rape her?"

Stuart's misery was rampant. His breaths were labored and convulsive; I was afraid he was going to collapse. "He didn't *need* to rape her. I took care of that for him."

"You raped Clara Brennan?"

"I might as well have," he said miserably. "Daddy kept saying that if I was really going to marry her, then we needed to be sure she could produce an heir. He promised that if it happened, and the next heir to the Colbert line was established, the stores would be mine when he died. So I did what he asked. Or what I thought he was asking."

"Rutherford urged you to impregnate her. Is that it?"

"Not exactly. At first he didn't even want me to date her, but when he found out I was and saw that I truly loved her, he told me I'd made a wonderful choice, that she was an exceptional woman. All he asked was that I be discreet."

"But you weren't, were you?"

He smiled and shook his head. "I wanted to show off, I admit it. Daddy got mad when he saw us in public. I was afraid he might make me stop seeing her."

"So you decided to curry favor by getting her pregnant."

He nodded. "Daddy was obsessed with the stores staying in the family after he passed on. He even made me put sperm in a sperm bank, just to make sure I would be potent when the time came. He wanted to test Clara as well, to make sure she was fertile; it was like we were royalty or something. Since I wanted to make love to Clara anyway, it was easy to believe that was what I should do."

He paused to reflect on his escapades. It didn't seem to produce a pleasant memory.

"I told myself I was doing the right thing," he went on softly. "I try to do that, you know. I don't get credit for it, but I try. It's just that the right thing always comes out wrong, somehow. I wanted it to be the best time there ever was for her but it was just a quick fix in the back of a car, and a month later she left me. Now she's left a *second* time. It took me twenty years to find her and now she's gone again."

The final phrase was desolate. He shook his head as though it had stopped working in mid-thought. "I should have walked away from it all a long time ago. Let Cynthia *have* the stores; she can wallow in them with my blessing. What do *I* care what happens to the fucking business?" He swept his hand across the desk as if to dispatch his life to the shag in the carpet. But there was nothing on the desk to dispatch.

"What happened to Luke Drummond?" I asked as he muttered something I couldn't hear.

"How should I know?"

"Didn't you track him down, too? In the process of finding Clara?"

He shook his head again, then grasped it with his hands and squeezed, as though to pinch off its output.

"How about his mother?" I asked.

He frowned. "Fern? What about her?"

"Why are you sending her three thousand dollars a month? Isn't it because she's raising your child?"

He shook his head. "I didn't *know* about the child, I told you."

"Then why the payments?"

"Because Rutherford told me to make them."

"You don't know why?"

"She used to work for him. I figured it was some sort of pension."

"Then why didn't he pay it himself?"

"Father's always been weird about money. He schemes and plans for months to cheat the IRS out of a nickel. I gave up trying to understand him a long time ago."

"Then why did you stop making the payments?"

He frowned. "How did you know about that?"

"Why?" I repeated. "Because you thought Clara had run off with Luke again? Because you figured Luke was living off his mother's stipend and that cutting it off was the only way you could hurt him?"

He sighed and nodded and sat back at his desk.

"She didn't run off with Luke, I know that much. So you need to start paying Mrs. Drummond again."

"Why?"

"To make sure Luke doesn't do something that will interfere with the new baby."

"But why would he—" He cut himself off, then slumped in his chair. "It doesn't matter. Don't you see? It doesn't matter anymore."

"Why not?"

"Because I'm calling the whole thing off. I'm not looking for Clara Brennan and neither are you. I'll call Russell and tell him to pay your fees to date but, from now on, you're off the case."

"It's not that simple, Mr. Colbert."

"You say she hasn't been kidnaped, which means she wants to be gone. So be it. I tried to do right and I fucked up. I *always* fuck up. So I'm going to take poor Millicent and move to Maui and live on the beach and forget all *about* retail clothing. Cynthia can have it all; I hope she drowns in it."

Steeled by fresh resolve, he got to his feet and marched to the door and waited for me to leave.

I held my ground. "What about the child?"

"Let Clara keep it."

"What if she doesn't want it?"

"That's her problem."

"That's not what the contract says. Under the contract, when she has a child, it's yours. Maybe you'd better be a man and do your duty."

"I can't," he said miserably.

"Why not?"

"Because it's tainted like the other one."

"What do you mean, 'tainted?'"

He shook his head. "I'm not talking about it anymore."

"What about Millicent?" I went on cruelly. "She's going to be devastated if this pregnancy doesn't work out."

"We've got other embryos on ice. We'll find another surrogate and do it again."

"You weren't willing to do that last week."

"It's different now."

"Why?"

"Because I don't give a damn, that's why."

"About the stores?"

"About anything."

He was as suicidal as anyone I'd ever seen. "How about the other person involved in this?"

"What other person?"

"None of this makes sense if it was Millicent's egg that got fertilized. The egg had to be Clara's. The question is, why?"

"I don't know what you're talking about."

"When you said the child was tainted, you meant it was just like the first time, didn't you? You meant that both times Clara Brennan got pregnant, it wasn't what *you* wanted to happen, it was what *he* wanted."

Stuart Colbert walked to the door and waited for me. "You're not to look for any more answers," he said heavily, manslaughter marbling his voice. "Do you understand? I order you to cease and desist."

I shook my head. "Six months from now, Clara Brennan is going to march in here and present you with a baby, precisely as the contract calls for. I don't care who or what was behind the surrogacy idea in the first place, but you're the responsible party and I suggest you be here to accept it. There's already one child out there you haven't been a father to; it's time for you to do what's right. If not for your sake, for your wife's."

I thought he was going to hit me. Instead, he went to the desk and pushed a button to summon security. I let him throw me out, not with muscle, but with misery.

When I got to the door, I turned back. "One more thing. Did your wife tell your mother about the surrogate arrangement early on? That the two of you were going to try to have a child in that way?"

Stuart Colbert bowed his head but I wasn't sure he was answering my question.

TWENTY-EIGHT

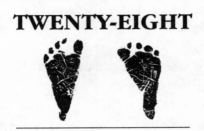

Everything should have been fine—I'd found Greta Hammond, or rather she had found me; the baby was alive and well despite my fears to the contrary; and Greta had declared herself willing and able to perform in accordance with the surrogacy contract: the child would be delivered in six months. The problem was that in the meantime, the world had turned upside down—Stuart Colbert didn't want the child and I was forbidden to find out why he'd had a change of heart. Which put Stuart in breach, and me in a quandary.

All I knew was that I couldn't leave it there. I'd decided that my principal in the case was Millicent Colbert, not her husband, and until she closed me down, I was going to see it through. Which meant among other things that I was going to have to find out why Rutherford Colbert had been so insistent that his son father a child by the last woman in the world he should have chosen as his partner. But before I did that, I had to protect my left flank.

On my way back to the office, I ducked into the St. Francis Hotel and used a pay phone to call Andy Potter. Andy is a society lawyer who uses me from time to time when his stable of blue bloods stumbles over a crack in the fast lane. We exchanged pleasantries, then made the ritual vow to do lunch. As soon as I could, I announced the subject for discussion. "Russell Jorgensen."

Andy paused to weigh the variables. "What about him?"

"That's what I want to know," I said.

"I thought you worked for him from time to time."

"I do."

"So?"

"So what's the lowdown?"

Andy paused again. The closer you get to truth, the more lawyers weigh variables. "I assume it's important," he evaded.

"Not really; I'm just killing time till the lottery numbers are posted."

"Sorry, Marsh. It's just that I don't like gossip. Especially about people on intimate terms with a courtroom." Another pause. "I assume my name won't surface in any way, shape, or form in whatever this is."

"No chance."

"I like Russell," he said after another pause.

"So do I."

"Is he in trouble?"

"I don't think so. But I'll know more after you talk to me."

"Russell's had a tough time, what with his kids, and his wife dying and all."

"I know."

"So what I'm saying is, there were reasons he did what he did."

There always are, even when what they do is murder. "What exactly did he do?"

When it came, it came quickly. "You know he's a nut about sailing."

My stomach did a responsive flip.

"Well, a few years back, some local swells were trying to mount syndicates to make a run for the America's Cup down in San Diego. The most prominent one was the Blackaller group, but one of the others was going to be skippered by a guy named Liggett. Well, this Liggett was a big talker and a good sailor but when he went trolling for money he didn't come up with enough to fund even one boat. So he put a move on Russell. And because Russell's wife had just gone through the cancer dance and he and his kids were a mess as a result, Russell was pretty vulnerable to anyone peddling a diversion and a good time."

"How much was he in for?" I asked.

"The name of the boat was going to be *American Enterprise*. Russell Jorgensen contributed a million five to put it in the water."

"Jesus."

"And then some. It was a pipe dream, of course. Hobnobbing with the international yachting crowd; hoping for a big return out of merchandise and licensing spin-offs if they were the winning boat; Russell learning enough and making enough contacts to get a shot at skippering a boat himself in the next cup series. It was Walter Mitty meets Alice in Wonderland."

"What happened?"

"About what you'd expect. The boat had some design flaws, mostly with the keel as I remember—damn thing wouldn't go in a straight line. And the financing started to unravel almost immediately—some grass farmer up in Willits had second thoughts about donating half his net worth to an enterprise that took place on saltwater instead of dry land. Liggett didn't even make it into the first round of qualifying—the whole thing went belly-up."

"Any return on investment?"

"The loss was one hundred cents on the dollar. And Russell's net worth suddenly turned negative."

"That seems dumb enough all by itself," I said. "Hard to believe there was another one."

Andy's laugh was curt and maybe a tad contemptuous. "Russell was like a guy at the craps table—doubled his bets to recoup his losses."

I sighed. "I don't really want to know, but what did he bet, exactly?"

"Remember back when the drought was at its peak and the reservoirs were at 10 percent of capacity and the whole Bay Area was on water rationing?"

"Sure. I took a bath in a thimble for a while."

"Right. Well, along came some guy with a new desalinization process—making seawater salt-free. The guy claimed he'd sold five units to the Saudis and that Montecito had paid millions for a process not nearly as good as his. All he needed was backing to sell his system to the coastal communities and the start-up investors would be making millions in two years' time."

"What happened?"

"Two things. Russell signed on for a million, and the next year it started to rain. Interest in desalinization pretty much evaporated and the general partner took off with all the money. Turned out the Saudis bought some desalinization plants all right, but not anything this guy was connected with."

"The bottom line seems to be that Russell is in big trouble."

"On top of losing the money, he got sued for fraud by the investors. Seems Russell went around touting this saltwater thing as a bonanza and the people who believed him are pissed."

"People who believe in bonanzas don't have the right to be pissed."

"This is America. We've got a God-given right to fuck up and blame someone else for it."

I laughed at Andy's uncustomary cynicism. "So what happened to the lawsuits?"

"Still pending."

"So Russell needs cash."

"Cash. Checks. Gold. Whatever."

I raised a new subject. "What about him and Cynthia Colbert?"

"What about them?"

"Are they an item?"

There came that pause again. "It's difficult to see how that could be relevant to anything."

"Come on, Andy. I can get it somewhere else."

"Okay, okay. It's no big deal anyway. He sees her on the Q.T., so the father and brother won't get bent out of shape by the situation. I know the guy who lends them his condo—they make quite a mess, he says; makes them pay for maid service. I hope you don't want to know where it is, because I'm not going to tell you."

It took fifteen minutes to walk from the St. Francis down Post Street and over to Embarcadero Four. Russell wasn't happy to see me but I wasn't happy to be seeing him, either.

The frown on his face looked as if it had been there since breakfast. "What's happening? Stuart just called—he said he'd fired you from the surrogate case."

"He tried."

"You shouldn't have seen him without me. I could have kept it from happening."

"You could have kept it from happening by telling the truth."

His frown darkened to the color of aged beef. "About what?"

"You and Cynthia, among other things."

"What about her? She's a client."

"She's a lot more than a client and you know it. If I were you, I'd get out of this thing while you've still got a shot at disputing a conflict of interest."

"What are you trying to say?"

"You've got a personal interest contrary to the surrogate thing and you should have disclosed it at the outset, and then bowed out and let someone else hold Stuart's hand for nine months."

Russell's chest swelled like the jib on his boat. "I have no conflict in this at all. Even if my interest in Cynthia does have a personal dimension, that doesn't mean I'm adverse to Stuart."

"Cynthia and Stuart have always been adverse. As soon as they got their own stores, it was time for you to choose sides."

"What do you mean?"

"I mean one or the other was going to be heir to a fortune. You've taken quite a financial bath in recent years, Russell—someone could make an argument that you're trying to make certain Cynthia ends up with all the marbles so you could get well at the altar."

The pain in his face was concentrated in the eyes and mouth and was framed by the scarlet of outrage. "I'm an honorable man. The idea that I'm trying to usurp Cyn's assets is insulting."

"Not as insulting as your behavior in this case."

"Now just a minute, I—"

"Come on, Russell. You even had her hit her mother up for money to lend you. Just tell me one thing. Did you tell Cynthia the name of the surrogate?"

When he didn't say anything, I had my answer.

"Did you also tell her that Stuart had selected the surrogate himself?"

"I . . . may have. But only because it was unusual behavior and I wondered if Cynthia had ever heard of the Hammond woman, which she hadn't. Why is any of this important?"

"I'm not interested in your retirement plan or your love life, I'm just trying to make sure that the surrogate arrangement isn't one of the chips in a game you're playing."

"*What* game? Name a single breach of fiduciary duty I've committed. Name a single thing I've done to obstruct the surrogacy."

I met his eye. "I just did. When Cynthia learned the name of the surrogate, she looked her up to try to buy her off. When she saw who it was, she informed the woman that Stuart Colbert was the contracting party. For some reason, that made the woman head for the hills." This time I was the one who issued the warning. "I'm getting close to learning why, Russell. Closer than you imagine."

His tone turned imploring. "I don't understand. Closer to what?"

"To knowing why Ethan Brennan died, for one thing."

"Will you get *off* that? It's over and done with. It was nothing to do with *anything.*"

"It's not over and I think you know it. It's being played out in the lives of the kids."

"I don't know what you're talking about."

"You know Greta Hammond and Clara Brennan are one and the same."

"No, I—"

"Come on, Russell. Cynthia's known it for weeks; she must have told you."

He couldn't meet my eye.

"I don't know why Greta was scared off when she learned she was carrying Stuart's child, but within twenty-four hours I'm going to and the chips will fall where they may. The child in Greta Hammond's womb is going to be presented to the Colberts two days after it's born, just the way they wanted."

Russell went to the window for his customary shot of confidence. "Stuart fired you, remember?"

"He's not the one who hired me."

"Well then, I—"

"Are you sure you want me out of it, Russell? Are you sure you want someone else rummaging around in all this?"

"It's not what I want, it's—"

"Even if you do fire me, there's an interested party in this besides Stuart and Cynthia Colbert."

"You mean Greta Hammond."

"Clara Brennan. Right."

He blinked. "Have you found her?"

"No, but I spoke with her yesterday."

His eyes widened to the size of bottle caps. "Where is she? What happened to her? What's she done with the baby?"

"I don't know where she is."

"But—"

"She called me."

He frowned. "Why?"

"To ask me to stop looking for her."

"You can't do that."

I smiled. "You just told me I had to."

He was flustered. "This may change the situation. What's the status of the child?"

"She says the child is fine."

"Really? Good. Then why did she disappear?"

"She was afraid someone was going to try to stop her from giving birth."

"Who?"

"She didn't say, but Luke Drummond is one candidate. I need to talk to him. Do you know where he lives?"

Russell shook his head.

"Stuart has been paying Mrs. Drummond three thousand a month for years. Do you have any idea why?"

Russell ran his hand through his hair, then collapsed in his chair. "God. This is like a video game. You solve one problem and another takes its place." He looked at me with intensity. "You have to find Clara."

"Why?"

"So we can monitor her. To make sure she follows the contract."

"She told me she would."

"We can't accept her word on it. She's already breached the prenatal portion of the agreement."

"She's getting medical care, she says."

"How do we know it's adequate?"

"Why wouldn't it be?"

Russell grumbled into silence.

I waited till he dared a look at me. "She said something interesting about you, Russell."

A brow lifted. "Me? What did she say?"

"I asked her if you and Cynthia were the ones who didn't want the baby to be born."

"And?"

"She said that wasn't it at all. She said that what you wanted was for history to repeat itself."

"What did she mean by that?"

"I don't know. But I came by to tell you that I'm going to find out. And to tell you to pass the word to your girlfriend not to get in my way."

TWENTY-NINE

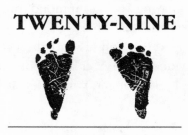

Hickory Avenue in San Bruno ran east and west between the Bayshore and Junipero Serra freeways through a nest of comparatively inexpensive postwar houses in a neighborhood not far from the Bayhill Shopping Center. The home that matched the address on the envelope I'd found in Greta Hammond's trash was a squat, beige bungalow with stucco walls, green composition roof, blue-trimmed arched doors and windows with wrought-iron overlays to give them a Mediterranean aspect while fending off prowlers as well. There was a view of the airport and the bay from the front yard, with Mount Diablo a hint in the hazy distance.

Although the house was well maintained, evidence of habitation was skimpy: the shades were drawn and the gate into the small fenced yard was closed against itinerants, as was the door to the adjacent garage. The only object that suggested joy or even occupancy was a warped wooden tennis racket buried in the grass in the side yard. The racket was an old Jack Kramer; two of its strings were broken. When I looked for a ball it could mate with I didn't find one.

I raised the latch and eased through the narrow gate, leery of guard dog or owner. When I didn't encounter either, I knocked on the door and waited to see what would happen. What happened was that the door was opened by a stout, gray-haired woman with a bowl in her hand and a scowl on her face. The glint in her eye was combative.

If she was who I thought she was, she had to be pushing seventy, but her taut gray flesh and kinetic blue eyes made her seem twenty years younger. "I suppose you're a lawyer," she said with a snide twist.

I shook my head. "I'm not a lawyer, I'm—"

"I told him I wouldn't stand for any more of this," she interrupted before I had a chance to say my piece. "So don't try to talk me out of it." Anger brought blood to her cheeks and several more years fell away.

"Told who? Stand for what?"

"Have you got the money? Just tell me that."

I shook my head.

"Then you know what I got to do. So just turn right around and march out of here. Go on. Scat. I've got no more to say to you than I had to the last one. I've got to get these biscuits in the oven before they set."

After her tirade she looked at me more closely. "What tried to skin you alive?"

"Your son."

She shook her head. "Who are you? Why would he do something like that?"

"I'm a detective. I've been working for Stuart Colbert. You didn't like the work I was doing, so you told your son to stop me."

She straightened her back and pouted. "Who says?"

"He does."

"What kind of work was it?"

"Trying to keep a baby alive."

She frowned. "Why would I care about that?"

"Because the baby belongs to Stuart Colbert."

She examined my face more closely, as though she was going to re-decorate it. "Is the boy going to be in trouble because of what he did to you?"

"Not if you cooperate."

She sighed and let go of something inside her. "I've been cooperating for twenty years."

"I know you have, Mrs. Drummond. But if you keep trying to interfere with the Colberts, Luke's going to end up in jail. And you will, too."

She let out all the air in her lungs and hugged the bowl to her bosom. "I guess you should come in."

The tiny home was confining and claustrophobic, as dark as a
cave behind its jaundiced shades. It was overstuffed with bulky furnishings, heavy and commodious objects made from oaks and leathers,
primarily in the mission style. The medicinal odors that pervaded the
house, and the hush in which they lingered, were a fit with the primary function I guessed it served.

She led me to two ladder-backed chairs that faced each other
across a wooden card table that was placed squarely beneath the
biggest window in the room, which was only the size of a suitcase. I took
a seat across from her—the chairs were caned and uncomfortable.
The jigsaw puzzle scattered across the table was sufficiently solved to reveal a bouquet of leafy flowers springing out of a painted china vase that
rested on a blue plaid tablecloth.

"I can't find the tip to this lily," Fern Drummond said as she sat
down, pointing to an irregular gap in a fragment near the top edge. "See
if you can spot it while we talk. Usually he finds them in a minute—I've
begun to think it's missing."

"How long does it take to do one?" I asked as I struggled once again
to get comfortable.

"We do two a week. We like to keep on schedule, though it's
hard to find new ones. He gets mad if it's not a new one."

"Is he here?"

She started to say something, then caught herself. "Who?"

"The person who does the puzzles."

She looked at me but didn't answer, still dubious of my motives. I
had doubts about them myself. "Nathaniel," I added when she didn't
speak.

She blinked and tried to dissuade me. "I don't know what you want,
mister, but if you knew Nathaniel you'd know he can't have anything to
do with anything."

"On the contrary. I think he may have everything to do with it."

"Nonsense. He's not even . . ." She searched for a word but couldn't find one that encompassed what Nathaniel was and was not.

"Normal?" I suggested.

She sighed and closed her eyes. "That's as close as any. He's better than normal, and worse than normal."

"What's wrong with him, exactly?"

"His brain's been bad since the day he was born."

"Is he getting any better?"

"Not a bit."

"It must be hard for you, having that kind of responsibility for all these years."

"It's not hard at all," she said with pride. "He may be different, but he's a saint. A godsend."

Which made him her entire universe. I hoped he would stay that way after I had done what I had to do.

"What does it matter what he is?" she was saying. "His mother won't come see him; his father doesn't know he exists; he never goes out except to bat his ball. How can he be important?"

"I'm not sure. Is he retarded?"

Her nose wrinkled and her voice turned prim. "They don't call it that anymore."

"I know they don't. Is he?"

She shrugged. "He does puzzles like a whiz. And sums—he can add better in his head than I can on paper. But he's backward in most ways."

"How?"

Her voice grew weary and matter-of-fact, as if Nathaniel had pieces missing just like the jigsaw lying scattered across the table. "He doesn't talk; he doesn't laugh; he doesn't cry; he doesn't do anything but work puzzles and watch me. Every minute of the day, he watches me. He knows me better than I know myself, I'm sure—it's probably a blessing he's mute." She shuddered at the prospect of Nathaniel acquiring the power of speech.

"I used to wonder what he thinks about the world," she went on, her newly candid voice eerily disembodied. "I used to wonder what he would have to say about it, if he could talk, and I used to hope that some day he would just blurt it out. What he thought about what he was and how he got to be that way, and what he wanted his life to be about. But now I hope I never know what's in his mind. I think it would be too awful."

Her estimate echoed in the house like the curse of a fiery sermon. "Has Nathaniel been looked at by any medical people?" I asked.

"Of course he has. In the beginning."

"What did they say about him?"

"They said we should put him in a home. Clara said so, too, before she left."

"Why didn't you?"

"Because it's not right. Because it's our burden to clean up after them."

"The Colberts?"

She nodded and fiddled with the puzzle picture. "But there's no need to talk about all that; it's over and done with."

"It's not over for Nathaniel," I said.

She nodded. "Poor Nathaniel. They keep saying he won't live much longer." Her laugh was irreverent. "They've been saying that since he was a babe in arms."

"When did you take custody of him?"

"When he was six days old."

"How old is he now?"

"He'll be twenty in two days. I'm trying to decide what to get for his present. I suppose another puzzle."

"A tennis ball might be nice."

She looked at me and smiled, and suddenly we were allies of some strange sort. "He lost the old one—a dog ran off with it." She shook her head. "He bats that ball against the house for hours. Drives me crazy, the thump, thump, thump, but he loves it. It's little enough to indulge him." A tear came to her eye, for a man-boy for whom life's highest pleasure was a lonely game of solitaire with a broken racket and a fuzzy ball.

"Where is he now?" I asked.

She glanced toward the rear of the house. "Sleeping. He sleeps twelve hours a day. It's a gift to both of us," she added, then offered me a psalm. "God Almighty gives us only as much as we can bear."

I asked if I could talk to him.

"What on earth about? He hasn't been off this block in twenty years."

"Does anyone come see him?"

"They do not. Not a single one. Luke takes him to the park, sometimes. But he makes Luke nervous, just like he made his mother."

Twenty years ago, Clara Brennan had run from Nathaniel and all that he meant, and now she was running from something else, something equally abhorrent. I was beginning to understand what it was.

A vehicle drove into the driveway and stopped. A door slammed shut with a sound that made me shudder. I expected to hear Luke enter through the back and emerge from the kitchen to confront me, but he didn't make an appearance.

"The money you get from Stuart isn't for Nathaniel, is it?" I asked in the lull.

I thought I might slip it in casually and get an unedited answer, but I didn't get an answer at all.

"Except for Clara and Delilah and Opal, no one knows Nathaniel exists, do they?" I went on. "You and Luke get paid to keep quiet about something else. Right? You know something about Rutherford Colbert and he pays you not to talk about it."

She looked at me defiantly. "So what if he does?"

"Concealment of a crime is also a crime."

"I never concealed nothing. No one bothered to ask me, so how can they say I concealed it?"

"What do you know, Mrs. Drummond? Something about Ethan Brennan's death?"

She was shaking her head by the time I had finished, addressing issues I hadn't raised. "We're not one of them; we never *will* be one of them," she proclaimed grimly, her mind on historic insults. "Folks think the Colberts and Brennans are so special, but we're better than they are. We raise our children, at least. And we keep our word."

"Are you the one who told him?" I asked softly.

"Told who what?"

"Told Rutherford that Stuart was dating Clara Brennan?"

"Why would I do that?"

"So Rutherford would keep Stuart from stealing Clara away from your son, which would give Luke a chance to marry into one of the families on Santa Ana. And a chance to inherit a part of the Colbert fortune."

Her lip stiffened and her eyes hardened to match the grain that ran through her life. "Stuart didn't have no business messing with that girl. Someone had to put a stop to it."

"But it didn't stop, did it? Even after you told him?"

She shook her head.

"Why not?"

"They're devils; all of them."

I wasn't compelled to rebut her. "I'd like to talk to your son," I said.

"Why?"

"If he tries to prevent the Colberts from having this child, he could get in big trouble."

Her eyes shone like candles. "Luke's been in trouble all his life; I never should have brought him to work at the big house. The rest of them, they go about their business all fine and dandy, laughing and playing and fornicating, leaving it to me and Luke to clean up after. I thought when Miz Colbert took to her bed, that would be the end of it. But I guess not. I guess it's never going to end, 'cause the Colberts can't leave well enough alone."

"What are you and Luke cleaning up, Mrs. Drummond? And why is it taking so long?"

"The wages of sin leave a big stain."

In the echo of her inflamed self-righteousness, I was about to ask what she was referring to when a door opened and the house became even smaller than before, inadequate and confining and ominous. The object that initiated the transformation filled the doorway like a boulder. It was a human object, obviously, but the outlines were ungainly and disproportionate: huge head and vat-like torso, stick legs, blunted facial features pitted with the leavings of acne, hair that seemed to have been ripped from his scalp in spots and dyed with shoe polish in others; hands that were large enough to hide a grapefruit. His pajamas were flannel, with pictures of footballs. His feet were bare and gigantic, like hairless paws.

"Unnh," he grunted with what seemed like anger, his voice as deep as a well, his eyes shallow and inexpressive.

"He wants his bath," she said to me, then went to his side and patted his massive arm and cooed in an effort to calm him. "Nice warm bath, coming up. My Nathaniel gets his bath right now. Doesn't he? Nathaniel gets all fresh and clean. Then we do the puzzle. I've got a new one for you. Yes, I do. A brand-new puzzle for Natty-Watty."

Oblivious to me and my errand, Fern Drummond grasped Nathaniel by his hammy hand and towed him toward the rear of the house. The boy lumbered after her like an upright wagon, panting eagerly through his pulpy, languid lips. I let myself out the front door, as eager to be gone as Nathaniel's mother had been some twenty years earlier, when her child was no older than the one she was carrying now.

Luke's truck sat in the driveway like a relic of a different age. I walked toward the only place he could be, which was inside the one-car garage at the back of the lot. The bay door was nailed shut and bordered with weather stripping but the door on the side stood open. I walked in without being asked.

Luke was still wearing cowboy regalia, though a different hat and boots. The inside of the converted garage was a match to his theme— western art, western furnishings, western music. He was sitting in a club chair covered in cowhide, boots on an ottoman, hat shoved to the back of his head, still as handsome as he had been when he was the favorite plaything of the young and restless on Santa Ana Way.

He was reading with such intensity that he was still unaware of my presence. I looked for a weapon but didn't see one. What I did see was a baseball bat in a corner by the door. I picked it up, then moved to where I could see what Luke was reading. It wasn't Louis L'Amour or *Arizona Highways*; it was *Women's Wear Daily.*

There were stacks of fashion magazines all over the place, in fact: *Vogue, GQ, Harper's Bazaar, Mirabella,* and others I'd never heard of, a horde of back issues piled to the level of the windows. I considered what it meant, then debated whether to break Luke's heart.

When I said his name he jerked with surprise. "Jesus," he said when he saw who I was and what I was holding. "How'd you find me?"

"I didn't find you, I found your mother."

He looked worried. "You tell her what I done?"

I nodded.

"What'd you do that for?"

"I hurt like hell, for one reason."

He grinned. "Look like hell, too."

"You're through playing cowboy with me, Luke."

He looked down at his boots and Levi's and the duds seemed to give him strength. "How you going to stop me; with that little bitty ball bat?"

"I'm going to tell you that I've told Stuart Colbert that if anything happens to me, he's to cut off your mother's funds. Permanently."

Luke shook his head. "The old man won't let him."

"The old man's half dead and Stuart's not feeling kindly toward him anyway. So keep your rope in the truck, and the rest of your tricks, too."

"Maybe I will; maybe I won't."

"And one more thing."

"What?"

"Stop looking for Clara Brennan."

"Why should I?"

My only leverage was his lifelong awe of the Colberts, so that was the tool I used. "Because she's doing a job for the Colberts and they want you to leave her alone."

"What kind of job?"

"That's none your business. But if you keep looking for Clara Brennan, I'm going to tell the Colberts about Nathaniel. I'm going to suggest they go to court and get an order that takes him out of here on the ground that you're not a fit parent. I'm going to suggest they terminate your rights and put him in a home, where his needs will be more fully met."

Luke was shaking his head with vigor. "You can't do that. I married her. That makes him mine."

"You think that will make a difference if the Colberts say they want him back? You think that will make a difference if their doctors prove he's not your son but Stuart's? They can prove paternity to a 99 percent certainty, Luke. You won't have a chance."

After he rubbed his face and thought about it, his resistance all but vanished. "Why don't you go on about your business and leave us alone?" he pleaded with an odd naiveté.

"Quit messing in Colbert affairs," I told him again, knowing that the Colbert business was his whole life, knowing that he had dreamed of running a store for years, knowing that he had a better chance of winning the lottery than proving the claim he had nourished since the day Nathaniel was born. "Quit or I go to court."

"I promise," was all he said when he said something. I decided it was enough.

THIRTY

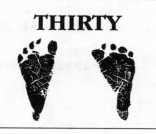

By the time I was back in the city it was dusk. I was tired and pained and sick of the Colberts and their messy secrets. But I thought I could wrap it up by the end of the evening, so I pulled into the lot at Stonestown and called Cynthia Colbert at the store for men. A tired voice told me she'd already left for the day, so I pulled back onto Nineteenth Avenue and pointed my car in the direction of Santa Ana Way and the core of the Colbert empire.

There was music coming from the house, a Latin salsa that belied the grim expression on Cynthia Colbert's face when she saw it was me on her doorstep. That she answered the door herself, wearing an off-the-shoulder something that made her neck and clavicles seem sculpted from French vanilla, indicated I wasn't the person she was expecting. The music and the hour and the light that drifted our way from the gardens and rendered everything soft and voluptuous made a part of me wish I was.

"What do you want?" she demanded nastily, ending my swoon in a hurry. "I'm expecting guests any minute."

"I need some more information."

"What kind of information?"

"About the old days."

She tapped her foot and crossed her arms and made her lightly tanned breasts bulge like twin soufflés above the rein of her sequined bodice. "At least you didn't call them the 'good old days,'" she observed sarcastically. "What do you want to know?"

"I'm interested in the period when your brother started seeing Clara Brennan."

"The summer he was home from Princeton. Junior year, I think. What of it?"

"You said before that your father knew what Stuart was doing."

She blinked and looked beyond me, at a long black car coming down the street, scouting for the party. "What difference does it make whether he knew or not?"

"I'm not sure. Did he?"

The car stopped next to the curb out front. Doors opened at my back, disgorging designer distractions most of whom sounded intoxicated. As I hurried to finish my business, I guessed that Cynthia Colbert's soirées were regarded as chores by the people who were summoned to them.

She didn't speak till I touched her on the arm. "You're asking if Rutherford knew Stuart was seeing Clara."

"Right."

She nodded wearily. "Of course he did. They tried to keep it secret, but Daddy knew; he knew everything that happened out here. He knew I'd slept with Luke Drummond three hours after it happened. For all I know he bugged all the rooms on the block."

"What did he do when he found out about it?"

"Me and Luke?"

"Stuart and Clara."

"He didn't do anything." Someone behind me emitted a squeal, as though she'd been pinched or slapped, and Cynthia yelled for her to behave herself till she got inside. "Now that I think about it," she said to me with a sliver of her attention, "he seemed upset at first, but later he seemed to enjoy it. Actually, he seemed to think it was funny."

"Funny?"

She nodded. "I remember one night Daddy and I were talking on the porch and Stuart and Clara drove by in his convertible and Daddy started to laugh. I mean, he didn't laugh that often, and this one was real. Then he said something about measure for measure. And then he got pissed because they had the top of the car down. It was kind of creepy; I remember that much."

"What do you think he was talking about?"

"I have no idea. I only realized recently that Daddy never liked Stuart much. I'd never admit it to his face, but baby brother always got the short end of the stick, at least until Daddy divided up the stores. Then he gave Stuart the best deal by far. I didn't understand it at the time but now I think he wanted to humiliate Stuart even further."

"How so?"

She adjusted her bodice and preened. "By showing the world that Stuart couldn't beat me at merchandising even with a head start. Anyway, I just assumed Daddy was happy about Stuart and Clara because Stuart was screwing up again."

"Screwing up how?"

"By falling for someone beneath him; by consorting with the hired help."

I smiled at her aristocratic sally. "You were doing the same thing, weren't you?"

"You mean Luke? I was only fucking him; I wasn't going to marry him."

"So Stuart was ready to take Clara to the altar."

"That's certainly what it looked like."

"Was she ready to go?"

"I don't know. Clara was playing it close to the vest by that time. I never knew what she was thinking, except it was usually something ambitious."

"I don't understand why your father thought what Stuart was doing was stupid. Clara was Ethan Brennan's daughter; her house was right next door. That's hardly the Tenderloin."

As the covey of celebrants staggered up the flagstone walkway, Cynthia's eyes darkened to match the hovering canopy of night. "Mr. Brennan had taste, I give him that. But to Daddy he was always a hanger-on. Just another Sammy Glick, clawing his way out of the gutter by trying to mimic his betters."

"Some people think Ethan Brennan was crucial to the business. That without him the whole enterprise would have gone under."

Her lip stiffened. "Those people are wrong. The only people crucial to Colberts are Colberts. Now, you'll have to excuse me. Marnie! That dress is to *die* for. If you tell me you bought it from Stuart I won't let you in. Nordstrom? Thank God."

Half a dozen revelers pushed past me without a greeting and exchanged kisses and hugs and smart chatter with Cynthia as she ushered them inside her home. The women were big-haired and bejeweled and stuffed like twice-cooked potatoes into shimmering skintight gowns; the men sauntered past in patent leather pumps that were topped with the accoutrements of black tie—ruby studs and red plaid cummerbunds were apparently the rage this season. I'd never been to a party like that in my life; I wonder if it had made any difference.

When Cynthia started to follow her guests, I grasped her arm to stop her.

"This is outrageous," she squealed. "You're *hurting* me. If you don't leave this instant, I'll yell for help. I warn you, Lance Millington is certified in martial arts."

"Third-degree plaid belt—impressive. I just talked to Russell," I continued into the fog of her ersatz bravado. "I know you and he are getting it on, as they say."

She sniffed. "Don't tell me; let me guess. You *fantasize* about us."

"I'm here to tell you that for both your sakes you'd better stay out of the surrogate arrangement."

Her laugh was as cool as the breeze off the sea a thousand yards below us. "Milly's bundle of joy? Don't you know us spinsters are tickled *pink* when one of our own bears fruit? It's so biologically reassuring."

"You weren't doing Millicent any favors when you told Clara that your brother was the intended father of the child."

This time she didn't bother to deny it. "That was then; this is now. I can't *wait* to see the new branch on the family tree."

"Why? Because you think it's going to look like Nathaniel?"

She canted a hip. "Who he?"

Her nonchalance was so thick it washed me off the porch and back down the walk toward the street.

"I'd ask you to join us," she laughed at my back as I retreated, "but these are fashion people. Unfortunately, Kmart didn't make an important statement this season."

I stood by my car until Cynthia went inside and closed the door, then walked down the block and knocked on the door to Delilah Colbert's Gothic hermitage. Although it was late and there wasn't a light in the place that was visible, Opal Brennan was still on duty.

"We asked you not to come back here," she said in response to my greeting.

"I know you did. And I know it's late. But we need to have a conversation."

"About what?"

"The man you were in love with."

"I—"

"The man *both* of you were in love with," I amended.

She looked at me with sorrowful eyes and a mouth that could no longer dispute me. "I suppose this can't be stopped," she said wearily. "I suppose you're determined to destroy even the little bit of dignity we have left."

"That's not what I want, Mrs. Brennan. All I want is a child to have a chance at a healthy and happy life."

"Whose child are you talking about?"

"Your daughter's."

"You're speaking of Nathaniel, I take it."

I shook my head. "I'm talking about the child Clara's carrying now."

I didn't expect it would be news to her and it wasn't. "I see," she said simply. "What is it you want?"

"Clara told you about it back when she agreed to become a surrogate, didn't she?"

Opal Brennan nodded.

"When did you learn Stuart Colbert was the surrogate father?"

"Last month. Millicent thought Delilah would be pleased."

"Since Millicent didn't know Clara was the surrogate, I assume you and Delilah put two and two together."

The hand on my arm was as light as a breeze. "Do you know where she is?" she asked, a worried mother for the first time since I'd known her.

I shook my head. "I'm sorry. But I've talked to her. She's well and she's not in danger."

Tears wet her eyes and lingered like contact lenses, gleaming in the light, distorting her view of past and present simultaneously. "Did she know Stuart was involved in this . . . whatever you call it?"

"Not at first."

"Thank God." She closed her eyes. "I suppose it's too late to stop it."

"Why would you want to?"

She reacted as though I'd cursed her. "I believe you know. I believe that's why you're here."

"I'm not sure if I do or not. But to make sure the child survives, I need to know who might want to hurt it."

Her face was gray with anguish. "Did you ever consider that it might be better if it *didn't* survive? To spare the world another tragedy?"

"You mean like Nathaniel?"

She closed her eyes and covered them with her hand.

"That's not my decision to make, Mrs. Brennan. Nor yours either, I don't think. Besides, I don't think that's going to happen this time. But to be sure, I need to know why Rutherford Colbert killed your husband."

She shook her head before I finished speaking. "It will serve no purpose."

"That's not necessarily true; for one thing, it might help your daughter stay out of trouble. I can keep a secret," I added when she didn't say anything.

I waited for her to decide. When she had, she stepped back and let me join her in the halls of the silent mansion that was home to a convent of two. As I waited for her to close the door, I glanced into the parlor and made a silent apology to the portrait that hung above the mantel like an icon.

I went through the washing and gowning ritual, then followed Mrs. Brennan to the antiseptic chamber where her companion held forth against the world and its many viruses. Delilah Colbert was exactly as I'd seen her last, for all I knew exactly as she had been for twenty years. Without being asked, I pulled up a chair and sat next to the bed. The women exchanged quick glances of censure, but neither of them did anything to stop me.

"How are you, Mrs. Colbert?"

Her eyelids were as thin and fluttery as tissue. Behind them, something dark and ominous seemed to seethe and threaten eruption. In furtherance of the threat, her voice was firm and didactic. "I'm alive. I'm content. I'm prepared."

"Prepared for what?"

"Death, of course. It's the only task that's left to me—preparing myself for judgment."

"How are you doing that, Mrs. Colbert?"

"Confessing my sins and asking for mercy."

"From whom?"

"The Lord our God, of course. Who else is there?"

"Your husband, for one."

"I ask nothing of him because I have gotten nothing from him."

"You betrayed him, didn't you?"

Her answer was firm and self-righteous. "Anything I did paled before his degeneracy and was justified by his faithlessness."

"I don't doubt it. But he's not racked with guilt about it; you are."

She seemed to look straight through her eyelids. "The state of my soul is my own business, Mr. Tanner. Not yours."

"If your salvation entails taking the life of another, I'm going to make it my business."

"I have no idea what you're talking about."

"Are you employing Luke Drummond to put a stop to the consequences of your adultery, Mrs. Colbert?"

"Luke? Why on earth would I have any use for a common laborer like Luke Drummond?"

"To keep Clara Brennan from bearing another child."

"Why would I want to do that?"

"So this child won't end up like the last one."

She shuddered in spite of herself and the satin gown fell off a shoulder that was as sharp as an awl at its tip. Opal Brennan hurried to replace its drape; in the process, our eyes met and she transmitted an urgent appeal, begging me to stop, to leave them to their lonely penance, to let the past stay shunned and silent. I wanted to do what those benighted women wanted, but it was too late for camouflage, or even kindness.

I smiled at Delilah Colbert, then took her hand in my rubber glove. "Who is Stuart's father, Mrs. Colbert?"

She turned toward the wall like a pouty child. "Please don't question me. I have atoned as best I could; I can do no more. Surely you understand that I am helpless."

"You may be helpless but I'm not. I understand most of it, I think. But it would help for you to tell me I'm right."

Delilah rolled back to face me. "Why do you need to know these things?"

"So I can save Clara's baby. So I can keep you people from making another mistake like the one that killed Ethan Brennan." I looked at the women in turn. "Stuart and Clara have the same father, don't they?"

Neither of them moved or spoke, each ceding to the other the province to voice their secret.

"The only possibilities are Rutherford Colbert and Ethan Brennan. My guess it was Brennan. Am I right, Mrs. Colbert? You and Ethan Brennan had an affair and Stuart was the child that resulted?"

She didn't acknowledge the questions.

"It was an affair, wasn't it? He didn't force himself on you, did he?"

Oddly enough, it wasn't his mistress who defended him, but his wife. "If you had been in Ethan's presence for one minute," Opal Brennan urged with passion, "you would not need to ask that question."

"So he really was as wonderful as people say."

She spoke with odd gentility. "He was a matchless man—considerate, generous, tender." She looked at the woman she lived with. "Delilah's husband was none of those things—quite the opposite, in fact. She was needful and in distress and she turned to my husband for succor. Delilah was inexpressibly lovely in those days, bewitching to everyone but her husband. Ethan was a kind man, but he was a man. He was unable to resist her appeal."

"That's Ethan above the mantel; not Rutherford."

She nodded.

"Did you know about the affair at the time, Mrs. Brennan?"

"No."

"You learned about it the day your husband died, didn't you? He told you just before he went over to kill Rutherford Colbert."

She lowered her head in admission.

There was still one motive that needed fixing. "I can understand why Rutherford killed your husband—because he'd just learned of the affair. I'm not sure I understand why Ethan went gunning for Rutherford."

When Delilah Colbert finally spoke, her head was cocked and pitiable, her voice tremulous and angry. "Rutherford took a more insidious vengeance than killing Ethan—that was too easy, and too incomplete. He wanted others to suffer as well and he wanted me to be reminded of the consequences of my behavior every day for the rest of my life. He made Stuart's life miserable, of course, but that wasn't the only price he exacted."

And right then I saw it, as clear as crystal, as evil as treachery. "Rutherford urged Stuart to pursue Clara and conceive a child."

"Yes," Delilah said.

"Knowing she was Stuart's half-sister. Knowing they shared the same father."

"Yes."

"Knowing their offspring might well be malformed and retarded. Knowing that would cause heartache to the Brennans ever after."

"Yes. Yes, yes, yes, yes."

Both women began to weep. Sobs buffeted their bodies; all I could do was end it as quickly as I could.

"Ethan knew he had fathered both children, of course," I said. "When his beloved Clara told him she was pregnant and who the father was, he went gunning for the man who had made it happen. But Rutherford had been warned he was coming and shot him down on the porch."

Delilah Colbert nodded, her eyes like black blood on white marble. "He took Ethan's life and ours as well. We have never recovered; we never shall. All we have is each other, the memory of a man we loved, and a faith that the sweet Lord will forgive us." She tried to smile but it wasn't enough to displace her deep despair. "Most days, it seems enough."

"But not always," I said.

"No," she admitted slowly. "Not always." She looked at me with uncertainty. "What do we do now, Mr. Tanner?"

"Nothing," I said. "Just keep it to yourselves."

"That's what we've been doing for twenty years."

THIRTY-ONE

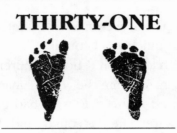

The lid I'd tried to put on the Colbert case must have fit, because it sat that way for six months: I didn't hear from Stuart or Millicent, I didn't hear from Cynthia or Russell, I didn't hear from the Drummonds, I didn't hear from the mothers, I didn't hear from anybody. Somewhere a baby was growing to term, somewhere a mother was eating pickles and ice cream and wrestling with morning sickness, somewhere an obstetrician was prescribing vitamins and performing ultrasound, somewhere an enthusiastic instructor was demonstrating the Lamaze techniques of pain avoidance. But that was somewhere else.

Just before Thanksgiving, I was driving down Nineteenth Avenue on my way to a lecture at S.F. State when I decided to detour down Santa Ana Way. All the houses seemed deserted but one—as I cruised past her home, Millicent Colbert came out the front door, looked up and down the block, then meandered to the sidewalk and turned toward St. Francis Circle, taking in some afternoon air.

She looked the same, yet different. For a moment, I thought she'd gained weight, but when she turned to me to cross the street, I realized that she had a pillow stuffed under her coat and was pretending to be pregnant for the benefit of her nosy neighbors. It was the saddest sight I saw all season.

Just before Christmas, which is to say just before the loneliest day of the year, I heard from Betty Fontaine. "Howdy, stranger," she began, an unaccustomed lilt to her words, an unusually melodic timbre in her voice.

"Hi, yourself."

"How are you?"

"Fine. I mean satisfactory."

She laughed. "That's worse than fine."

I admitted it. "You sound uncommonly peppy this evening."

"I know. I am."

"May I know why? Or do I have to guess?"

"Guess."

"A man."

"More."

"A good man."

"More."

"*The* man."

"Bingo. At least I think so. Guess where we're going for Christmas."

"Pismo Beach."

"Farther."

"Palm Springs."

"Farther."

"Puerto Villarta."

"Farther."

"Patagonia."

"Calcutta."

"Why didn't I think of that? Christmas and Calcutta. I try to capture that scene on all my cards."

"It's not as nutty as it sounds."

"It couldn't be."

"There are some lovely things in Calcutta, Frank says."

"There are lots of things in Calcutta. Most of them are wearing rags and sleeping in the streets."

"As opposed to here, I suppose."

"Touché, Ms. Fontaine. Take lots of pictures. Bore me with a slide show. Write a travel piece for the *Chronicle*."

"I don't think I'll have the energy."

"Why not?"

"Guess what we're going to do in Calcutta."

"Play whist with Mother Teresa."

"We're going to make a baby."

"Out of what?"

"Out of the usual stuff, stupid."

"*That* kind of baby. Well. That's great."

"Thank you." Her voice positively bubbled. "It really is, isn't it?"

"Yes, it is. Congratulations. Who's Frank?"

"He's a lawyer."

"Then let's hope he's like Calcutta."

"What's that mean?"

"It means let's hope he's better than he sounds."

"Well, he is. So wish me luck."

"Luck."

"If it's a boy I may name it after you, you know."

I laughed. "You sound like Clinton before the NAFTA vote."

"I'm serious, Marsh. You're an important person in my life."

"You're important to me, too, Betty."

"I know I am. That's why we should talk once in a while even after Frank and I . . . We will, won't we? Talk and stuff?"

"Sure."

"So you'll call me sometime?"

"Till the first time Frank answers the phone. Then I won't call anymore."

"You can call me at work."

"Fine."

She sniffed. "This is where I came in. See you, Marsh. Have a nice holiday."

"See you, Betty. 'Good screwing' seems an appropriate send-off but it sounds sort of gauche."

"You'll get over me, Marsh. You really will. Just like I got over you."

And just like that, Betty Fontaine was out of my life.

When a relationship breaks and you're the breakee and not the breaker, a portion of the bond remains long after the termination has been announced. It lingers for years, sometimes, when there's been no defining incident that triggers the separation—no brutality, no betrayal, no basis for the break but cold analysis and clear-eyed projection. The persistence of the bond is not always apparent, however, and its benefits often survive unnoticed, except in retrospect. It's only when Saturday night seems unbearably lonely, Sunday afternoon agonizingly long, Monday morning achingly pointless, that you know the link is finally severed and that you are, yet again and indisputably, physically and emotionally alone. From whence comes despair and desperation and ultimately, if you're lucky, a quick laugh and a fresh face that looks a lot like salvation.

All of which is to say that when the phone rang one Saturday night in early February, I wasn't in very good shape. And it only got worse when I learned who was calling.

"Are you ready?" she began without preamble, as though I'd ordered a pizza and she was down at the door to deliver it.

"Ready for what?"

"The baby, of course."

"Ah. The elusive Miss Brennan. I've been wondering when I'd hear from you. When's the blessed event?"

"Yesterday."

My larynx double-clutched. "It's here?"

"It's nibbling at my breast even as we speak. You can probably relate to that, just as I can relate to the fact that the relationship is going to be temporary."

I didn't know how to defend myself, or even if I wanted to, so I retreated to the bloodlessness of etiquette. "How are you feeling?"

"I'm sore as hell; those Lamaze people need a reality check. It hurt like a son of a bitch."

"I've heard it's not nearly as bad as an ingrown toenail."

"You must have heard it from a man."

I laughed. "How's the baby?"

"Fine. Six pounds, two ounces."

"Small."

"Petite."

"You need to bone up on your nomenclature—I don't think that's a compliment to a boy."

"Well, I won't have to deal with nomenclature or diapers or anything else, will I? I'm just a brood mare in this deal. So round up the usual suspects and meet me at high noon the day after tomorrow."

"Where?"

"The big house."

"Rutherford's?"

"Right."

"Why there?"

"Why not?"

It didn't seem wise to debate her. "Who else is invited? Stuart and Millicent, I presume."

"Mommy and Daddy Colbert. Right."

"Anybody else?"

"Cynthia and Russell."

"Why them?"

"Because I said so."

"I'll see what I can do. How about the grandmothers—Opal and Delilah?"

"Get your facts straight, Tanner—only one of them's a grandmother to *this* one."

I was embarrassed at my confusion of provenance. "How about the Drummonds?"

"I think we can leave them out of it, don't you? They've got one of my children already."

The ice in her voice was depthless. "Should we have a doctor on hand or anything?" I asked.

"Just tell Millicent to bring whatever she needs to tote it home. I'll provide a blanket and a carrier. Noon on Monday, Tanner."

"Noon on Monday." I paused and took a sudden plunge. "I'd like to talk to you afterward. Do dinner or something."

"I think saying a permanent good-bye to the creature I just brought into the world will be enough entertainment for one day, don't you?"

THIRTY-TWO

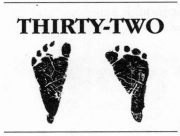

I felt like an attendant at valet parking. Two by two, the Colbert siblings and their mates came out of their doors, looked up and down the block, saw me serving as sentinel in front of Rutherford's homely mansion, locked their doors and then their arms, and walked my way beneath a soggy winter sky. Two by two they asked if she was here yet and two by two I told them that she wasn't. Nervous, apprehensive, jittery, as leery of each other as they were of the bouncing baby boy the surrogate stork was bringing them, they trooped inside the elder Colbert's castle as though they had been sentenced to hang and Rutherford was providing the gallows as a public service.

All except Millicent. Millicent Colbert was as frisky as a kid at a carnival, squirming, smiling, giggling, and grasping a pink plastic bag stuffed full of baby things as though it held the launch codes to the missiles and atomic bombs. I liked her for her ecstasy and hoped nothing I had engineered was going to dilute it.

Stuart and Millicent went inside the house, then Cynthia and Russell joined me. Cynthia didn't greet me or even slow down, but Russell lingered to talk.

"Have you seen her?" he asked with a hint of the conspirator about him.

"No."

"Are you sure she's coming?"

"Reasonably."

"Is anything else going to happen?"

"Like what?"

"Like accusations, allegations, protestations."

"Against you?"

"Against anyone."

I slapped him on the back, prepared to forgive his transgressions. "I can't speak for everyone but *I* certainly don't intend to be so boorish. As long as Clara gets her fee, I don't see why she'd act up either. Do you have her check?"

He patted his breast pocket. "Postdated three days, so the child can be examined by a physician."

"Examined for what?"

Russell indulged in lawyer's oratory. "Health problems attributable to prenatal neglect. Nutritional deficiencies. The kind of thing that would vitiate the agreement. Since she willfully evaded the contractual safeguards, I feel it's incumbent to make such tests."

I laughed. "Give the role a rest, why don't you? I don't think there's going to be a problem."

"We'll know in a few minutes, won't we?" He looked up and down the street, then regarded me somberly. "I assume this is your final function in this matter."

"As far as I know," I agreed.

"Well, good." Russell glanced at the house. "How's the old man this morning?"

"Don't know. Haven't seen him."

"A complex individual."

"And a ruthless one."

He started to dispute me, then stepped toward the house, then turned back. "I'm resigning from the firm," he said.

"I thought you might be."

"I'll be handling Cynthia's affairs, and a few other clients', but I'm cutting way back. Giving up the rat race."

"And the view."

His smile was wan and attenuated. "And the view. I'm trying to persuade Cynthia to let Stuart have the men's stores as well and open her own shop. Something exclusive. Something manageable."

"Good luck," I said.

He thanked me, then started toward the door again, then offered an addendum. "I'm sorry it got complicated, Marsh."

"So am I, Russell."

"And I'm sorry . . ." He didn't seem to have the vocabulary to apologize more specifically. "But it looks like it's going to work out, so no harm done. Right?"

"Right."

"All's well that ends well."

"So I hear."

"At least the sailing was fun. Right?"

"Right."

"Let's do it again someday."

"Let's."

Russell waved awkwardly and manically, as though he was about to sail off to the Lesser Antilles, and went inside the mansion. Eight minutes later, a battered Volvo sedan turned into the street, slowed to a crawl, then parked halfway up the block. Two minutes after that, a woman got out of the driver's side and walked to where I was standing. She was dressed in tan twill slacks and a blue cotton sweater. If there was anyone else in the car, I couldn't see her from where I stood.

"Good morning, Ms. Webber," I said as she approached.

She had no time for pleasantry. "Are they there?"

"All present and accounted for. Is Greta in the car?"

Her expression shifted into neutral. "Greta isn't here."

I swore. "You got all these people here for *nothing*?"

"Not at all. Greta isn't here, but the baby is."

My heart jumped to double time for an instant and I glanced at the suddenly suspect vehicle down the block, complications confounding me once again. "How will they know it's hers? I mean theirs? The one called for by the contract?"

Linda patted her purse. "I've got the birth certificate right here, complete with palm and foot prints, plus a Polaroid photo to match. If that's not enough, there's a videotape of the birth in the car."

My heart returned to normal cadence. "I guess that'll have to do. Shall I go get him?"

She shook her head. "I'll do it."

She strolled to the car as casually as a border inspector, then opened the passenger door and leaned inside. After some maneuvering and manipulating, she emerged carrying a bright white wicker basket and walked back to me down the center of the street, as if to herald the birth to the neighborhood. The basket swung loosely at her side; on occasion she glanced at its contents, which seemed to come wrapped in a fuzzy pink blanket. A wave of relief ran through me, allowing various interior knots to loosen, even though a shopping basket seemed an odd vehicle for a baby. But what did I know about it?

She brought me the basket the way she would bring me bullion and placed it on the sidewalk at my feet. I looked into the mound of covers that rose and fell beneath the arc of the braided handle. Two tiny blue eyes looked back at me from within a round red face and a shiny wide forehead. Then one pudgy little hand reached up and did something I chose to interpret as a wave.

"He likes me," I said.

"Can we get it over with, please?"

Chastened, I stepped away from the basket and let Linda pick it up, then led her up the walk toward Rutherford's forbidding lair.

They were all in the parlor but Rutherford. No one was saying anything; no one was looking at anything animate; no one was happy but Millicent. When Linda and I entered the room, Millicent emitted a tiny squeal, then covered her mouth with her hand, then tugged on the arm of her husband. "She got the color wrong," she whispered nervously, halfway between laughing and crying. No one seemed to hear her; it felt like the start of high mass.

Stuart had something other than color on his mind. "Where's Clara?" he demanded of me.

"She's not coming."

He leaped to his feet and made fists. "I suspected as much. This is nothing but a charade. She's an extortionist. She never *intended* to—"

Millicent stood up and put her hand over her husband's mouth. Stuart reacted as if his spine had been severed. I gave his wife a silent ovation.

"We have the baby," I said quickly, pointing to the basket at Linda Webber's feet. "And we have documentation." I recited the details except for the videotape. "There's further proof if necessary."

Stuart and Russell exchanged glances. "It won't be necessary," Millicent Colbert said before either of them could voice objection.

Russell only shrugged. Stuart regarded his wife as though she had just floated down from Venus.

I looked at Linda Webber. "I guess you can hand it over."

She shook her head. "Not till *he's* here."

"Who?"

"Mr. Colbert. Greta said to be sure Rutherford Colbert was here when I made delivery."

I looked at Russell. He scowled and shrugged and went into the hall and disappeared. Two elongated minutes later, he returned, followed by a man piloting a motorized chair and trailed by a private nurse.

The nurse was so lovely it seemed unlikely she possessed any practical skill at all. The man was her cadaverous opposite, withered and wizened and bleached, the hairless limbs extending from his blue pajamas as thin and tenuous as plastic straws. His cheeks were sunken, as though gouged out of his face by a chisel; the bones above them were as sharp as shelves. His hair was white and sparse, his eyes as blue and piercing as if they'd been repainted that morning. His bare feet occupied a pair of slippers incongruously, the way fish would occupy a nest.

A yellow canister was strapped to the back of his chair. A clear plastic tube led from its nozzle up the back of his head where it divided, the twin tendrils circling his skull and disappearing into his nostrils, feeding a continuous diet of oxygen to his ravaged lungs. As I inhaled a fresh batch of air myself, I could smell the cigars and cigarettes that had put him where he was.

Except for myself and Linda Webber, his audience was rapt and reverent. When he spoke, the words seemed to be formed not by tongue and tooth but by bellows and sponges and leaky balloons. "Where is she?" he wheezed.

"Clara's not here, Mr. Colbert," Russell Jorgensen said quickly. "But the child is. That's all that matters, when you get down to it."

Rutherford's eyes darted on and off each one of us, leaving as quickly as they came, as though our vitality offended him. His glance lingered only when it landed last on Linda Webber and her basket.

"She has documentation," Russell added, and extended his hand for Linda to hand it over.

She dug a paper from her purse and handed it to me. "The money first," she said.

Russell got the check and handed it to me in turn. I exchanged it for the birth certificate, then passed the check to Linda. She read it and looked at Russell. After he explained about the postdating and the medical exam, she frowned and shrugged. "Whatever."

When Linda Webber made no move to surrender the baby, I grasped the basket and carried it toward Millicent. She reached to receive it with both hands, as eagerly as she would embrace absolution.

"Him," Linda Webber said at my back.

I turned to see a finger pointed at Rutherford Colbert's pigeon breast. "You're supposed to give it to him," she elaborated.

Millicent started to say something but Stuart hushed her audibly. I took the basket to Rutherford and placed it in his bony lap. The nurse hovered close enough to intervene if he declined or dropped it, either of which seemed likely. When I turned back to Linda Webber, she was gone.

I looked at Stuart and Millicent and then at Russell Jorgensen. "I guess that's it," I said.

Russell nodded absently, his eyes roaming the birth certificate. "I guess so."

"It's been nice knowing you," I said to Stuart and Millicent, mostly to Millicent.

"Thank you very much for your time and trouble, Mr. Tanner," Millicent said warmly. "I have to admit I was worried there for a while."

I smiled. "Me, too."

"Oh, I can't just *sit* here," she blurted, and hurried to the wheelchair and gazed down into the tidy basket that perched on her father-in-law's lap like a new fedora. "Can I hold you?" she asked the baby. "I know he's your granddaddy, but *I'm* your *mom.*"

She reached in the basket and extracted its fuzzy contents and cradled it in her arms the way women know to do from birth, then began to bill and coo. The nurse and I were the only others who were smiling.

Suddenly Millicent sniffed and giggled. "You need changing, don't you, little man? Yes, you do. Well, I have some diapers right here." She went to her bag and fished for a Pamper.

"Let me do it," Russell said.

"What?" said Millicent and I in unison.

"Let me change it."

Russell went to her side and reached for the baby. "But . . ." Millicent sputtered.

"I've got two kids; I've changed more diapers than you have freckles. Here."

He grabbed the diaper from her hand, then took the baby from its mystified mother and cradled it with one hand and spread its blanket on the floor with the other. With an easy flourish he laid the baby on its back in the middle of the precise pink square that was bordered by a satin ribbon. He did seem practiced in the procedure and a moment later he was tugging a dirty diaper free from the baby's upraised bottom and handing it to Millicent to dispose of.

"Just as I thought," he said.

I frowned; Stuart Colbert looked down at the baby; Millicent peered over Russell's shoulder. Rutherford's chair rolled forward, to the accompaniment of his labored gasps and the rustle of the nurse's skirt as she hurried to follow his progress.

"God fucking *damn*," Stuart said, then looked fearfully at his ailing father. "Someone messed up, Daddy."

Millicent searched out her husband, then bent this way and that to see what they were talking about, for fear there were suddenly grounds for horror. "What's wrong? Stuart? Russell? What's wrong with my *baby*?" Millicent was near hysteria and I was pretty jarred myself.

Stuart swore again. "It's a *girl*. That's what's wrong. It's a fucking female."

"Bitch."

Rutherford Colbert coughed twice, then swore again, then spun his chair around and rolled out of the room in a hurry, the nurse a supernumerary in his wake.

I looked at the baby, naked and squirming and soiled, then looked at its contractual mother. She was standing motionless in the center of the room, stunned and terrified, holding a dirty diaper by the tips of two fingers without even realizing she was doing so. The image hit me like a club. I backed out of the room and ran to my car and drove as fast as I could to the sea, empty of all but panic.

I walked Ocean Beach for over an hour, then drove to Golden Gate Park and wandered its grounds for an hour more. My thoughts careening from the invasion of likelihoods, my needs and desires at civil war, I was confronted with questions I had dodged for years. Without warning, I was forced to act and not react, required to define myself and my future in the space of the next few hours. Since I didn't know what else to do, I went to the car and placed a call.

After three secretaries and two nurses had filtered out my purposes, he came on the line.

"Dr. Bradshaw?"

"Yes?"

"My name is Tanner. I'm calling on behalf of Mr. Colbert."

"Yes?"

"Mr. Rutherford Colbert, that is."

He audibly relaxed. "How may I help you, Mr. Tanner? And please convey my appreciation once again to Mr. Colbert for his most recent gift to the clinic. As usual, we do appreciate it. Truly."

I told him I'd be happy to convey the message. "I'm calling about the procedure you performed some nine months ago. I'm sure you know to what I'm referring—the insemination of the Hammond woman."

"Of course. What about it?"

"The child has been born and is about to be delivered to the intended parents. Mr. Colbert believes it likely that questions may arise as to its genetic origins. He wants me to confirm that the confidentiality in place originally will remain in full force and effect."

"Of course. But I must warn you as I did the last time, that the barrier may not hold up in the face of a court order."

"There's a physician/patient privilege in this state, is there not?"

"Indeed there is. But who is the patient in this instance, Mr. Tanner? If you ponder that question for a moment, I believe you will see the difficulty."

I saw more difficulties than he could possibly imagine. "I want also to confirm that Mr. and Mrs. Stuart Colbert's embryos are still being preserved intact."

"Yes, they are. Three of them, as ordered."

I thanked the doctor for his time. Still dazed by developments, unclear of my desires and suspicious of my motives, I drove back to Santa Ana Way and parked the car in the middle of the block and stewed for yet another hour as darkness made its daily claim on the city.

Kids came home from school, maids trudged to the bus stop, mothers whizzed by on their way to the market, all without regard for me. I got out of the car twice, then got back in. I started the engine, then turned it off. I pounded the steering wheel, I slumped in the seat and closed my eyes and tried to ward off the world, I swore and prayed and begged and bargained with entities toward which I was generally agnostic. Head throbbing, heart pounding, alternately awash in sweat and sentimentality, I picked up the car phone and dialed once again.

"Ms. Webber? This is Marsh Tanner. I need to see her."

"What?"

"You heard me. I want to see Greta. Face to face; just the two of us. Some time within the next week. If she doesn't agree, I'm going to come looking for her. And she's not going to be happy when I find her."

"She doesn't want to talk to you."

"I don't care what she wants."

My voice must have mirrored my state of mind. "I'll see what I can do," she relented.

I tossed the phone on the seat and got out of the car and walked to the Colbert house and pressed the bell. As I waited for a response to my summons, I remembered that the last man who had rung that bell to challenge Rutherford Colbert about the subjects I was about to vent myself had been gunned down before he could do so.

THIRTY-THREE

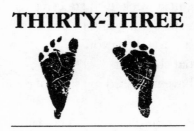

The nurse who had been on duty some four hours earlier opened the door to confront me. She was still lovely and her uniform was still immaculate, but both her allure and her coiffeur had wilted in the interim. I was the worse for wear myself.

The arch to her brow and the purse to her lips suggested she brought her employer as much competence as comeliness, so I marshaled my best moves. I told her my name and reminded her that I had been there earlier, then asked to see Mr. Colbert. Without so much as a blink, she told me he was indisposed.

"I think he'd better dispose himself."

She shook her head. "I'm sure you have a compelling reason to visit, Mr. Tanner, but the events of the day have been taxing, as I'm sure you can appreciate. An audience is out of the question."

"He's going to be taxed a lot more than he is now if he doesn't see me. And stop pretending he's the pope—he's just a rag salesman who got lucky."

She sniffed and started to close the door—that had been happening a lot lately.

"I don't know what that business with the infant was about this afternoon," she said officiously, "and I don't want to know. But the experience put Mr. Colbert temporarily in extremis and he needs time to regain his equilibrium."

"What's your name?"

"Deborah."

"Is Mr. Colbert on medication, Deborah?"

"I'm not at liberty to say."

"Can he understand what's said to him? Can he process information?"

"Certainly he can. Why?"

"I've got more medicine to administer to him and he might as well take it now. That way when he does regain his equilibrium, he can keep it for a while."

She crossed her arms beneath her sprightly breasts. "Even if it was medically appropriate, which it isn't, I'm not at all sure he would be willing to see you." There was enough hauteur in her voice to let me press her without compunction.

"Try him. Tell him I'm here to talk about his grandchild. On second thought, make that plural. Tell him I'm here about his grandchildren."

She checked the symptoms of my determination—wild eyes, bared teeth, bulging jaw—and compared them with her patient's vigor. "I'll speak with him," she concluded. "Please come in."

She admitted me to the foyer, directed me toward an antique church pew along one wall, then went down the hall to consult her superior. While I waited, I noticed details I hadn't appreciated the first time I'd been there.

The house was even more opulent than I'd sensed that afternoon, but it was a faded and outmoded grandeur, not an active one, as though the furnishings and appointments had been assembled during a madcap weekend some fifty years before and neglected ever since. But the tapestries and landscapes and stained glass that occupied eye level, the burly chandelier overhead and the thick and burnished balusters of the sweeping staircase, gave the house an air of gravity that suggested history and consequence. The exquisite detailing of the coat rack and commode and church pew that shared the foyer, as well as the wainscoting that enclosed them, emitted an air of eminence that had clearly been the owner's intent. His current inclinations were far less laudable.

Deborah came to fetch me five minutes later. "I'm sorry for the delay—he wanted to get dressed before he received you."

"Understandable for someone who made his millions in the fashion business."

She blinked. "Of course. I never thought of it that way." She was glad to have an uncertainty crossed off her list. "Please come this way."

She led me toward a room in the center of the house that had once served as a den and now seemed more like a mausoleum. The walls were lined with books and maps, the floors were polished broad-gauge fir, the furnishings were out of Washington Irving and Edith Wharton. It was perfect down to the Tiffany lamps and brass spittoon, which meant it was as artificial as the breathing mechanism being employed by the man seated in his wheelchair behind the leather and gilt of a Queen Anne desk, wearing a pinstripe suit and a gaudy silk tie and looking as though he wanted to dispatch me the way he had dispatched his colleague some twenty years before.

"You're nothing," he said as I sat in an opposing wing chair. "I hired and fired a dozen guys like you in my day." His words remained a soggy rasp that transported us back in time to a scene out of Chandler or James M. Cain. I thought of General Sternwood and had to suppress a smile, then took a deep breath and launched my opening statement.

"I assume you know that I got involved in Colbert business when Russell Jorgensen hired me to evaluate a woman named Greta Hammond, who had agreed to serve as a surrogate mother for your son and his wife."

He didn't move or speak or breathe. I wondered if the oxygen tank made it unnecessary to do any of those things at normal intervals.

"So?" he grunted in a wooly monotone.

"Your daughter told me that you know everything that happens out here, so I also assume you know that Greta Hammond was really Clara Brennan and that Stuart didn't choose her as his surrogate at random; he hunted her up and picked her on purpose."

"So?" he whistled again.

"What I'm trying to say is that I know what you know, Mr. Colbert, but you don't know what I know. So that's what I've come to tell you."

"Why would I care?"

"Because I know enough to cause trouble. I know enough to wreck your family and your business, both."

"How?"

"By making your private life public."

What he saw in my face made him decide not to quibble. "What will stop you?"

"Your promise to leave the status quo. I know you were expecting the baby to be a boy and I know you're upset that it wasn't. I don't know how that happened or why, and neither do you, but I'm telling you to accept the situation as it is and let Stuart and Millicent raise the girl the way they planned. Whether she succeeds to a part of your empire isn't important—it's your estate and you can do what you want with it. What matters is that she has a normal happy life. I need you to promise not to fuck it up."

His hands made lumpy fists on the arms of his chair and his lungs sucked for more air than the plastic tubes had been engineered to transmit. "Who are you to tell me how to treat my family?"

The utterance of an entire sentence seemed to expend the energy of a mile run. He slumped in his chair, eyes closed, chest heaving, gasping like a fighter between rounds. Moving briskly and impassively, the nurse took his pulse at his neck.

When his eyes were open I answered his question. "I'm someone who's been hip-deep in your family history for nine months. I've learned things I didn't want to learn and I've been obstructed to the point of assault by people who didn't want me to do my job." I smiled in a way that would aggravate him. "When that happens, I get real intent on results, Mr. Colbert; I get eager to earn a gold star. I was hired to make sure this surrogate thing works out and I'm going to do just that. Part of the way I'm going to do it is to convince you to quit trying to re-arrange reality to suit your private purposes."

"Nuts," he said, but he was still searching for air, not passively accepting it, and his pigmentless flesh had colored to the pink of his gums.

"Now I'm going to tell you what's going to become public knowledge if you don't do as I say." I looked at the nurse, then back at Colbert. "You may want her to leave the room for this part."

He looked at me for several seconds, then lifted his hand off the chair and waved it once. After a hostile glance at me, Deborah left the room without a word. Even on the edge of pulmonary crisis, Rutherford was lord of the manor.

"Here's what I know," I said. "And what I know I take to the cops and the business press and the financial community if you don't stop messing up your offsprings' lives."

He was too intent on breathing to obstruct me, so I started my trip through his past. "Forty years ago, your wife had an affair with your right-hand man, Ethan Brennan. Stuart was the product of that affair, which makes Stuart and Clara Brennan half-siblings. You didn't find out for almost twenty years, not until Fern Drummond told you about it in order to get you to make Stuart stop courting Clara so her son could have a chance at romancing Clara himself."

His eyes closed and his lungs made noises. I couldn't interpret their significance but it didn't look like he needed the nurse.

"When you found out your wife had been unfaithful, one of the methods of retribution you concocted, other than to frame Ethan Brennan for embezzlement, was to do the opposite of what Fern wanted—far from urging him to break it off, you encouraged Stuart to court Clara ardently, which, like the dutiful son he was, he did. You told Stuart to keep the relationship secret, because you knew Ethan Brennan would stop it if he knew, but kids get reckless when they're in love, and Brennan got wind of the romance. When he found out you were the instigator of the relationship, he came gunning for you, whereupon you shot him down."

I looked for a reaction. What I saw was a mind struggling for memory and laboring at denial and revision.

"I think Luke learned what Brennan planned to do and he warned his mother and she warned you. Fern Drummond knew you could have defused the situation if you'd wanted to, but you didn't; you preferred to see Ethan Brennan die. Fern saw you shoot him in cold blood and you've been paying her hush money ever since."

His poisonous glare transmitted far more conceit than contrition. "That last part I probably can't prove," I admitted. "Not unless Fern talks, which she won't as long as you keep buying her off, which I don't have a problem with provided you follow instructions."

Colbert knew that if he got too excited it could kill him; I felt the heat off his bottled rage. I laughed and made it worse for him. "I gave you more credit than you deserved, actually. I assumed the money for Fern was to support Nathaniel, since you were responsible for the genetic collision that caused his problems. But you didn't give a damn about Nathaniel once he'd served his purpose, which was to inject a hot shot of guilt and grief into the veins of the Brennan family. You were just trying to save yourself."

This time the reaction was more vigorous—a hiss of borrowed breath and a squint to his eye that forecast vengeance.

"The one thing I couldn't figure," I continued nonetheless, "was that if Stuart and Clara produced a retarded child the first time, why would you want them to risk it again? Ethan Brennan is dead, your wife and his wife live like Carmelites, so you haven't had to deal with them in decades, and you made Stuart's life as miserable as you could after you learned who had sired him. So why repeat the pass at incest?"

His smile told me I wasn't going to get an answer. Mine told him I didn't need one.

"There are at least two answers to that," I said. "One is that Nathaniel's not part of your gene pool after all. Everyone thinks Stuart is Nathaniel's father, even Clara, because he'd been trying so hard to impregnate her, but my bet is that Stuart is sterile. I don't think he knows it, but even if he does, I doubt that he told you because that would be just one more way he didn't measure up. The fertility people must know—they must have found out when Stuart went down to donate sperm twenty years ago. They even faked a vasectomy to help you cover it up when Stuart began to suspect he had a problem. That was the germ of your plan, the knowledge that your son couldn't have children. The rest of it was hatched when you came down with emphysema and were face to face with your own mortality."

I looked for an admission or an objection but didn't get either. "If Luke Drummond is Nathaniel's father," I went on, "then Nathaniel isn't the product of incest, like everyone thought, but of some genetic tic in the Drummond or Brennan lines. It can be proved one way or another if it has to be, but at this point the only one who gives a damn is Luke—he still thinks he's going to inherit the Colbert stores as some sort of guardian for Nathaniel."

I paused to make sure he was with me. "So much for grandchild number one, who probably isn't your grandchild after all. Now for grandchild number two: the baby in the basket. Except she isn't your grandchild, either."

Colbert paused to adjust his tubes but the additional air didn't cheer him. When he was finished tinkering, I spoke with an arrogance that matched his own. "What you need to understand is that I know the baby in that basket wasn't your grandchild, Mr. Colbert; I know that baby is your *child*."

I waited for him to absorb my deduction. When he had, he mumbled something guttural and disparaging, then reached in a drawer in his desk and pulled out a gun.

It was an Army-issue .45, a war souvenir no doubt, as lethal-looking as anything Colt ever made. Despite his frailty, Rutherford jacked a round into the chamber as easily as I can comb my hair, then leveled the weapon at my chest. I was afraid and he knew it, but the tremor in his hand told me he was afraid as well.

"What's that going to solve?" I said as blithely as I could manage. "How many people do you think you can shoot in cold blood and get away with it? It's not like the old days, Mr. Colbert. Titans of commerce don't get cut any slack by the cops: titans of commerce get spread all over 'Hard Copy' and *The National Enquirer*."

I gave him time to test my prediction. "They don't have pretty blond nurses in San Quentin, Mr. Colbert. They've got burly black orderlies who'll wheel you into a corner and ignore you the rest of the day unless you fall out of your chair and maybe even then. Is that the way you want it to end? If it is, pull the trigger. Because it would be what you deserve."

After two heaving breaths, he lowered the gun and put it where it came from. When his hand emerged from the drawer, it crawled like a tortoise to the edge of the desk and pressed a button. I hurried to finish before Deborah came back and threw me out.

"It wasn't Stuart's sperm in that petri dish; it was yours. In fact, there wasn't a dish at all. When you got sick you decided the only way to ensure that your name and your business would live forever was to leave your empire to a person who combined the genes that had made it successful in the first place—yours and Ethan Brennan's. Brennan wasn't around but his daughter was, so you arranged the surrogate charade to concoct the perfect heir. You've put enough money into the fertility clinic over the years to persuade your buddy Bradshaw to abandon his ethics—he performed an artificial insemination instead of the *in vitro* fertilization Stuart and Millicent planned. Stuart thinks the sperm was his, and Millicent thinks it was her egg, and both of them are wrong: all three of their little embryos are still on ice." I looked into his jaundiced eye. "But if you do the right thing, they won't be the wiser. And neither will the cops."

Nurse Deborah came in and stood behind her charge, ready to do battle with his lungs or with me, whichever seemed more hazardous. But Rutherford didn't issue instructions.

"You set this surrogate thing in motion from the beginning," I went on. "Stuart is so used to doing your bidding he doesn't realize he's doing it anymore—he still thinks it was his idea. But using Clara as the surrogate had to come from you because she's the only one who could give you what you needed, which was a set of genes with Brennan imprinting to mate with your own."

"How much do you want?" he said, as insultingly as his monotone could manage it.

"All I want is for you to leave well enough alone and make the Drummonds do likewise. Don't try to find Clara; don't tell Stuart or Millicent about their baby's true biology; don't disown the child either emotionally or physically. Be a doting grandpa; no more, no less."

He sighed heavily and his head sank toward his chest as if the tubes were suddenly transmitting lead. I added some final instructions.

"Buy her dolls or computers or chemistry sets or whatever little girls play with these days. Fund a fancy birthday party; put her on your knee and bounce her; carry her picture in your wallet and show it to friends if you have any; and cut Stuart enough physical and emotional slack so he can become a good father. You do all that, Mr. Colbert, and you won't hear from me again and you can suck on that pipe in peace."

It took a while but he finally nodded; at least that's what I interpreted the movement to be. After some invisible prompt, Nurse Deborah wheeled him out of the room. As I let myself out, I wondered if the old man would ever know that the revelation I'd experienced in his home some four hours earlier suggested that the story I'd just told him had been true at one time, but had recently become a lie.

Two days later, I got a message. "Palace Hotel," it said in the terse voice of Linda Webber. "Garden Court; tomorrow noon. Be alone."

THIRTY-FOUR

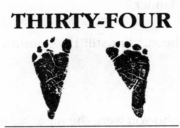

The Palace Hotel—now the Sheraton Palace—is one of San Francisco's oldest landmarks. The largest hotel in the world when it opened in 1875, it was destroyed in the fires following the 1906 earthquake, rebuilt in 1909, and remained one of the West Coast's major hostelries until the middle of the century, when a combination of competition and recession deficits resulted in a deterioration of its amenities. On the brink of closure, the Palace was rescued in the mid-eighties by a foreign consortium that purchased the hotel and then spent 150 million dollars to refurbish it. All to the good, as far as I could tell, especially since the heart of the restoration campaign was the jewel at the center of the hotel, the Garden Court, which the new owners had returned to its former elegance and beyond.

The surfaces of the fabled restaurant were bright with coats of fresh enamel. The gold leaf sconces above the polished marble columns that supported the dramatic arc of the domed glass ceiling gave the place the stamp of royalty. Augmented and accented by a series of chandeliers and mirrored doors, even the light itself made the atmosphere magical and otherworldly.

Clara Brennan was already at a table when I arrived, a solitary island in the center of the busy room, sipping a glass of wine and looking far too composed for someone who had just delivered and then surrendered a child. Her cheeks seemed fuller than before, and her hair less lustrous, but those were the only traces of motherhood I could spot, although I guessed a more lasting imprint was invisible.

I pulled out a chair and sat down. She raised a brow and toasted me with her goblet. "Mr. Tanner."

"Ms. Brennan."

She shook her head. "I'm still Hammond to everyone but my mother."

"Good."

"Why?"

"Because that's who you were the night we made love."

She sighed with a mix of pain and anger, regret hanging between us like a drape. At a loss for words, she fiddled with a button on her denim dress. When a waiter scurried by, I ordered a beer.

After he left, we exchanged awkward smiles, then looked quickly away, the way you do after a peek at the sun. I asked how she was feeling.

"I'm fine. All things considered."

"It was an easy birth?"

She shrugged. "Comparatively, I suppose."

"Compared to Nathaniel, you mean?"

A streak of anguish through her eyes made me sorry I'd made the reference. "Compared to most women."

"Are you living on Kirkham Street again?"

"Not yet." She paused to provoke me. "But when and if I do, you aren't going to know about it."

I nodded in surrender to her terms. "Do you need anything?"

Her chuckle was less a laugh than an editorial. "I need just about everything. But I don't expect you to provide it."

"I could help."

"No, you couldn't."

In the middle of our face-off, the waiter brought my beer. I raised my glass. "To the baby."

She lifted her goblet and smiled crookedly. "To the baby."

I rubbed at a sting in my eye. "It's odd that we don't even know her name."

"It's odd that we won't know anything else about her, either. Not one thing. Not ever." She sipped her wine and raised the menu, less to read than to hide behind.

"It's mine, isn't it?" I asked softly, my body tensed against the answer.

"What makes you think so?" The question floated from behind her shield, innocent, innocuous, insidious.

"The circle on your calendar got me thinking. I thought at first you were highlighting our night together, but what you were really doing was calculating menstruation and ovulation. Right?"

The menu didn't move.

"Then, when the baby got changed at the mansion, something about the way Millicent was holding the dirty diaper suggested what you'd done."

"What did that have to . . . oh. The condom."

"What did you use, a turkey baster?"

She lowered the menu and looked at me. Tears climbed her eyes; her cheeks were mottled with crimson. "Do you really want to know?"

"About the turkey baster?"

"About the baby," she corrected fiercely.

I started to nod my head, then didn't. I thought I already knew the truth. I thought I'd come to terms with it. I thought I'd constructed the necessary rationales and provided myself with sufficient defenses. But Greta was offering an out, in the form of ignorance and ambiguity, and I'd made use of such aids before.

"It's a serious question," she said as I ran my options through my mind yet again. "It's not a pleasant thing, knowing you have a child being raised in someone else's home. Even if there are reasons. Even if there isn't any choice. It's still not fun. It's still something you think about every day of your life. It's still something that makes you wonder if you deserve to be called a human being." She blinked at a globe of tears and made it shatter. "Does that make any sense?"

I nodded.

She swiped at the side of her nose. "You must have considered whether to have kids at some point. Right? There must have been a time in your life when that was an issue."

"Once or twice." And more recently than you know, I thought but didn't say.

"And you obviously decided against it. So why decide differently now? It's not like you did anything wrong. You did what you were supposed to do to keep it from happening and the only reason it did if it did was because I tricked you. If it did happen, you didn't know about it. If it did happen, it was with a woman who was living a lie and who did it for reasons you had no knowledge of. So why buy into something that came out of that? Think about it. Because I'm here to tell you that once you buy in, you buy in for life."

"I believe you," I said, because I did and because she needed me to.

"You're looking at me like I'm some sort of monster."

I shook my head. "I'm not looking at you, I'm looking at me."

When I didn't say more, she turned mean. "You could have stopped it, or tried to, at least. You used to be a lawyer; you could have gone to court and tried to void the contract and asked for a determination of paternity and claimed parental rights of your own. You could have kept me from handing her over and cut the Colberts out of it. You could have, but you didn't. You didn't even try."

"No. I didn't."

"I think that says something."

"Maybe so."

She leaned back in her chair and crossed her arms, her smile both triumphant and disparaging. "Millicent will make a good mother."

"Yes."

"And Stuart will be okay too, probably, once the old man's out of the picture. He may even become a decent human being."

"That would be nice."

"She'll have a lot of advantages you can't afford to give her."

"True."

"The whole arrangement might collapse if they find out what you think is true is true."

"It's possible," I agreed.

She finished her wine. "So what's the verdict? I'll do whatever you want. You want the truth, I'll tell you."

I found myself trying to do damage. "You were wrong about almost everything," I said without knowing why.

"How so?"

"The baby wasn't Stuart's. *Neither* baby was Stuart's."

Her eyes became jade stones, hard and inscrutable. "Bullshit."

"Truth."

"How the fuck do *you* know?"

"Stuart was sterile."

"Says who?"

"Says his father; says his first wife,." I extrapolated.

"Then who . . . ?" Her mind couldn't travel in time or grip the contingencies.

"Luke the first time; Rutherford the second."

I might as well have punched her. "*Rutherford*?"

I nodded. "His sperm; not Stuart's. Your egg; not Millicent's. He set it up with the clinic people. Stuart doesn't know, by the way. Stuart doesn't know lots of things."

Greta Hammond closed her eyes and hugged herself, as though we were deep in a bone-cold cave and the ceiling overhead was ice. "Rutherford won't quit till he destroys us all, will he? First Daddy, now me. And sooner or later Stuart, too."

"He'll quit now," I said with more certainty than I felt. "I told him what I knew and read him the riot act. He might have stood up to me ten years ago, but now he's too sick and he knows it. So no one will know about all this unless you tell them."

Her breaths were as labored as Rutherford's when I ordered him to abandon his plan. "I hope to God you're right," she said, then tried to lighten her psychic weight. "Not that it matters at this point, I suppose."

"It matters," I countered, "because *she* matters. She may be the only thing that does."

"What is this, a guilt trip?"

I smiled. "Precisely."

Her lip curled. "Well, guess what? I choose not to play. I wish some of the stuff that happened hadn't happened, but it did and there's nothing I can do about it. So don't try to load shame and humiliation on *my* plate; I won't take a bite of it."

"You don't have to. All you have to do is one thing."

"What's that?"

"Play ball with Nathaniel once in a while."

She leaned forward and shook her head; her voice was as raw as my flesh after the night with Luke Drummond. "Don't pull that atonement shit with *me*, Tanner. You don't have the right."

"What did you do, tell Luke that if he married you and took the child, sooner or later it would inherit the Colbert bucks?"

"Fuck you."

"It's what he believes, you know. He reads *Women's Wear Daily,* for Christ's sake."

She wrinkled her nose in disgust. "Let's cut to the chase. This isn't about Nathaniel, this is about a baby girl. Do you want to know whose she is or not?"

In the grip of an urge neither noble nor rational nor predetermined, I fished out my wallet, threw some bills on the table, and stood up. "I'm full," I said. "Enjoy your lunch. Enjoy your life. Just keep me out of both of them."

"You don't have any idea what I've been through," she sneered. "You can't judge me."

"I can judge both of us," I told her, and left the hotel by the door to the alley.

Thirty minutes later, I was back on Santa Ana Way. The woman who opened the door was laughing so hard everything above her waist was jiggling. I asked her if Mrs. Colbert was in.

"She's busy."

"With the baby?"

Her nod created waterfalls of flesh and the vectors from her smile threatened to burst her cheeks. "That baby is the best thing that ever happened in this house."

"I'm sure it is," I said. "Please tell Mrs. Colbert I'd like to speak with her." I gave my name and waited.

"She says to come in," the housekeeper said when she returned. "And don't mind the mess—I'm about to get on it."

She led me to a room off the kitchen that had once been a pantry but now was a playroom. The temperature was close to eighty; the smells were of fresh paint and talc. There were enough toys lying around to fill Santa's sleigh twice over.

Millicent Colbert was wearing yet another Laura Ashley but now there were wet spots at the shoulder and breast and one of the buttons was missing. She was down on the floor, eye-to-eye with her tiny infant, who was lying face down on a quilt clad in one of those footless sleepers that cinch at the bottom, the kind Sweet Pea used to wear. Every few seconds the baby would raise her head to look at the strange apparition that was her mother, then make a face that approximated a smile, then put her head back down for a rest before she took another look.

"Madonna and child," I said in the middle of Millicent Colbert's lilting croon.

She rolled to her back and looked up at me. "Mr. Tanner. How nice."

"Just wanted to see how things were going."

"They've never gone better. I couldn't be happier, and neither could Eleanor." She couldn't keep her eyes off the child, so she rolled onto her belly and bonded some more.

"Eleanor," I repeated.

"We decided last night. Stuart wanted Gwendolyn."

"I'm glad you won."

She rolled back to her back. "Why don't you join us? There's plenty of room."

"Not this time." I was breathing so hard I felt faint. "But I would like to come by once in a while to see how she's doing. I've developed a paternal interest in Eleanor, for some reason."

"As well you should," Millicent said happily. "Without you, we might not have gotten her back. Clara was acting so strangely."

"Yes, she was."

"Do you know why?"

"Not completely. But she won't bother you again."

"I hope not."

"Don't worry. So how's Grandpa Rutherford behaving?"

"He's being . . . cute, I suppose you could say. He sent over a playpen and a stuffed animal." She pointed at a rabbit the size of a bear.

"So you don't mind if I peek in once in a while?"

She reached out a hand so I could help her up. "I *insist* on it. In fact, we have a favor to ask you."

My stomach made a fist. "What is it?"

"I was going to do this formally but, well, I was talking to Stuart and I, we, would like you to be Eleanor's godfather. Mr. Coppola ruined the term with his film, of course, but nevertheless we're serious about it. Will you agree to serve us in that capacity, Mr. Tanner?"

I felt myself redden. "I'm not sure what a godfather does, exactly."

"He supervises religious instruction, I believe. And sponsors the child at baptism."

I drew in as much air as my lungs would accept. "That doesn't sound like something I'd be very good at. Now when she's ready for membership in the 49er Faithful . . ." The mechanics of my smile didn't work.

Millicent put her hand on my arm. "Do consider it, will you, Mr. Tanner? We truly would like to honor you in some way."

"I'll give it some thought." As soon as I could, I bid mother and child good-bye.

I did think about it. And then I did research on the subject, to the point that I discovered that when E. M. Forster was asked to serve as godfather to the son of some close friends, he declined the invitation.

After I read the catechism that described Forster's difficulty in deciding the right thing to do, I called Millicent Colbert. "I've been reading about godfathers," I said when she came on the line.

"What have you found out?"

"Mostly it has to do with religion, like you said. But E. M. Forster said that one of the roles of godfathers is to tell their godchild 'about the things that they have liked in life.'"

"How nice."

I paused. "I think maybe I could do that for Eleanor: tell her about the things I have liked in life. Not so much about God or anything abstract. But about black-faced sheep. And *Peter and the Wolf.* And *The Bobbsey Twins.* And strawberry junket. And playing catch. I think I could do something like that once in a while if you want me to."

"I think that would be wonderful."

"I think so, too," I told her. Wonderful, and excruciating.